INNOCENCE
SOLD

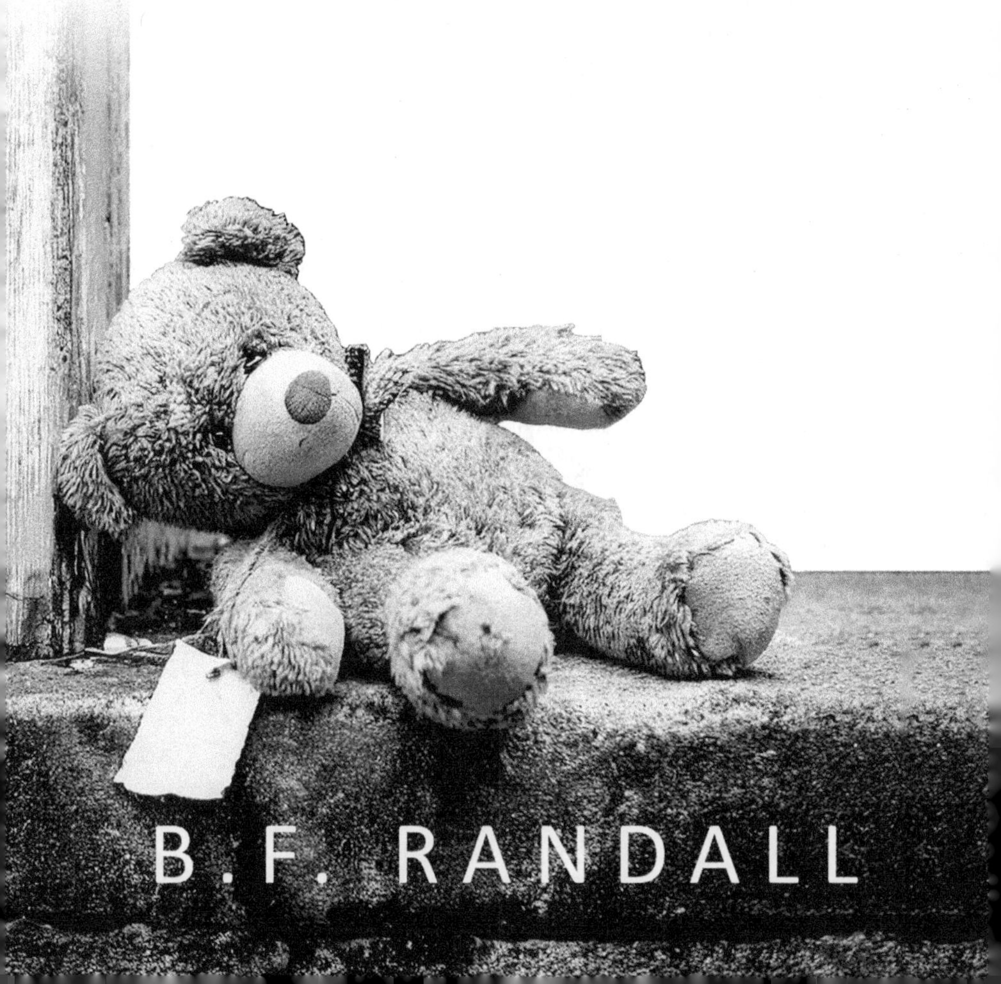

B.F. RANDALL

Innocence Sold

Iron Stream Fiction
An imprint of Iron Stream Media
100 Missionary Ridge
Birmingham, AL 35242
IronStreamMedia.com

Library of Congress Control Number: 2025934645

Scriptures taken from the Holy Bible, New International Version®, NIV®. Copyright © 1973, 1978, 1984, 2011 by Biblica, Inc.™ Used by permission of Zondervan. All rights reserved worldwide. www .zondervan.com The "NIV" and "New International Version" are trademarks registered in the United States Patent and Trademark Office by Biblica, Inc.™

Cover design by twolineSTUDIO.com

ISBN: 978-1-56309-788-1 (paperback)
ISBN: 978-1-56309-789-8 (ebook)

1 2 3 4 5—29 28 27 26 25

"B. F. Randall has done it again! With his varied experiences in life, he has given us another bestseller. *Innocence Sold* is one of those stories that grabs your attention within the first few pages and never let's go. It has plenty of twists and turns of a whodunit with a pleasant mix of humor and intrigue, all the while showing us how his relationship and belief in the Lord guides Sergeant Richards through difficult times, both personally and professionally. Another great read!" —**Gregory S. Agresta**, Chief of Police, Martinez, CA (Ret.)

"B. F. Randall is a masterful storyteller whose unique background in policing, pastoring, and chaplaincy breathes authenticity and depth into every page. In *Innocence Sold*, he channels a lifetime of service and compassion into a powerful, unforgettable novel that shines a light on one of the world's most urgent and hidden crises—human trafficking. With heart, insight, and gripping realism, Randall exposes the dark underbelly of society while celebrating the courage of those who refuse to look away. This is more than a story—it's a call to awareness, action, and hope." —**Jan Makowski**, Vacaville Police Department (CA), Lieutenant (Ret.)

"B. F. Randall has that unique ability to write stories that capture your imagination and to pull you into that world. *Innocence Sold* draws you into and through burglary, kidnapping, child trafficking, conspiracy, and murder, not to mention life, love, faith, and commitment—in other words a life from today's world. As you read, you are walking in their shoes." —**Charles P. McDaniel**, Deputy Chief of Staff, Training (Ret.), IL&ETC, National Guard Professional Education Center

"The story of Officer Richards brings to life the experience of an author who has lived and done what he writes. His books bring a realistic view into the life and career of Ofc. Richards as he navigates his daily law enforcement and family routine. This book grabs you from the very beginning and keeps you turning the pages. B. F. Randall has incorporated God's work into this novel with mastery and precision. I highly recommend this book. Great job!" —**Steven V. Lambeth**, Senior Special Agent (Ret.), Homeland Security Investigations (HSI)

"Once again, author B. F. Randall leaves you with a hunger for more with each turn of the page. In *Innocence Sold*, we follow Sergeant Richards through more of life's challenges as seen through the eyes of a law enforcement officer continuing his journey in faith. As he continues to learn and grow with his faith, being a good man, father, husband, a leader within OPD, and life itself, B. F. Randall shows us once again that God has plans and a purpose for us. For those walking the same path as Sergeant Richards, this story resonates and brings hope that men can be whom God has called them to be." —**James Strasser**, Federal Correctional Institution (FCI), Edgefield (SC), Captain

"*Innocence Sold* explores one of the darkest crimes mankind can inflict upon another, child trafficking. It also highlights the dedication, determination and faith needed by law enforcement and frontline agencies to combat modern-day slavery, and the exploitation of the innocent through force, fraud, or fear. The faith displayed by Bob Richards, and the men and women in Randall's story, is vital in the real fight against human trafficking. B. F. Randall reminds us that God's protection is bigger than any crime man can commit or harm he can conceive." —**Tanya Thompson**, A21 Advancement Specialist, Global *Restore* Efforts

"Imagine yourself as a parent on a wonderful outing with your young children. The kids are playing or exploring, and your attention is distracted for a moment. When you turn back, you experience the sudden fear and panic of not finding them where they should be, but worse . . . never finding them at all! B. F. Randall takes us on a heart-pounding trip into a parent's worst nightmare, and when Sgt. Bobby Richards gets assigned to the case, he discovers how deep the rabbit hole goes! Get ready for another book that is hard to put down!" —**Brad M. Maty**, SMSgt, USAF (Ret.)

Dedicated to Roberta, my wife, partner, companion, and friend. Thank you for standing by me through every chapter of life. I would not be able to do it, nor would I want to, without you.

And to those who are simply known by their uniform and badge, who bravely venture into the unknown in pursuit of justice, thank you. Your willingness to serve and protect is the foundation upon which our freedom is built.

CHAPTER ONE

"Bobby . . . Bobby, wake up," came the sweet voice of my bride, followed by a sharp poke in my back. "You said you wanted to be up by three. It's three, get up."

"Yeah, yeah, I'm up, I'm up."

Dragging my butt out of bed was and continues to be one of my greatest challenges. There is, quite literally, no more comfortable place upon this earth than my bed at the moment I have to wake up. Rolling over, I was going to kiss and thank my beautiful alarm clock when she began to snore loud enough to shake the shingles off the roof. I thought it best to jump in the shower, grab my coffee, kiss her good-bye, and hit the road. She's a deep sleeper and any unnecessary disruption could risk having to call a roofer.

This sabbatical is what I call "me time," that brief opportunity everyone needs to get away and clear their head. Rosie calls it my "thankful time." When I was younger, I would head for the mountains for a few days. Now I just spend the day at some park or retreat pondering the paths my life has taken. Getting on the road well before the sun rises allowed me to reach my destination early enough to avoid the crowds and enjoy the solitude watching the sun birth a new day.

1

Clearing the rainbowed arches of the MacArthur Tunnel, I maneuvered through the light, early morning traffic heading into San Francisco along US Route 101. Just before reaching the Golden Gate Bridge, I took the exit to the Marin Headlands. About two thirds of the way up I pulled over onto a gravel parking spot tucked into the hillside. Getting out, I realized that I should have brought a warmer coat. A thick layer of morning fog had drifted in off the Pacific into the Bay, as the deep tones of distant fog horns blew. All that could be seen were the tops of the Golden Gate's towers, and across the Bay, the points of the Transamerica Pyramid and the Sutro Radio Tower.

It was June, and most of California basked in the warmth of summer, but this was San Francisco, and a breeze off the cool waters of the Bay sent a chill through many unsuspecting tourists and forgetful natives alike. The view and the nip in the air were why I came here. It was a place where I could reflect, because as the fog slowly cleared, exposing Coit Tower, so did the memory of my yesterdays.

I once lived in that City by the Bay, attended elementary and junior high school, and later attended the University of San Francisco. My mother and I had a two-room cold-water flat in the Mission District, at 16th and Valencia streets just down from the old Roxie Theater. We didn't have hot water or a central heating system, yet we were comfortable. A single, large bathroom in the hallway provided hot showers and restroom facilities for the three apartments on the second floor. Individual electric space heaters in each room provided all the warmth we needed despite the periodic power outages. Life was good then. My only concerns were making sure I had enough Brylcreem for my hair and finding out if the girl I liked, liked me.

As the sun rose, creating a luminous glow over the eastern horizon, the morning haze began to burn off. Seated on a bench carved out of a redwood log and covered in etched hearts, initials, names, and promises, I watched as the city gradually came into view. The Golden Gate stretched from Marin to the shores of the Presidio, where I had spent a few months in Letterman General Hospital following a tour in Vietnam. Once released back to duty, I served my final six months in the army as a member of a military police honor guard, performing funerals for those less fortunate than myself.

Today I was taking my "thankful time" to sit gazing out over the Bay and wondering what the future would hold for me. After thirty years of service, I was ready to put my badge in a memory box and hang it on the wall. I promised Rosie that I would stop playing cops and robbers and would spend the next few decades exploring the world with her and the grandkids.

The day began to warm up, and the traffic coursing back and forth across the bridge had slowed to a crawl. I got up, stretched, and strolled along the historic bunkers, once used to protect the port of San Francisco from hostile ships. Now abandoned, they whispered to the hearts of those passing by that they have a story to tell.

Looking around, I reflected on one of the few times I brought the boys up here. Little Joe was eleven, Sonny was nine, and Critter was six. They wanted to run around and check out the bunkers. There was really no place for them to go, so we said sure, but they had to obey the "Richards'

Rule": *Don't go where you are out of our sight.* If they couldn't see us, then we couldn't see them.

A tour guide with a group of Japanese sightseers caught our attention as he stepped up onto a concrete bench and began to tell his audience the history of the Headlands and its bunkers. We only listened for a few minutes, and when we turned around, Joe and Sonny were gone.

"Where's your brothers, Critter?" I asked.

"They went over there," he said, pointing toward a small mound of earth at the end of the road.

"I don't see them. Where did they go?" Rosie asked, showing some concern in her voice.

"They're here somewhere, baby, it's okay. Besides where could they go?" I said in a calm almost joyful tone, showing no real concern. "Rosie, you two stay here, I'll go get them and be right back."

They were probably playing hide-and-seek, so I began my search heading toward the far end of the small peninsula. I searched through the surrounding bunkers and concrete foxholes, continually calling out each boy's name but getting no response. Once I cleared the area, I was confident that they had returned to their mom and were no doubt in tow. Taking a shortcut over a small hill, I spotted Rosie standing with her back to me among a crowd of tourists.

"Rosie," I shouted and began to jog.

Rosie turned toward me, and I could see the boys were not with her, and the expression on her face had morphed into grave concern.

"Bobby, where are they?" she said, as her lower lip began to quiver. I grabbed her and held her tight. "It's only been about fifteen minutes. They're here, they're here."

Looking over her shoulder I spotted a 1950s Volkswagen minibus, painted in wild psychedelic colors, with wooden bumpers and large painted peace signs covering all the side windows. It was parked oddly under a small grove of trees, blocking any view from those passing by. As I stared at the van, a feeling of dread and alarm coursed through me, a feeling I couldn't explain to the department shrinks. It was the same feeling I got when I heard my friend Alford Jackson say Curtis Mitcham's name over the radio just before Mitcham killed him.

"I'll be right back," I said. "Wait here." Stepping around her, I walked quickly toward the van, stopping just short of the left rear where a small portion of the painted peace sign had chipped away. Looking inside I could see a mattress, blankets, and an assortment of pillows, but no people. Scattered on the floor were beer cans, food wrappers, and a large green bong. Hearing voices, I stepped around to the other side and was met by two long-haired, unkempt men and two spaced-out, disheveled women, all clad in typical well-worn paisley and tie-dyed garb. On a long log, front row center, sat an audience of two, listening to whatever this pied piper was pitching.

"Hi, Daddy," Sonny said with a big smile.

"He's telling us a story," Little Joe chimed in.

"That's nice," I said, looking over the motley crew. "Time to go, boys, come on."

"Not yet, Daddy," Little Joe said.

"Joseph, it's time to go, now."

The bigger of the two men stood slowly and said, "Leave them alone, man. They got a right to be here."

"These are my sons, and we're leaving." Turning to the boys, I lowered my voice, "Boys, look at me. Get up and move . . . now."

The tone of my voice and the look in my eye were all that was required. Little Joe took Sonny's hand and the two jumped off the log and walked quickly to me.

Leaning down, I pointed to where I had left Rosie, "Joseph, take your brother over to Mom. Go now."

Without a word Little Joe picked up his pace, almost dragging his brother behind him. He knew that when I called him Joseph, I meant business.

Now both men were on their feet. "Hold up, buddy, how do we know they're your kids?" the storyteller said.

"Yeah, they don't look like you. I don't think they are your kids," the big guy said as he moved slowly toward me.

I looked back to see that the boys were running toward Rosie as she opened her arms. Reaching into my pocket, I took out my ID and badge. Raising it, I let my Members Only jacket fall open, exposing my holstered Browning 9mm.

"I think that's far enough, gentlemen." Wide-eyed they stopped their forward movement, but anger was beginning to flare in their eyes.

"We're not going to get hassled by no pig," the story-teller growled.

"We're up here enjoying the day, just like you. Now, I can thank you for finding my boys and we both go our way." I said rising and slowly sliding my right hand under my coat. "There's no point in doing something stupid and ruining a beautiful day."

A myriad of scenarios raced through my mind as my heart began to pound like a jackhammer. Taking a slow, steady breath, I relaxed my posture, tilted my head slightly, and put on a smile. It was my expression that spoke of who was in control, unless of course these two toads could hear my heart ripping its way out of my chest.

"What's it going to be, gentlemen?"

My *Dirty Harry* moment was interrupted when both the women jumped to their feet. "Stop it. What's wrong with you two? Stop it or Mary and I are leaving."

"Okay, okay," the storyteller said. "You're welcome officer. I'm glad we found your kids for ya."

"Alright, well you folks have a good day," I said backing away. Once behind the van I turned and jogged over to Rosie and the boys. Walking to the car, I watched as the van backed up and pulled onto the road. As it passed us, the woman named Mary leaned out of the passenger window, "Goodbye, Mr. Policeman. It was a thrill to meet ya."

Laughter could be heard inside the van as they maneuvered around tourists. I noted the Oregon license plate and planned on running it later. I had a sneaking suspicion we would meet again.

When we got home, Rosie and I sat the boys down and spent the evening talking about the danger of strangers. We did the best we could to avoid frightening them, but we knew some measure of fear was required to plant a sense of caution in them. I haven't found any books on how to instill in the two younger ones a level of wisdom and understanding that they could grasp. The greatest fear in the hearts of most parents is not being able to adequately teach our children how to recognize danger and protect themselves.

Although we had a wonderful day, there was a need for discipline. The boys failed to follow the Richards' Rule of staying within sight. They had long known not to talk to or follow strangers. On Saturdays, our normal routine before bed included popcorn and an episode of *My Favorite Martian*. Not tonight. Tonight, it was straight to bed.

Although it had been an enjoyable day, it was also a scary one. I never told Rosie the whole story; it would only have kept her up at night. I often wonder what would have happened if things had gone differently. I played the scenario over and over in my head, working out different ways the situation could have gone and been dealt with. Every cop, doctor, pilot, and plumber does this. It helps to prepare them for the unexpected.

When bad things happen, a cop doesn't have the luxury of time afforded judges, juries, or the general public, nor can they choose not to get involved. The average cop will experience challenges and events every day that most people will never experience in a lifetime.

I was uniquely blessed to have had Alford Fergus Jackson, better known as A. J., as my training officer. He shared his life and wisdom with me and taught me the importance of mental role play. He passed on his understanding of the streets and showed me the importance of fear, how it increases adrenaline and heightens our senses, but how it must never be shown. Our calm bearing and controlled demeanor could be instrumental in quelling even the most chaotic of situations.

A. J. was a cop's cop. He had over thirty-five years on the streets of Oakland and knew the city and its inhabitants like no other. He was my training officer, my mentor, and he became my best friend.

Responding to a motorist's assist, a simple call of a truck broken down, and its driver lying on the grassy knoll nearby, A. J. was gunned down by Curtis Mitcham, a man we had arrested for burglarizing a local grocery store years earlier.

It was a call that should have been mine. I was on the opposite side of town when I heard him say Mitcham's name over the radio, and I knew there was going to be trouble. By the time I arrived, Mitcham was gone, and A. J. lay dead. The greatest regret that continually haunts me was that I couldn't get there on time. I wasn't there to help him, to keep him alive.

He died nearly two decades ago, and his killer was removed from this life six years ago in San Quentin's gas chamber. I would like to think that it was all behind me, but unfortunately, unlike the morning fog, it never simply fades away.

Retrieving my thermos, I returned to my favorite bench with its spectacular view and watched as the maddening flow of commuter insanity created a flickering ribbon of red lights threading its way into the city. Sipping my coffee, I took in what unfolded before me and inhaled deeply the brisk, briny morning air. Closing my eyes, I sat back and allowed my mind to drift like the light white foam on the waves of the Bay. This is why I had come here this morning, to remember. To allow the reflections of days gone by to fill my spirit with appreciation. For me, the only way to properly move into tomorrow was to take time to embrace my yesterdays, both the good and the bad. It had been a good ride, filled with joy and heartache, neither of which would I ever exchange.

CHAPTER TWO

On the door of each officer's locker hung a twelve-by-twelve leather pouch in which various communiques, reports, and assignments were left for the officer's attention. In mine was a folder from Sergeant Atwood congratulating me on my new assignment—one I did not request—and asking me to hang over a couple hours.

Police Chief Robert Boon had been diagnosed with atrial fibrillation, a progressive heart disease that affects the pumping of the heart muscles. His prognosis was poor, so he took an early retirement. In the interim, while the commissioners and city council interview candidates for the police chief position, Captain Jorden Walker was appointed Acting Chief.

Walker is the perfect example of the *peter principle*, which states that a person will eventually be promoted to the level of their incompetence. He was known to be a good patrol sergeant some years back, but when he was promoted to Lieutenant, and later to Captain, he became a notorious suck-up, creating a number of policies, rules, and procedures merely to draw attention to himself. Most of his ideas were short lived, usually because of a lack of administrative interest. This idea, however, was a good one, but unfortunately, it too would most likely die a quiet death.

Sitting behind two six-foot folding tables put end-to-end in the back of the squad room, I waited for Sergeant Atwood, Walker's personal gofer, to come to the podium and present Walker's most recent stroke of genius.

"Good morning," Atwood said. "This morning, there will be a weapons inspection. Before you leave this room, you are to line up at one of the two tables in the back where Senior Officers Richards and Johnson are seated. Remove and clear your service revolver, along with any firearm you carry on duty."

A loud groan along with a few choice expletives filled the air.

"That's enough," Atwood said angrily. "This inspection will be a regular event, conducted whenever Captain . . . I mean Acting Chief Walker, deems it necessary. Senior Officers Richards and Johnson will inspect and record the serial numbers of your sidearms."

Stepping around the podium for emphasis, Atwood said, "It has been noted by the range master that some of you are using an unauthorized firearm to qualify every six months. From now on, you will qualify with the firearm you carry while on duty. If your weapon requires maintenance, you will be required to submit to a second inspection." Stepping back, Atwood turned the podium over to Sergeant Tom Allen, Shift Watch Commander.

"Okay, gentlemen, first things first, from where you're seated, slowly remove and clear your firearm, keep it pointed to the floor and your finger away from the trigger housing. I have a busy day ahead of me and don't have time to explain to your wives the meaning of 'friendly fire' or why you're not coming home for dinner."

The inspection revealed that most of the weapons were well maintained and needed little attention, but there were a few that went way beyond the need of a mere cleaning.

Officer Stanley Ratchet had served for twenty-five years as traffic control and resource officer for our local elementary schools. He was well known, deeply loved, and the son of Mayor James Ratchet, who held the office longer than any other, from the late 1940s through the mid '60s.

With a smile, Stan placed his Sam Browne belt on the table in front of me. It held his handcuffs, mace, additional bullets, and a holstered Smith & Wesson Model 625. "Here you go, Bobby."

"Thank you, Stan. Please step over to the side, remove your service revolver, and make sure you have cleared it."

He stood there motionless, with a dopey grin, saying nothing.

"Is there a problem, Stanley?"

"Well, uh . . . yeah. I can't do that."

"You can't do what?"

"Well, I can't get my gun out of the holster."

Taking the Sam Browne, I got up and moved to the side of the table, away from a line of frustrated officers, and pointed the firearm to the floor. I unsnapped the safety strap, gripped the butt, and pulled. It wouldn't budge. Aside from it being extremely dirty, I couldn't see what was keeping it from being removed from the holster.

"How long has it been like this?" I asked.

"I don't know," he said scratching his head. "Truth is, I can't remember the last time I took it out of the holster."

"How have you been qualifying?"

"Oh, I haven't done that in years. I usually don't even attend briefings, but I got a note that said I had to attend this one."

Pulling back the leather along the top of the holster, I could now see what held the gun in place. After years in the rain, never being removed, let alone fired or cleaned, it had rusted firmly to the rivets and metal clip that held the holster together. Stanley was in need of more than a simple weapons inspection, and that fell way outside my scope or authority.

"Stan, there are live rounds in there so I'm going to send this to the range master to see what he can do with it. You need to see Sergeant Allen and let him know what's happened. Make sure to let him know that you need to qualify."

"Okay." Stanley shrugged.

Although that moment with Stan was dumbfounding, it was also enlightening. Was I really any different than Stan? Like the gun, had I become vulnerable, resting comfortably in a holster I had created for myself? I tended to lose sight of my limitations when held securely by routine and lack of any challenge. Like Stanley, I believed I was equipped to handle what came my way, but I wasn't. I had become comfortable in my routine and avoided the maintenance that was required. I was starting to rust.

Stanley had spent his entire career being the representation of safety and security, but in truth, he may not have been able to provide it, and he didn't know it. Fortunately, it was a simple inspection that exposed how ill-prepared he actually was.

Over the years, I had come to know many of my weaknesses and strengths best by being exposed to what I would prefer to avoid. During my tenure in the army, I learned that good soldiers are made through well-planned and persistent training. However, instruction would not make a warrior; that only came from experience. Warriors weren't made at the range but in combat. This was also true for cops. The academy would teach them about being a police officer, but it's the street that would make them cops.

Little did I know that this truth would soon be played out.

The early morning shift was quiet with just a few of the usual calls to referee volatile family reunions and to remove a few inebriated bumper-car drivers from the city's darkened streets. Even the bars were reasonably tranquil, with little of the usual mayhem that bubbled out onto the sidewalks at bar dump.

"Xray-3, Dispatch."

"Xray-3, go ahead Dispatch," I said.

"We received a call from a concerned parent that her two sons, Clifford, thirteen, and Brandon, fifteen, had snuck out of the house and are believed to be heading to San Francisco via the Dumbarton Rail Bridge. SFPD has been advised and will begin the search from their end."

"Ten-four, Dispatch. How did they get to the bridge?"

"Not sure. They left a note for their sister stating that they were heading that way."

"Dispatch, do we know how long ago they left home?"

"Negative, believed to be within the last two hours."

"Got it. Charlie 3, meet me at the foot of the bridge, on the right side of the tracks. We'll work our end from there."

Charlie is the call sign of an officer in training and the number that follows is the trainees TO. Charlie 3, known as Axel, acknowledged my request by two clicks on his radio. Axel Heart was one of our newest officers, born in the city of Oakland and raised in the Fitchburg District, the most crime-ridden area in the city. He decided to enter law enforcement while in high school after his big brother was killed in a drive-by. He hadn't talked about it and seemed to want to avoid the subject all together. The case remains open.

I had been his training officer for nearly eight months, and I could see that he was more than capable of hitting the bricks on his own, but policy kept him attached to me at the hip for at least another four months. He was a quick learner, sought instruction, and was willing to take directions. He truly cared for those he met on the street and was a devout believer who began every shift with a prayer. At the end of his day, he would head across the parking lot and shout "Thank you, Lord, for keeping us safe!"

Standing at the entrance to the railroad bridge, Axel walked up and handed me a flashlight and my portable radio. "I've lived here all my life, Bobby, and I've heard all the stories about this bridge, but I've never gone much farther than this."

"There's a lot of stories, some are true," I said, looking up. "The last time I walked this bridge we had a full moon. It lit the place up like noonday, but not tonight. Black as pitch."

Dropping his head, Axel began to pray, "Lord, protect those boys, and lead us to them. Protect us and those coming from the other side. Amen." It was brief, but it said it all.

"Okay, what I'm going to tell you, you may already know but listen up any way. This is a single track, six-span bridge. Each span is one hundred and eighty feet long and a minimum of eighty-five feet above the water at high tide. We're going to cover three of those six spans, and SFPD will meet us in the middle, unless the boys are found first. Dispatch is contacting the railroad authority to get the schedules of oncoming trains and to stop them if possible. Be very careful and watch your step. The bridge is suspended on iron trusses and girders with steel mesh open to the water below. Over the years, maintenance crews have removed large sections of the mesh, so you'll have to maneuver around the holes." I looked up into his eyes and said, "There are no nets. Remember to keep your flashlight always trained three steps in front of you and move slow. Got it?"

"Yes, sir."

"Okay, so what do you want, left or right?"

"Left, I guess," Axel said reluctantly.

A loud creaking sound resonated in the still night air as we stepped out onto the first section of mesh. "One foot down and 540 to go, and then we walk back," I said with a snicker, but got no response from the other side.

"Clifford! Brandon!" we shouted as we methodically moved forward. "Clifford! Brandon!"

Axel was keeping up well so far, and up to this point the only openings in the bridge floor were on my side. We were a third of the way through the second span when the sound of an excited voice shouted from my portable radio, "Xray-3, Xray-3, come in!"

"Axel, hold up, stop where you are, don't move." Keying the radio, "Go ahead, Dispatch, this is Xray-3, what's up? Have they found the boys?"

The voice screeched, "Negative. Negative. We just got word that a ten-by-ten northbound train is heading your way. They can't raise the conductor and it will reach you within eight minutes. You have to get off the bridge now!"

"Got it, call you back," I shouted into the mic as I skipped cautiously over the tracks to Axel's side of the bridge.

"Axel, we have a train coming, a big train. We're going to have to get off the track now."

His eyes as wide as dinner plates, he looked back from where we had come. "Get off the track? What are you talking about, get off the track? Where are we supposed to go?"

"Calm down and listen. We don't have much time. We need to climb over the side railing. If we remain on this side of the rail, we'll get sucked into the train. Now climb over the railing."

Axel was frozen in place. He was gripping the top of the rail and staring down at the waves below. His mouth hung open as he gasped for air.

"Axel, move!" I yelled as I stepped over the rail onto a five-inch piece of the bridge's flooring that protruded outside of the railing. Moving slowly toward him, I slid my feet inches at a time until I was next to him. I looked down and saw nothing but air between me and the waters of the Bay. Holding onto the rail with my left hand, I gripped his forearm as tightly as I could with my right, pulling him to me.

"Axel, I can't find those kids without you. I need you, now come on."

He didn't move, just stared intently at the waters below. He gripped the rail with such force I thought he would bend it. Off in the distance the haunting sound of a locomotive's whistle signaled early morning commuters of the train's approach.

"Okay, okay," I said, trying to avoid shouting at him. "Stay there, right there, but you're going to be responsible for all those reports I'll have to write," I said, turning away from him. "Not to mention the mess you're going to make all over that train."

Tilting his head, he took his eyes off the water and looked at me.

"Get your butt over that rail, rookie," I said in as commanding a tone as I could muster.

Closing his eyes, he slowly raised one leg over the rail, stepped down onto the small metal protrusion I was on, then lifted the other leg. Once he was on the outside of the trestle, I demonstrated what was next.

"Okay, put your arms under the top rail and crouch down. With your forearms, pull yourself into the railing. When the train goes by it will also pull you in, but don't loosen your hold. The pull will only last while a boxcar is going by. It slackens between cars and will be gone at the end. Got it?"

Nodding, he did as he was told, and together, nearly a hundred feet above the San Francisco Bay, we were suspended like a couple of bats off Dracula's chandelier.

Within minutes the northbound Iron Horse greeted us by shaking and rattling the bridge so violently we knew it was about to collapse. The sound was deafening as it passed. I couldn't believe how long it took for a ten-by-ten, or hundred boxcar train, to clear this bridge. I was getting weak and feared falling backward into the frigid waters. If the fall didn't kill me, the hypothermia would. I glanced over at Axel as he held tight to the rail, his lips moving in prayer. I didn't have his youth or strength, but I did have what he was resting upon, faith in God.

Closing my eyes, I began to pray. I needed miraculous intervention, to hold tight and simply trust in Him. It is through trust that my faith is built, and it's in times like these that my trust is put to the test and my faith strengthened. I'm not in the holster anymore. I'm now in the hand of God.

Finally, the last car passed, leaving us clutching the rail and listening as the distinctive clacking sound of steel wheels rolling on the tracks slowly faded in the distance. Cautiously we climbed back over the rail, collapsing onto the mesh in silence.

After several minutes, without a word, we stood and began to walk back to our cars. We didn't speak because we knew what the other person was thinking. There was no point in continuing in our search. If the boys were on the tracks, they couldn't have survived what we just went through. Had we gotten there earlier, or moved faster, or thrown caution to the wind, we might have been able to save those boys, boys that were close to the ages of my sons. All I wanted to do was get home to them.

"Dispatch, this is Xray-3 and Charlie, any word from SFPD?"

"Negative, at this time. I have the train authority on the line and will get an update soon. Are you two alright?"

"We're good, just a little rattled. We're clearing the bridge now and will be standing by for follow up."

At the end of the bridge, we split up and went to our respective vehicles. I opened the door and looked back to see Axel hunched over the front fender of his car vomiting with such force I thought he would cough up a lung.

"Are you okay?"

"Yeah, yeah . . . I'm good," he said, waving me off.

"Axel, it's okay man. We've all been there."

"No, no, I'm good . . . I'm good."

Straightening up, he turned to me. Even in the dim illumination of a streetlight, I could see he was pale and the expression on his face was of absolute terror.

"I'm sorry, Bobby, I just have a really, really bad fear of heights."

"You have a fear of heights? Like ladders and stuff?"

"Yeah, but it's a lot worse than that," he said as he turned away and wretched once again.

"You should have . . . ah never mind."

Yes, he should have told me, but he took control of his fear. His concern for those boys was greater than his concern for himself. He'd have to get some balance with that, but he was going to make for a good cop.

"Xray-3," came the somber voice of Lacy Smith, Dispatch Supervisor.

Seated in my car, I watched Axel get into his, and when the radio squeaked, he looked over at me. He knew as I did, this was going to be bad news.

"This is Xray-3, go ahead, Dispatch."

"Xray-3, the parents just called in to tell us that the boys were found smoking in a friend's basement. We're advising SFPD now."

"Thank you, Dispatch. Show me and Charlie out on Code-7."

"Ten-four, enjoy."

Pulling out, I waved to Axel to follow me to the Pancake House for some lunch. I knew he needed something in his stomach. En route I used the time to again thank God for His hand of grace and protection. I also asked for Clifford and Brandon's father not to be an advocate of the new form of discipline that Doctor Spock had been pushing called "time out." When junior acts up, just send him to his room for some time out. I, for one, was hoping for a little more "hands-on" involvement by dad, but despite my frustration, I was thankful for their safety.

CHAPTER THREE

Sliding behind the wheel, I clicked my newly installed seat-belt, put the key in the ignition, and prepared for every one of the 280 horses under the hood of my canary yellow 1972 Dodge Charger r/t to get a serious workout. All I wanted was to get home and spend a little quality time with my boys before they headed off to school.

I couldn't get this morning's escapade on the Dumbarton Rail Bridge out of my head. Those boys were the same age as my sons. It could have easily been Little Joe and Sonny out there, strolling along in the dark without a care in the world, just looking for a little adventure. The odds of Clifford and Brandon surviving their journey, had they been there, were zero to none.

Pulling into the driveway, I maneuvered around a collection of bicycles and skateboards that would one day be exchanged for a varied assortment of automobiles. Getting out, I stood at the car door for a moment and admired the beautiful creature in the window. Rosie, the Commander-in-Chief of the Richards Clan, stood by the kitchen sink cleaning cereal bowls and packing lunchboxes. Looking up she spotted her prince, smiled, and invited me to enter the

Richards Realm with a wink and a tossed kiss. It was good to be me.

Rosie was able to arrange her weekends to fall with mine, Sunday and Monday. Her Saturdays were short, just a few hours in the morning setting things up for the coming week, and my weekend began when I got off at 8:00 a.m. Saturday, giving us almost a three-day weekend together every week.

Today was the Marina International Festival of Winds at the San Francisco Marina, with music, vendor booths, food, and a sky filled with elaborate and creative kites that boggle the mind. It was a beautiful day, with clear skies, warm weather, and a slight breeze. Every year Grandpa Joe would make the boys a kite, and today was perfect for a test flight.

We ended up having to park two city blocks from the marina, but once we got there with our ice chest, blanket, umbrella, and gear, we were able to find a great spot near all the activities.

It was a wonderful day, and the picnic made by the queen was beyond expectations. The troupe made new friends and spent most of their time getting Grandpa Joe's kites to fly. Me, I found that a full tummy under the warm sun and an ever so light breeze off the Bay was a perfect combination for a nap. While Rosie struck up a conversation with a couple ladies next to us, I pulled my sombrero over my eyes and began engaging in a momentary horizontal life-pause. I was asleep in seconds.

"Bobby!" I knew the voice, but I was confused by the tone and volume. "Bobby, wake up!"

"What? What?" I said, pushing my hat back. "What's going on?"

"You have to get the boys. Hurry, go get them!"

"Why?" I asked, noting that the sun was no longer directly overhead.

"Go find the boys. The police are coming, someone lost a child. Bobby, go find ours. Hurry," her voice began to splinter with emotion as she looked franticly in every direction.

I jumped to my feet as my brain registered that moving was more important than asking questions, and ran toward where I had seen them last.

"Bobby, over there," Rosie shouted behind me.

Sliding to a stop, I turned to see Rosie pointing toward the narrow beach area by the water.

"Boys, get over here . . . now," I shouted.

Climbing over the small breakwater that separated the small beach from the grass, they ran over to me. "We saw you, Dad, we kept the Richards' Rule," Little Joe said, as Casey took my hand.

"Yeah," Sonny added. "We could see you, so you could see us."

"Thanks, guys. We have to get ready to leave now."

By the playground, several police cars had lined up, and within minutes officers, cadets, and volunteers were receiving instruction and beginning their search.

Packing up, I was about to ask Rosie if she would mind if I lent a hand, when she looked at me and said, "Help me load this stuff and the boys in the car, then go and see how you can help."

I approached what appeared to be the command post, showed my identification, and said, "My name is Bob Richards. I'm with Oakland PD. Is there any way I can help?"

"Sure," a tall, muscular young officer said as he appeared from behind one of the cars, extending his hand. "Richards, was it?"

"Yes, sir," I said, noting lieutenant's bars on his collar and the name plate showing "Lt. Lloyd Plaxton."

"How long have you been with OPD, Richards?"

"Nine years, sir."

"Good, so you have skills. Step over here a moment," he said, handing me a clipboard and a pen. "Starting at the swings in the playground, catch as many people as you can and get their names and contact info, starting with yours. Cover as much of the marina as you can, then get back to me. We'll follow up with them later."

I spent the next hour and a half working my way around the perimeter of the park, getting names and numbers from parents and picnickers who had more questions than I did. The rumor mill was in high gear and working overtime. Almost everyone had a take on what happened, from the cops making a big deal out of a kid walking home without telling his parents to street gangs kidnapping kids for ransom.

Although the festivities weren't over and the sky was still filled with kites, there wasn't a child to be found that wasn't at mom's or dad's side. The playground and what had been a busy soccer field were empty.

Handing Lieutenant Plaxton his clipboard I had to ask, "Sir, there's a lot of scuttlebutt about what's happened. Some are saying that there's been a big increase in kids being snatched in the city. Any truth to that?"

Pulling me to the side, Plaxton said, "Don't pass this on to anyone, we don't need any more hysteria than we already have. Admin is putting together a public announcement that will hit the press tomorrow."

Two officers approached and Plaxton waved them off. "Yes, there has been a spike in missing children. This one is an eight-year-old boy. The missing kids are all boys, ranging in age from six to ten. White, Black, Hispanic, or Asian, it doesn't matter. Whoever is pulling this off is smooth, the kids just disappear. This boy was with his fourteen-year-old sister getting ice cream at one of the food venders. She turned to give her brother a cone and he was gone."

"Wow. Feel free to give me a call if there's anything I can do to help from our end of the Bay," I said as we exchanged business cards. I wanted more information about the abductions, but I knew an active crime scene wasn't the place.

Heading back to the car I saw Rosie and the boys sitting on a blanket playing a card game with a deck of cards we always kept stuffed in the trunk. "Hey, guys, sorry it took so long."

"That's okay, Dad, it gave me time to prove that I am the champion at Crazy Eights," Little Joe said.

"That's because you cheat," Sonny grumbled.

"That's enough. Scoop up the cards and let's hit the road," I said, extending a hand to Rosie and helping her to her feet.

Giving her one end of the blanket, I took the other and we began to shake out the grass and leaves when I spotted an old van with large peace symbols covering the side windows. Dropping the blanket, I ran as fast as I could to the corner to get a better look, but it turned the corner and disappeared. I thought of jumping in the car and chasing it, but that would only put my family in danger. Besides, it was the Festival of Winds, every street, alleyway, and bike trail around the marina would be jammed. It would take a while to just get the car on the road.

Once we got home, I rummaged through a mountain of sticky notes that I kept in a tray on my desk. I was about to quit when I remembered a folder where I had tossed notes over the years. There I found a crumpled sticky note with the number of an Oregon license plate once spotted on an old van, similar to the one I spotted at the park. Calling SFPD, I left a message and the number on Lieutenant Plaxton's answering machine.

The weekend was beautiful but quick. I went in early to work a double shift, covering for Scott Johnson who had a special evening out, escorting an eleven-year-old princess to a gala event. It was the annual Calvary Chapel's Father Daughter Ball, something I will never be a part of, unless my boys provide me with some granddaughters.

A note was clipped to the pouch on my locker from Dispatch Supervisor Lacy Smith to see her before I went out on patrol.

"What's up, Lacy?" I said, stepping into her cluttered office. It looked like a paper company and crayon factory exploded. She was the proud grandma of four little girls and two boys. All of them were either in preschool or kindergarten, and if you asked Lacy, they were all destined to be artists. The proof hung on every inch of available wall space in her office.

"I had Chief Walker's wife on the phone for twenty minutes. She's hysterical. Said there's a large rattlesnake in her yard. I tried to calm her down, but she insisted on talking to the watch commander. Sergeant Miller told me to give it to you. Do you mind taking the call?"

"No, but why would it matter?" I shrugged. "Any idea why he wants me to handle it?"

"Don't have a clue."

The chief's residence was a typical single-story western-style home at the end of a long, shaded driveway. Its natural stone walls, flat brown roof, and covered porch blended seamlessly into the hillside, providing a perfect place any self-respecting rattler would love to call home.

After ringing the doorbell and knocking several times, the lace curtain over the oak and glass door pulled back slowly, and Mrs. Walker's right eye peered out at me. I was about to assure her that snakes can't knock or ring doorbells but noted that the expression on her face said levity wouldn't go over well.

"Have you killed it?" she asked.

"No, ma'am. I just got here."

Without Mrs. Walker opening the door, I listened to a rendition of an encounter between man and beast so horrific, no one along the California coast was safe.

"Mrs. Walker, please go into your kitchen and get a drink of water," I said through the door.

I stood surveying the prospective places Mrs. Walker's nemesis might be hiding when she returned with glass in hand. "What do you want me to do with this?"

"Take a drink, Mrs. Walker, then take a deep breath and find a comfortable place to sit down." After a couple of minutes I asked, "Are you sitting?"

"Yes," came a shaky voice.

"I assume your husband is not at home."

"No. He's at a meeting." She began to sob.

"Okay, Mrs. Walker, just stay put and I'll be back in a few minutes."

"Please hurry . . ."

The yard in front of Chief Walker's home was a monochromatic, nondescript river of tan rock. With the exception of a few cacti and a large desert marigold, there was little place for a snake the size Mrs. Walker described to hide. For that matter, the county of Alameda was too small.

I walked around the side yard to see if I could spot the elusive creature when the rear door flew open and out stepped a small lady of about fifty, with a 12-gauge shotgun under her arm and her finger on the trigger.

"Mrs. Walker, it's Officer Richards," I said, raising my hands over my head. "Please put the gun down."

"Where's the other officers?" she asked, looking around the yard.

"I'm here as you asked. Please put the gun down. I'll take care of your snake problem."

Turning back toward the house, she let the shotgun drop onto the deck. Once she was inside, I retrieved the gun, jacked the slide open, and noted it was fully loaded, with a round in the chamber and the safety off.

Standing at the screen door I called inside, "Mrs. Walker, where did you last see the snake?"

"In the front yard. I was trimming the hydrangea. It was under it."

"Okay, stay inside and I'll take care of it. Can you open the garage door for me from the inside, please?"

In the garage I grabbed a shovel and a four-foot piece of PVC pipe. As I walked out, the lady of the house was standing behind the screen at the front door.

"Are you going to shoot it?" she asked.

"No, ma'am, but I'll get it out of your yard."

"Officer, you have to shoot it. I insist that you shoot it. It may come back."

"Mrs. Walker, if I shoot at it with all this rock around here, I'd probably miss. It will ricochet and hit one of your neighbors. Trust me, when I'm done, he won't be coming back."

Rustling the marigold with the PVC, I listened for the customary rattle but heard nothing. After several more pokes around the base of the shrub, I spotted movement, then the head of a three-foot-long garter snake.

"I got it, ma'am. I'll get him out of here for you."

"I want you to shoot it. I demand that you shoot it."

I thought of picking it up and dropping it off in the Oakland redwoods, but that wouldn't satisfy the missus. I had a feeling that if I didn't take care of this guy, short of shooting him, it was going to come back to haunt me.

With a swift down stroke, I removed Mr. Wannabe-Rattler's head, then deposited his vital remains in the trash can and advised Mrs. Walker of the outcome.

"Would you put our can out by the road? They will pick it up tomorrow."

"Yes, ma'am."

"Officer, you don't think it can get out of there do you?"

"No, ma'am. It's dead."

I drove back to the PD thinking of what that little lady went through today, and what she will go through tonight. I can picture her lying on her bed staring at the ceiling, listening for noises outside, getting up and constantly going to the window, checking the trash can for any sign of movement. It's horrible to be enslaved to fear.

For a brief moment my mind took me back to my time in Vietnam and my first night at basecamp Alpha, just outside of Vung Ro Bay. I and another neophyte were given guard duty in the listening post, a hole in the ground with a few sandbags around the outside edge and partially covered with camouflage netting and tree branches. It was located one hundred yards out from the camp's perimeter, equipped with a radio wired to the guard posts that was not to be used unless we were under attack. I remember wishing I had a 60-caliber machine gun, but instead I had a flare gun and a 7.62 M14 rifle.

Our job was to sit quietly and listen for any sound of approaching enemy soldiers. We couldn't see anything, but as the night wore on, we heard everything. It got so quiet, our heartbeat sounded like a base drum. Every cricket and field mouse that rustled a leaf was the enemy. The biggest danger we faced was our fear. Monsters tend to get bigger in the dark.

I sat at the table in the back of the squad room as the events of the day were presented to the oncoming grave-yard shift. It had been a reasonably calm evening, but it was Friday, so the bars were full of potential that was yet to hit the streets. I bent over to pick up a warrant folder I had dropped when all of a sudden, a deep baritone voice shouted, "Attention."

I stood quickly, connecting the corner of the table with the back of my skull. The pain shot to both ears as I glanced toward the doors as they flung open and in walked Chief Jorden Walker.

"Take your seat, gentlemen and ladies."

"Chief, it's good to have you here. What brings you out this late?" Sergeant Miller asked.

"Well, I wanted to talk to one of these officers. Something took place today that I feel needs to be addressed and dealt with directly."

The tone in his voice made everyone in the room sit up a little straighter. All were going over what they had said or done, waiting for the other shoe to drop. It had to be either day or swing shift because graveyard was just getting started and hadn't had time to screw something up.

"That sounds serious, Chief. What seems to be the problem?"

"I want to speak to the officer that went to my home today and killed the snake in my front yard."

I knew that he had come to congratulate me for a job well done and applaud my bravery in the face of potential danger. The chief's gruff manner was just the way he communicated. It was all good, even better than good, but he went on before I could step forward to receive my accolades.

"Every year just before fall, I used to get mice around my home. I had tried everything, and nothing worked. One day a rodentologist professor friend of mine told me how I could rid the problem without leaving a bunch of dead mice around. Go buy a garter snake, he said. So, I went to the pet shop at the Concord Mall and ordered a snake. That prize rodent exterminator is now in two pieces in my trash can."

A chill ran down my spine. I could deny it and say it attacked me, or I dropped the shovel. No, those wouldn't work. Then again, he is, or at least was, a spineless reptile, so I wondered how suicide would go over? A giggle was heard in the back of the room, then a snicker, I had to move before they erupted.

Standing up I approached the podium to face him. "Sir, I'm sorry for the unfortunate and premature death of your . . . uh . . . snake. I was requested to respond and eliminate what your wife thought was a rattlesnake."

Leaning over the podium, Chief Walker looked at me. "Officer Richards, did you not recognize that Snickels was merely a harmless garter snake before you maliciously struck him down?"

Looking across the room he went on, "I will not pursue action against you for the blatant, premeditated murder of Snickels if, and only if, you promise to never, and I mean never, let my wife know how he came to reside in our yard. If you or any of your IM force get a similar call to my home, you will not kill my vermin liquidator. Do I make myself clear?"

"Yes, Chief," I said, as it echoed around the room, followed by a chorus of laughter.

Grasping my hand, he shook it firmly. "Thank you, Officer Richards, well done," he said as he headed for the door. "Be safe out there, ladies and gentlemen."

CHAPTER FOUR

"Bobby, you're wanted on the phone," Rosie called out from the kitchen.

"Get a name and number, I'll call when I'm done," I said, pinning my silver badge onto my dress blues. In a few hours, that badge will turn to gold.

"It's a Lieutenant Plaxton from SFPD."

"Okay, I'll be right there."

I picked up the phone and asked, "Lieutenant, what can I do for you?"

"Wanted to give you a heads-up on that plate you gave me," Plaxton said. "It's from a van stolen out of Portland. It was found stripped and burned, missing its plates just outside of Redding."

"I've had that number on a sticky pad for some time. Just never got around to checking it out," I said.

"An APB has been put out on the van. We've gone through a decade of witness statements in missing children reports. In two of the more recent ones, an old van is mentioned. It's a stretch, and hippie vans are a dime a dozen, but we're going to give it a shot. Richards, we need you to think back to when you saw the van and write a thorough statement of the encounter you had, with a detailed description of both the men and the women. It's a good lead, Bob. We're going to run this out and see where it takes us. I'll keep you in the loop."

"Thank you, Lieutenant. I'll have my statement to you in the morning."

After I hung up, I just stood there looking into the bathroom mirror wondering if some child's abduction would have been prevented if I had only run that plate back when I first wrote it on my hand.

I couldn't shake the what-ifs that were rolling around in my head, and Rosie could tell that there was something wrong.

"Bobby, I don't know what it is, and you don't need to tell me, but try to put it aside for now if you can. This is a special day," she said, looking into my eyes. She gently kissed me and took my hand. "Come on, we don't want to be late."

In the council chambers of city hall, I stood at attention beside three other officers in front of a packed house. I glanced slightly to my left and caught the smile that made my heart beat, my partner in life, Rosie. Seated to her right, in the front row, were my three sons, Joseph, Stefan, and Casey. Behind them sat Joe and Alberta Hensley, my in-laws, and beside them was Betty Jackson, my best friend's widow.

At the podium stood recently appointed Chief Jorden Walker, proclaiming the merits of Oakland's finest and spewing promises of safer streets, aggressive crime suppression, and a more professional police presence. If I didn't know any better, I would have thought he was still running for the office.

Following nearly forty minutes of self-promotion, Lieutenant Oliver Lewinsky was called forward. After addressing his history with OPD, Chief Walker handed a set of captain's bars to Lewinsky's wife, Carol, who pinned them on his collar and kissed his cheek. This was followed by Steven Miller's wife pinning a lieutenant's bar on his lapel. Rosie then stepped to the platform and removed the silver badge pinned to my chest. Turning to Chief Walker, she exchanged it for a gold badge and a set of silver chevrons.

Looking into my eyes she said, "I'm proud of you, Sergeant Richards," then pinned the chevrons onto my collar and the badge to my chest. Giving me a peck on the cheek, she whispered into my ear a promise of a sweet rendezvous later. Yeah, it was good to be me.

Following the ceremony, the Richards crew along with Betty, Scott Johnson, who also received sergeant's stripes, and his wife, Charlotte, retreated to the Hensley Ranch to gorge ourselves on Alberta's incredible cooking.

It was a good day, but without A. J. at Betty's side, it was somewhat bittersweet. He was the man who had taught me what being a cop was all about. He once told me that peace can only exist if order exists, and order without compassion is nothing more than brutality.

Police officers carry many titles, most are defamatory, but three are descriptive and accurate and define who we are and why we have been entrusted with the safety of our community. We are Public Servants, Peace Officers, and Law Enforcement Officers, in that order.

We must remember that we are here to serve the community, not to rule it. We are to ensure that peace prevails by establishing a safe and secure environment. A. J. would often remind me that we were not to simply enforce the law but to apply the law ethically and morally. A gentle word and a soft touch were always the best way to approach a situation, but we had to be on our guard and ready to react if necessary.

I retreated to the backyard and sat on the swing Grandpa Joe had built for the boys and watched Sonny and Critter toss a football around while Little Joe struck up a conversation with a neighbor girl. I thought of how instrumental A. J. had been in helping me to be more than a cop, to be a good man. I only hoped I could pass that onto my sons and those under my charge.

"What are you doing sitting out here, Sergeant Richards?" Scott said.

"Just hanging out, Sergeant Johnson," I replied.

Slipping into the other swing, Scott said, "Well, we made it, Sergeant. Now what?"

"We should be getting our assignments in the morning," I said. "I put in for graveyard watch commander. I've worked nights for so long I don't think I could sleep once the sun sets. Besides it works out well with Rosie's schedule and getting the boys to school."

"I asked for traffic division, but being the junior sergeant I doubt I'll get it."

"You've got history there and you've gone through all the training. I think you have a great shot at it."

"Okay, gentlemen, soup's on!" shouted Alberta from the back door. The food was wonderful, and the evening was the usual warm and happy environment afforded by all who entered the Hensley household. I had planned on cutting the evening short because of the work that awaited me, but as usual the clock got away from us.

The next morning, as I walked into the police department, I couldn't help but notice my reflection in the glass doors. Slowing my pace I admired the three gold and blue chevrons on my sleeves. Inside, several officers that I had worked with congratulated me and tossed in a few jokes about abandoning real police work and not being one of the good guys anymore.

On my locker door Lieutenant Miller had placed the request form I had completed for a graveyard shift assignment. At the bottom was a smiley face sticker and his signature. On an orange sticky note he wrote. "Welcome aboard, Sergeant. It's good to see you in command. Stop by my office when you can. Miller."

I would assume a new position that had been rumored around the PD for the last year. I would be one of the newly appointed relief sergeants who would cover all six districts, filling in for watch commanders who were off due to illness, vacations, training, and the like. I was given my request and would be working from midnight to 8:00 a.m. Scott received his wish as well and was now one of the two traffic division supervisors.

I couldn't be happier. I was still on graveyard shift, had my regular days off, and got to explore and experience all the city while getting to know all the "zombies." *Zombie* was a title of endearment given to those of us who liked to work the graveyard shift.

"Lieutenant Miller, you wanted to see me?" I said, standing at his open door.

"Yes, come in, Sergeant, and have a seat. Bob, I just wanted to give you a heads-up about something you probably already know. It has been our practice that when a watch commander was off, the senior officer on that shift assumed the role of WC. That hasn't always worked well, and that's why we are creating the Relief Sergeant position. It's new and so are you, so you may get some flack. Be ready for it."

"No problem, Lieutenant. It may take a while, but it will become the norm. It's needed."

On the following Monday, I arrived an hour early for my first shift in District 3. The watch commander was on vacation so I would be here for at least a week. District 3 is a widely diverse community, both socially and culturally. It is where the Alameda County Seat is located, as well as the largest number of hospitals and medical centers in the Bay Area.

During the briefing I introduced myself and received a cold reception. It would take a while for this cadre of officers to open up to the fresh meat who showed up with authority. They were a brotherhood, and any new faces had to earn their place in the family.

One officer in particular who sat in the back corner of the room demonstrated his disdain for me by rolling his eyes and giving sarcastic grunts. Once I had given out the beat assignments and handed out the warrant folder, I turned my attention to him and politely asked, "Officer, what is your name?"

"I'm Senior Officer Michael Vaughn."

"It's good to meet you, Senior Officer Michael Vaughn." It was clear who I had bumped out of the acting WC position when no sergeant was available. "Do you have a question, Senior Officer Michael Vaughn?"

"Yes, Sergeant Richards, I do. How long are you in grade? Those stripes look new."

"Well, let me see," I said looking at my watch. "Looks like about twenty-two minutes. How am I doing so far?" This brought some laughter, but not from Senior Officer Michael Vaughn.

"That's what I thought," he said. "You might want to get comfortable in your office. We can take care of the street."

"That's a great suggestion, thank you. Okay, gentlemen, let's go to work. Be safe out there."

Following the briefing, I took the opportunity to explore District 3. Cruising the darkened streets, I watched as the shadows of the homeless and the desperate drifted in and out of abandoned buildings and alleyways, searching for a night's lodging or the next fix. Every emergency room I passed was lit up with red and blue flashing lights. And from the sound of approaching sirens, more bright lights were on the way. Despite the number of emergency rooms in the district, they all appeared to be overflowing with victims of stabbings, shootings, accidents, and the common cold.

My Motorola squawked calls for service to the various beat officers and assigned cover where needed. Nothing stood out that would require my response, but I drove by anyway. The usual family fights, drunks, and customary fist-icuffs outside of the local pubs, everything was on course. The morning was off to a good start.

I had spent a couple hours exploring my new and temporary turf when my radio crackled, "WC-3, are you available?"

Keying the mic, I said, "That's affirmative, what do you have?"

"Xray-1 and Xray-4 went out at the county hospital's J ward on a disturbance call. We just received a call from an orderly who says there's a lady threatening hospital staff. Are you available to respond?"

"Affirmative, I'm en route."

I arrived within minutes outside the J ward entrance. Through the large window in the lobby I could see several orderlies, a couple of nurses, and a police officer standing in a circle around a woman in a formal gown.

Inside, the chaos was deafening. Everyone was yelling at the woman and jumping out of her way as she ran around swinging a stiletto high-heeled shoe at anyone who got near. On the floor, up against the reception desk, withering in pain, lay Senior Officer Michael Vaughn, with a black stiletto-heeled shoe driven deep into his thigh. His face contorted in pain as he begged for someone to help him, but the only one getting any attention was the yellow-clad whirling dervish in the center of the room.

"Ma'am, please calm down. We want to help you, but you need to calm down." My words got lost in the shouts that seemed to do nothing but encourage her. Stopping momentarily, she turned slowly with her shoe raised above her head, glaring at her prey, seeking out and sizing up her next victim.

The stiletto heel of her shoe was made of steel and honed to a point to be used as a dagger. Its back edge was sharpened to a razor's edge for slashing. It's been reported that the female members of Satan's Servants, a central California biker gang, commonly sport these deadly glamour gliders.

I grabbed the closest orderly, turned him to face me, and shouted over the pandemonium, "Get over there and take care of that officer."

He hesitated, looked at me, and began to turn away. I pulled him back and yelled, "Get your butt over there now or you'll be the next to go to jail." That seemed to hit home.

Keeping an eye on the crazed woman, I took the arm of the nurse to my right and said loudly in her ear, "Go help that orderly, now." Her response was immediate. All she wanted was an excuse to get out of there.

"Lady, you need to stop, please. We're not going to hurt you. Calm down, we're here to help you," I said as softly as I could, but again my words were lost in the commotion.

The rampage resumed as she ran within the circle of hospital staff, trying to impale anyone she could reach. Stopping, she suddenly reversed direction, catching everyone off guard. A heavy-set nurse tried to retreat but was only able to raise her arm in time to protect her face. The stiletto slashed across her forearm spewing blood in every direction, leaving her defenseless as she fell to the floor weeping.

With our prom queen's back to me, I stepped into the circle and signaled to the officer to step over and stand a few feet to my left side.

"Hey," I shouted. "Over here."

Turning, she glared at the officer as if she was about to eat him. Her face took on an unearthly expression, and her eyes reflected a darkness that sent a chill down my spine. It had a similar effect on the young officer, causing him to instantly step back.

Opening her mouth wide, she let out a blood-curdling scream and lunged toward him with the shoe raised above her head. Her second step put her parallel to me, so I shifted forward and, with what my dad called a haymaker, connected my fist just below her left eye. Her feet came out from under her, and when she hit the ground her yellow evening gown flew up, blossoming like a sunflower.

Several observers, whom I presumed were doctors, had taken refuge in the hallways and ventured out and rendered aid to the nurse and our demonic prom queen.

"Officer, what's your name?" I asked.

"Gary Hicks, Sergeant," he said, breathing hard and staring wide eyed at the results of the morning's events.

"Officer Hicks, cuff her and get those shoes. Make sure she gets the medical attention she needs, then book her for assault with a deadly weapon. This is your arrest so make sure you get statements and info from all the witnesses, me included."

"Yes, Sergeant."

What happened next really set me back. A few of the orderlies and nurses started yelling, even cursing at me for the action I had taken to quell the woman who was trying to skewer them. The same woman they all refused to touch.

"You didn't need to hit her, did ya?" shouted a nurse.

"Do you have any other suggestions, other than shooting her?" I asked.

"What about mace? You could have used mace."

I headed toward the hall to check on Officer Vaughn, stopped, and said, "You might want to spend a little time checking the rules you folks put into place, that we have to live by. The hospitals, and I presume you, have forbidden the use of chemical mace within your facilities."

I found Vaughn in the emergency room, awaiting surgery. No major damage, but he'd be off work for a couple weeks. The shoe was removed and put into a plastic bag and given to Officer Hicks to book into evidence.

"How are you feeling, Senior Officer Michael Vaughn?" I asked as I stepped into his room.

"I'm fine, Sergeant, but it really hurts. Thank you."

I came up beside the bed as he reached out to shake my hand. "Listen . . . uh . . . just call me Mike, okay, and . . . uh . . . I'm sorry about being a butt in briefing."

"No problem, Mike, I understand. Maybe you could help me cut through the ice with the other guys."

"You got it, Sergeant."

The rest of the morning was quiet, and after meeting and debriefing the oncoming day shift watch commander, I was called into Captain Oliver Lewinsky's office, commonly referred to as "the Big O."

Seated behind a large, cluttered oak desk was a massive human being clad in a uniform that required more navy blue material than was needed to cover the Hindenburg.

"You wanted to see me, Captain?"

"Well, Richards, you've kicked up quite a bit of dust on the first night of your first shift as a sergeant, haven't ya?" Picking up a couple of phone messages, he stared at me with a look that said the new chevrons on my sleeves were about to take a hiatus.

"I have received a couple complaints about the way you handled a young lady who was in distress and merely needed medical attention. What do you have to say for yourself, Richards?"

"I believe the report Officer Hicks will submit along with witness statements, my account, and the physical evidence will bring clarity to what took place. I'm confident that my actions were justified, and I would not hesitate to respond and react in the same manner if confronted with the same set of circumstances."

We sat in silence as the Big O looked over the notes and then reached down and pulled up even more.

"Richards, I have two messages that say they feel you overreacted," he said without looking up, followed by another long dramatic pause.

Then he continued, "I have five more and two direct conversations with hospital administrators, who thanked OPD for the exceptional way in which you handled the situation." A smile covered his broad face. "Well done, Sergeant Richards. Good to have you on our team. You're dismissed."

"Thank you, sir," I said and exited quietly and quickly before any other calls came in. My daddy always said, "Get out while the getting's good."

CHAPTER FIVE

My first shift as a watch commander went reasonably well. I still had a job, and I still had my stripes. Not bad for a rookie sergeant.

"Sergeant Richards," came the familiar voice of Susan, the front office receptionist. "Sergeant, I have a message for you from an Alberta Hensley. Said she was your mother-in-law. Asked you to come by to see her before you went home. Said it was very important and sounded like it too."

"Thank you, Susan."

As I walked up to the house, Alberta stepped out onto the porch with a tall, frosted glass of sweet tea in each hand. She sat across from me and began to rock slowly, saying nothing, just looking me in the eye. A polite, emotionless smile formed. "Bobby, I love you."

"I love you too, Alberta," I said in a tone that expressed truth. As long as I have known her, she has asked to meet with me only twice. The first time was when I asked her daughter, Rosie, to marry me. She had questions, a lot of questions. The second time was shortly after the day she, her husband, Joe, Rosie, and our boys were held hostage in her basement by Curtis Mitcham. That time she hugged me, thanked me, and prayed for me. I couldn't imagine what this meeting was going to be about.

"Bobby, it's important that this conversation is held in confidence, until it's necessary for others to know."

"Sure, Alberta. Are you okay?"

"Yes, I'm fine. It's Rosie I'm worried about."

"Rosie? Why? Everything is going great. She's been promoted to senior finance director at Walsh, Harper & Smith, and the boys are healthy and doing really well in school."

"I know things are working out well for you both, and I couldn't be more pleased. I'm sorry I made it rough for you in the beginning. I was just afraid that you might hurt her. I was so wrong. I know now that you are the man God made for her."

She dropped her head and began to cry.

"Alberta, what's wrong? You can tell me. I promise to keep it between us."

Looking up, her tears continued to flow. "Do you remember what we went through when Joe was diagnosed with prostate cancer? The doctors, tests, and surgeries, then the counseling and therapy. It was as much hell for me as it was for him. I never left his side, not once."

"Has it returned? I know he gets an examination every six months. Did his last one show something?"

"Last week when we all stayed in Monterey, Rosie and I had gone out to the pool while you, Joe, and the boys went out to the beach. We used our room to change in, and while Rosie was gathering her bra and tank top, I noticed an unusual lump on her left breast. I asked her about it, and she said it was just fatty tissue. Although I knew truth to be something Rosie held tightly to, something deep inside of me set off an alarm that this was more than just fatty tissue."

Reaching over she touched my hand and said, "You know me, Bobby, I can be somewhat pushy if need be, and this was what I felt to be one of those 'need to be' situations. So I pushed until she gave in and shared that she had actually noticed the lump several weeks earlier while taking a shower, and that so far, she hadn't gone to see the doctor."

Wiping away tears with her napkin, she said, "Bobby, she had all the normal excuses, her work schedule, your work schedule, the boys' activities, you know the usual stuff. I wanted to accept that at face value, especially when she assured me that it was nothing and that I shouldn't be concerned. Something inside of me was saying it's much more."

Alberta's eyes once again filled with tears as fear took hold of her heart. First her precious Joe, and now perhaps her only beloved daughter was potentially facing the trial of a lifetime.

As she spoke, I began to feel like I was in a Hitchcock movie where the character falls backwards off a cliff and the scenery around him begins swirling as he plummets toward the ground. My mind and heart moved closer and closer to the edge of panic as deep-seated fears bombarded me. Why hadn't she told me? What could she possibly have been thinking? She was my wife, the mother of our sons, and she hadn't taken time to even call her doctor.

Then in the sudden shock of "what might be" and how this would impact our family, it dawned on me that I had lost sight of what Rosie must be going through and why she had chosen not to make that call. I knew it wasn't out of oversight, neglect, or carelessness. That wasn't Rosie's character. She was always on top of things, especially something like this.

Before these thoughts could fester any further, I heard Alberta's soothing voice cushioning my mental freefall. "Bobby, Rosie is acting out just as she did as a child. It's nothing, and it will go away. When she was ten years old, she fell off her bike and hurt her left wrist. We didn't know about it for nearly two days. I went to her room and pulled back the covers to wake her up. She had wrapped her wrist with a towel. Both her wrist and hand were swollen twice its size. X-rays showed that it was broken, so she spent two months in a cast up to her elbow. This is Rosie's way of maintaining control of the situation. I know she would never intentionally jeopardize her health or the welfare of her family."

If Rosie wouldn't or couldn't move forward, I knew that I could. The look on Alberta's face told me she saw down deep into my soul and knew that whatever emotion was driving my response, it wouldn't result in the ending I envisioned.

"No, Bobby, that will only cause you both more heartache than you need. Nothing has been confirmed yet. Please don't let your emotions get the better of you. You know our little Rosie and she needs time to handle this her way."

Taking hold of my hand, Alberta looked up at me as her eyes filled with tears. "You and my little girl are one, so go home and act like it. I'll meet you there before she gets home, and we'll put together dinner for you both. I will pick up the boys from school, and they can spend the night with us. I'll see that they get to school. Tonight, you talk, you plan, you pray, and you cry together if necessary. Control that man of action in you, and don't get frustrated. Rosie isn't stupid. She's just a little girl that needs love, support, and compassion."

Although it took every ounce of strength within me to hold back, I knew that she was right. Rosie and I were one and God was in our lives. I took a deep breath, composed my thoughts, and allowed Alberta's advice to sink in.

It was a painful but blessed night that lasted until the sun rose. Rosie and I talked for hours, sometimes crying, even laughing at times as we held each other on the patio chaise, praying fervently for God's perfect will to be accomplished. We watched as the horizon exploded in brilliant colors of gold and blue ushering in a new day. Although the circumstances hadn't changed, somehow, we had. With a renewed understanding that regardless of what might lay ahead we would be able to face it head-on. We're not alone; we're in God's hands.

I took the next three days off, and Rosie called in sick, so we were good to catch a few needed winks. Alberta made an appointment for us with Dr. Larry Chamberlan, our family doctor. He delivered Rosie when she was born and was there when our boys came into the world. He was a good doctor, a good man, and a good friend.

After the usual formalities and small talk, Dr. Chamberlan called in a nurse to draw blood. Nodding to me he said, "Bobby, would you mind stepping out and taking a seat in the hall for a few minutes while we conduct an examination? Nurse Nichols will remain and assist me."

"Sure," I said, though I didn't want to leave her side. It was one of the longest twenty minutes in my life. When the doctor finally reappeared, I searched his face for any positive indication that his examination had merely confirmed

Alberta's belief that it was nothing more then fatty tissue. I saw no such sign and rose to my feet to follow him back into the exam room and to my precious Rosie. I searched her face as well, hoping for her positive retort, "It's all good, Bobby!" There was only silence as Rosie smiled her familiar warm smile that always brought me to a state of calm.

Extending her hand for me to hold, Rosie said with an unwavering and confident tone in her voice, "Sit down, Bobby, and let Dr. Chamberlan explain what he found."

Dr. Chamberlan leaned in toward us both and looked me directly in the eye. "There appear to be two nodules in your wife's left breast. The right appears to be clear, however I want to take scans of both, along with the lymph nodes around the area. Depending on what we find will determine if we need to take a biopsy."

"Okay, Doctor, what do we do after that?" I said, trying to maintain a calm demeanor.

"Right now, we don't need to concern ourselves with 'what if.' We don't need to deal with results we don't have. I want you to go back to your boys and enjoy your life. I will call you as soon as the results are in."

I heard myself thank Dr. Chamberlan, and I pulled Rosie close to me as we headed for the office door. He said something else about not worrying, but somehow the words sounded like they were coming from such a distance, I couldn't make them out. My only concern was Rosie and how the news was affecting her. The ride back home was more silence than conversation, and I could see Rosie's eyes were moist with tears although none of them had fallen onto her cheeks. Rosie was not one to jump ahead to the worst possible outcome in a situation, and this time was no different. Still, I knew my girl better than anyone, and I knew this had hit Rosie harder than she was letting on.

Finally, Rosie broke the silence. "Our God is bigger than the outcome, Bobby, and He will still be on the throne regardless of the test results. I don't want you to worry. Now, let's get home and have a nice dinner with our boys."

Reaching over she put her small, warm hand on my neck, giving it a light squeeze. Somehow, I knew we'd be okay, no matter what the test results might reveal. When we got home, the smell of Alberta's cooking filled the air, sealing that feeling of assurance. I sat back and watched as the Richards horde attacked their mother's fear with the greatest weapon of all, love.

* * *

I had slept for a couple of hours and woke to the sound of a football bouncing off the outer wall of my bedroom. Rolling over, I covered my head with the pillow but couldn't ignore the incessant barrage of incoming footballs. Then another sound caught my attention, a hair dryer. Who was using Rosie's hair dryer?

Throwing the pillow off, I rolled onto my back. "Hey, who's in my bathroom?"

"Me, silly, who did you expect?"

"Rosie, what are you doing home? You're supposed to be at work."

"I'll go in later. I got a call this morning from Dr. Chamberlan. He got the results from the scans and tests and wants to talk to me."

"Okay," I said, swinging off the bed and grabbing my pants off a hanger in the closet. "What did he say? Did he give you any results?"

"No. He just said he got the results back and that I needed to come in to talk."

Her voice began to crack, and I watched as she gripped the sides of the sink, bent over, and began to weep. Wrapping her in my arms, I pulled her close to me as she buried her face in my chest. There were no words to say. It wasn't a time for words. After several minutes, she gently pushed me away, wiped her eyes, and continued to prepare for her appointment.

* * *

Sitting in Dr. Chamberlan's office, an intense silence fell over the room as he thumbed through a stack of papers. Rosie took my hand and held it so tightly the blood drained from my fingertips, but that was okay. Looking up at us, Chamberlan's eyes reflected a hopeful sadness. With a few words, this elderly gentleman told us what we didn't want to hear, while expressing a hope that we desperately needed.

"Rosie, your biopsy showed that the lumps in your left breast are cancerous, but I believe we have caught it early. In 1971, President Nixon signed into law the National Cancer Act that has established national cancer research centers. You live in a very special time because major advances are being made in radiotherapy, chemotherapy, and surgery."

He stood up and walked around his desk and sat on its edge in front of us. "Rosie, you and Bobby need to make some very serious and difficult decisions as to how you want to address this. At present, the customary approach is radical mastectomy. It is the most extreme approach, but it has shown to be the most effective. There are, however, an increasing number of women choosing less invasive methods. Assuming the cancer hasn't spread, the option of a combination of both surgery and chemotherapy is available. There is a fair chance it hasn't spread in your case because it has been caught early. You and Bobby go home, read over the information, talk, pray, and get back with me in a few days and we can discuss everything more fully."

We were given a suitcase of material to read, and a new appointment was made, giving us a week to digest it. Rosie took on the task of getting to know what she was facing and the options that were laid before her, like she does with every challenge that comes her way. It wasn't long before she was explaining to me what was about to happen in medical terms that I couldn't begin to understand. It always made her laugh when I would look at her with the wide-eyed, head-tilted expression of a confused puppy. It brought a degree of levity to what could easily have been very depressing. When the day arrived for her appointment, I knew Rosie was ready, and regardless of the result, Jesus, Rosie, and I had it covered.

Dr. Chamberlan rose to his feet and gave Rosie a warm embrace, then he shook my hand, looked me in the eye, and said without a hint of hesitation, "We've got this, Bobby."

Confident that my love and attraction for her would not waver in the slightest no matter what physical alterations were required, Rosie chose the combination of both limited surgery and chemotherapy as Plan A. If there was any sign during the surgery that the cancer had spread then Plan B would go into effect, a radical mastectomy. As much as we disliked the necessity of this choice, there were four men at home who could not live without her.

She went back to work and made sure that everything was covered while she was off convalescing. She would receive calls, answer questions, and give directions from home. I made arrangements with the other watch commanders to cover my shifts over the four days Rosie would be in the hospital. When she was released, Alberta and Joe would take over while I went back to work. I can't imagine what people do who don't have a family to support them, and a God of compassion to lean on. The night before the surgery Rosie and I called the boys into the living room for a family powwow. Although the boys knew their mom had cancer and what we were facing as a family, Rosie wanted one last time with us all so that any last-minute questions or fears could be addressed. There were a few tears as expected, and Little Joe's prayer for God to provide wisdom and guidance to Dr. Chamberlan moved us all. Rosie assured the boys that although there were some changes coming, one thing would never change, her love and devotion for each of them. She was their mom, and she loved them to the moon and back.

With tears in our eyes, we circled around this beautiful lady and each of us laid our hands on her shoulder as I lifted my eyes and heart toward heaven. "Father, I know You are in total control of this situation and Rosie's cancer didn't catch you by surprise. You know the end of this matter as well as its beginning, and we commit your precious child, our mom, and my bride fully into Your care. Thank You, Lord, for loving our Rosie even more than we can imagine. In the power of Your name, we pray."

With that, five voices sounded a heartfelt, "Amen."

Following a round of warm hugs and expressions of love, the Richards clan closed the door that night on one chapter of their family journey, eagerly looking forward to a safe and healthy conclusion of the battle that lay ahead.

After Rosie was released, and the seven days of recuperation that followed, I got back to work. Sadly, we had to go to Plan B. Alberta took up residence in the guestroom, and Grandpa Joe took responsibility for the boys. It was hard to return to work, but it was also good because Rosie needed a break from me hovering over her.

CHAPTER SIX

The watch commander over the District 2 graveyard shift was taking a couple weeks off to help his wife introduce their newly born twin girls to their new home and family. These two young ladies rounded out the girls in their family to five, all beautiful and well mannered, ranging in age from three days to six years. I'm surprised he didn't take a couple months off. I would have shot for a year. Thank you, Lord, for boys.

I always enjoy working District 2 because of its diversity. Some of the finest restaurants in the Bay Area, and the best hot dog stands in the country are in District 2. It is also the center of Oakland's upscale retail district and where the newest hotels are located.

There are four large upper-middle-class housing tracks, each with its own preschool, elementary, and middle school, as well as a new public high school that's under construction. On the northeast section of the district is a very large park that is a dedicated nature reserve, with jogging paths and bike trails. It's fenced and gated and it closes at dusk. There are, as expected, those who ignore the signs and sneak into the park to set up camp, but they are quickly run off by privately hired park rangers. There have been a few assaults in the area, but most of the real crime is done by hungry birds and squirrels stealing picnic lunches.

The only real downfall of District 2 was Abel Glasser. Whenever I'm filling in for the watch commander of District 2, I know I'll probably have to deal with him. I remember first meeting Glasser in the squad room during briefing. It was when Sergeant Helmer was our watch commander, and he always began our shift by introducing new officers, cadets, reserves, dispatchers, and clerical staff. He wanted them to know that they were part of the team. It wasn't just the officers on the street, like you see in the movies. We all played a part in serving and protecting our community. He emphasized their importance by frequently saying that without any of them, the job simply wasn't going to get done.

The night of Glasser's first tour of duty, Sergeant Helmer began by introducing two recently sworn officers, new members to the graveyard shift.

"Gentlemen, we have two new additions to our early morning romp. A lateral transfer from LAPD, Officer Abel Glasser." In the far side of the room, a large guy with a military-style haircut waved his hand as if swatting away flies.

"You all know our next addition. She has been with OPD for eight years and has requested the opportunity to work patrol, Officer Chelsey Defo." Chelsey stood and gave a gentle wave to all in the room.

"Abe, why don't you tell us a little about yourself?" Sergeant Helmer asked. "What brought you up North?"

"Well to begin with, Sergeant, my name is Abel, not Abe, and able is what I am. I've worked the streets of LA for five years and wanted to go someplace a bit quieter for the next five."

"Well, welcome to the quiet streets of Oakland. Try to stay awake out there. Things can get pretty boring, especially for an experienced LA cop, like yourself," Helmer said a bit sarcastically.

Turning his attention to Chelsey, he said, "Officer Defo, tell us a little about yourself."

She stood and was about to speak when Abel said, "That's something you won't see in LA, women cops on patrol."

"Officer Glasser, you had your two minutes of fame. Now we want to hear from someone else. Since you are unaware of the protocol, let me bring you up to speed. When I talk, you don't. Do I make myself clear, Officer Glasser?"

"Yeah, loud and clear, Sergeant," he said with a snicker.

Glasser came with an attitude and a huge chip on his shoulder. He made no friends, nor did it appear that he wanted to. His experience in LA proved to be limited at best, yet for some reason he continued to work the street without receiving any direction or discipline. Truth be known, I doubt it would have done any good.

Voyaging through the dark alleys and mall parking lots, I listened to the usual chatter on the radio and caught the familiar voice of Abel Glasser making a traffic stop. Being close and not hearing any response from other officers willing to provide him cover, I rolled his way.

I spotted Glasser's vehicle on 7th Street West. He had pulled over a black 1951 Ford and was conducting a field sobriety test on a possible drunk driver. I was on the eastbound side of the street, so I had to go a quarter mile to get around the center divider. When I pulled up Glasser had a young man handcuffed and pinned against his car with one hand as the other was reaching for his mace container. The thin figure pushed up against the car was a boy of about eighteen, and he didn't appear to be resisting, simply had a broad grin on his face.

"Glasser, stop," I yelled, but he was already in a forward motion.

Aiming the canister and saying something only the boy could hear, he pressed the button on the top and a steady stream of liquid mace poured out, directly into Glasser's eyes. He had somehow turned the small container around in his hand.

"Aaah!" he screamed, dropping the canister and letting go of the boy.

The young man never made a move, just broke out in laughter. With eyes as red and swollen as ripe tomatoes, Glasser leaned against his car and began rubbing his eyes with his sleeve.

Taking the boy's arm, I pulled him away. "I'll put him in my car, and don't rub your eyes anymore. You'll only make it worse."

Just as I reached my car, Glasser let out a shout, "Okay, punk, how do you like this?" Stepping away from the car, he raised his size-fourteen boot and stomped on what appeared to be the boy's watch, crushing it under his foot. Strangely, this merely caused the boy to laugh hysterically, to the point of tears. I let go of him as he slid down the side of my car, heaving for air and laughing uncontrollably.

"Officer," he said, trying to catch his breath. After several gasps he looked up at me, struggling to get the words out. "I don't have a watch."

A two-man back-up unit arrived, and after putting the pieces of Glasser's watch in his shirt pocket, I instructed one of the officers to drive Abel back to the PD so he could wash out his eyes. The other officer would take custody of the boy and book him on a DUI.

With everyone gone, I kicked back and waited for a tow truck to impound the Ford. Yep, everything was back to normal.

It was a struggle for me to understand why Abel Glasser was allowed to continue working as a police officer for the city of Oakland. He was an absolute screwup. His ego and arrogance not only showed itself to the public but also endangered them and the other officers.

On one occasion I heard about officers being called out to a disturbance in the upscale neighborhood of Release Valley. Upon their arrival they were greeted by a dozen irate and angry neighbors equipped with flashlights and cameras, shouting at what appeared to be a blow-up snowman, like the ones you see at Christmas. It turned out to be Glasser in his tighty-whities and a T-shirt two sizes too small. He was standing over four whimpering boys ranging in ages from eleven to thirteen. Clipped on the waistband of his undies was his badge, and in his hand was his .357 Magnum service revolver.

"Handcuff them," Glasser demanded. "Put them all in juvenile hall. I'll write up the report in the morning."

"For what, Glasser?" one of the responding officers asked.

"Malicious mischief and trespassing."

He pointed to all the evidence, which was four rolls of toilet paper. It appeared the criminal intent of these wannabe hoodlums was to maliciously and feloniously attack Glasser's begonias by draping toilet paper on them.

Fortunately, the Big O happened to live on the next block and intervened. He was told of the call by his mother-in-law who lives with him and lies awake at night reading crime novels and listening to her police scanner.

The Big O stepped into the fray, ordered Glasser to go into his house, put his gun away, and put on a pair of pants. The responding officer took the boys' information and released them to their parents. When I heard what little attention this incident received from the brass, I had to ask. So I arranged for an appointment with my friend, and boss, Lieutenant Steven Miller.

"Come in and have a seat, Bobby. How is Rosie doing and those young men?"

"She's doing much better, thank you."

"So, what brings you into the hallowed halls where lieutenants reign?"

"I'm here about Abel Glasser."

"What kind of crap has he gotten into this time?"

"None, at least nothing that I knew about. My question is why he's made of Teflon. Nothing sticks to him. I know he's been written up, but nothing seems to ever happen to him."

"Okay, Bobby, I'll fill you in, but it doesn't leave this office, got it?"

"Got it. Understand, I'm not looking to jam him up. I'm just concerned that he might get somebody hurt."

"I understand. I don't believe he's going to be with us too much longer. We just want to make sure we have enough documentation to close the book on the governor's brother."

Stunned, I just sat there. When his words settled in my head, I said, "He's the governor's brother? Our governor? Are you telling me that Governor Wainwright is in the same bloodline as Abel Glasser?"

"Yep. Well, he's a half-brother," Miller said, shaking his head. "Abel's transfer from LAPD to OPD was a favor for the governor. Remember the Omnibus Crime Control and Safe Streets Act of 1968? When Congress passed legislation establishing the Law Enforcement Assistance Administration, each state's governing body determined where the money and assistance went. Thanks to Governor Wainwright, OPD got a big bite of that pie. Glasser was our way of returning the favor."

"So, we're stuck with him?"

"No, but you might want to be thankful. We were able to hire twenty-two new officers because of that grant, and you were one of them."

"So, I owe my career to Abel Glasser. Ouch," I said, rolling my eyes.

"There were two conditions Wainwright asked for," Miller went on. "One, never put it out that Glasser was related to him, and second, if his conduct became unacceptable, release him."

Sitting back in his chair, Lieutenant Miller held up a thick manila folder as a smile formed across his face. "He was offered a position with the Imperial County Sheriff's Office, overseeing a substation in a place called Slab City.

I'm not sure how they heard about Glasser, but my guess, it's another favor being fulfilled."

"I've never heard of Slab City. Where is it?"

"Ever hear of Salvation Mountain?"

"Yeah, isn't it a hill some guy made out of junk and painted it with religious symbols and scripture verses? I think it's down south, real close to the Mexican border."

"That's it. Salvation Mountain is at the entrance to the city. Population one hundred and fifty, but it can balloon during the winter months."

"Is he going to take it?"

"He came in here boasting about the opportunity to step up into what he perceived as a chief's position. I didn't correct him, but I did point out that one more complaint and he'd be unemployed. Bobby, you know it's only a matter of time and he'll screw up, so keep this under your hat. Let's just let him go out softly."

"I will. Thank you for taking the time."

Stopping at the door, I turned back and asked, "Sir, what kept Glasser from shouting from the rooftops that he was the governor's brother? He's so boastful I can't imagine him keeping that under wraps."

"Money," Miller said. "The family is loaded, and it's all wrapped up in some kind of trust. Wainwright has full control as to who gets what. If Glasser doesn't toe the line, he doesn't get a dime."

Walking back to my office, my head began to spin. I was having a hard time grasping that the governor of California and Abel Glasser drew life from the same bloodline. I hadn't always agreed with the decisions Governor Wainwright had made, but I'd never questioned his intelligence or integrity.

Officer Glasser was another story all together. The fact that he held his tongue and didn't use his relationship or abuse it, showed that he was more of a man than I took him for. Then again, it may be demonstrating how desperate he was for a financial free ride.

Over the last year working as the relief sergeant, I had been able to meet almost every zombie working the grave-yard shift. I had driven or walked every street, avenue, alley, and gravel road within the city limits. It was a city of extremes. There were those who were impoverished to the point of starvation, and the wealthy who were equal to royalty. Residences varied from gated palaces to cardboard boxes, and clothes were tattered rags or designer gowns.

It's all here, I thought, every culture, creed, and creation, and they're mine to care for as best I can. That was when the Motorola chirped. Little did I know that I was about to encounter one of those precious souls relegated to my care whose circumstances were daunting to the imagination.

"Dispatch to WC-3."

"Go ahead, Dispatch," I responded.

"Xray-6 went out on a possible medical assist at the Empyrean Towers on 13th Street. He's asking for your assistance."

"Ten-four, I'm en route."

The Empyrean Towers was a century-old, dilapidated hotel that had been condemned for years because of safety concerns, yet it continued to accommodate a full house. Because of its condition it was known as "Hotel Hell."

Parking between a firetruck and the EMT vehicle, I secured my car and went through a large wooden door that hung loosely off its hinges. Inside, I looked down a narrow hallway that cut through a series of pup tents and wood pallets. Midway down the hall, a tall, thin man of about fifty waved to me and shouted, "They're upstairs, at the end of the hall. Room 217."

"Thank you," I said, jogging past him and up a flight of steps that creaked and groaned as I ascended.

"Back here, Sergeant," Officer Jeff Winer said, waving to me at the end of the hall.

Stepping into the room, I was overtaken by the stench. Reaching into my utility pouch, I removed a small twist-top container of mentholated Vaseline and put a touch on my upper lip and passed it on to Jeff.

"Put a little of this under your nose."

I asked where the EMTs were, and Jeff pointed to a door on the right side of the room. I looked back to see that he had almost smeared the whole container under his nose, all over his mustache, and partially around his mouth. He was having a hard time with the smell, almost as hard a time as he was going to have trying to get that stuff off his face.

Inside the room, lying on a king-size bed that almost filled the room from wall to wall, was the biggest human being I had ever seen. On either side of him EMTs worked feverishly, attaching and examining a portable EKG machine and inserting an IV. Next to them stood two firemen watching intently.

"What do we have, Jeff?"

"The big guy has had a stroke, and the EMTs say they have to get him to the hospital because he keeps having small, repeated strokes. The problem is he's nearly six hundred pounds, and there's no way to get him out of here. If we don't get him to the hospital, they believe he'll die."

"What's his name?"

"Earl Quantel. He's lived here for the past eight years."

"Any family?"

"None that we know about. He hasn't been able to communicate."

"Okay, Jeff, go through his things and see what you can find. There has to be somebody feeding this guy."

Approaching the firemen, I said, "Gentlemen, I'm Sergeant Richards, do you have a plan on how we can get him out of here?"

"There's no way we can get him down the steps," one of the EMTs said. "Even if we had the manpower, he's too big to fit through the stairwell."

"How about the windowed French doors and side panels? If we take the doors off their hinges, it may be big enough," I said, pointing to the back wall. "I don't know how we get him through it, but if we do, do you have a ladder that can hold him?"

"Nope." The fireman shrugged. "I'm surprised the floor joists in this dump are holding him up."

Turning to Jeff, who was going through the drawers of an old, scuffed-up dresser, I asked, "Jeff, have you found anything?"

"Yes, Sergeant," he said, holding up a stack of opened letters. "He has an aunt and an uncle living in Walnut Creek. I have their address, but no phone number."

"Okay, contact Walnut Creek PD, fill them in, and have them swing by the address and make a notification."

"Sergeant, I don't think there's anything we can do," one of the firemen said. "I mean, he really did it to himself."

He may have been right, but I couldn't help but feel sorry for Earl Quantel. He might be responsible for his condition that had imprisoned him in this room, but God found sufficient cause to give him life. I'm not so sure I had the right to write him off.

I noticed Earl watching the firemen and listening to their conversation. They weren't being cruel, but the way they were discussing the situation dehumanized him. I wondered how he saw himself. At what point had he given up and lost hope? You could see it in his eyes. It wasn't despair but acceptance, a resignation of the soul. I leaned down at his side, and he turned slightly to look at me.

"Earl, we're going to get you out of here. We're going to get you to a doctor, so just hang in there," I said.

A slight smile formed on his face, but the reflection in his eyes spoke his heart. He knew nothing was going to change even if we did get him out of there. He did not fear death; he desired it. Life itself had reached a point where it was too much to bear.

Walking out into the hall, I went to the far end and looked through a window that overlooked Highway 80. I wasn't going to give up on him, although I had a feeling that most of those in his life already had. Closing my eyes, I sought an answer to an impossible question, and there was only One who could provide the answer.

"Lord, how do we get this man to the hospital?"

CHAPTER SEVEN

My silent prayer was interrupted by the sound of sirens. My attention was drawn to the highway where a white specialized industrial fire engine, equipped with fire suppression apparatus to fight refinery fires, headed north, running Code-3. Refinery! That's it.

I ran back into the room. "Anyone know if Earl has a phone?"

"I don't think so," one of the EMTs said.

"I'll be back. Keep him alive," I shouted over my shoulder, then ran to my car.

"Dispatch, this is WC-3, drop to Tac 2."

"Ten-four, WC-3."

I waited a few seconds then switched to Tac 2.

"Dispatch, I need you to patch me through to Shell Refinery Maintenance. Ask for J. Johansen, Maintenance Supervisor."

"Got it, WC, stand by."

After ten minutes, the baritone voice of Jack Johansen, Maintenance Supervisor, came on the line. "Bobby, it's been some time since I've heard from you. I'm told you have a problem; how can I help?"

I filled Jack in on the situation, and it got quiet on his end of the line.

"Jack, you still there? Jack?"

"Yeah, yeah. I'm here. I'm just trying to figure out what to do. Give me the address."

Within thirty minutes a bright yellow crane truck, known as a boom truck, was parked at the end of the street. Capable of lifting heavy steel and concrete to significant heights, Earl Quantel should not be a problem. Now it's just a matter of getting him out.

Clearing the police, EMT, and fire vehicles from in front of the building, Jack maneuvered his oversized Tonka toy into place. Suspended from the end of the crane's boom was a steel pallet a little larger than Earl's bed. It hung flat, secured by a cable on each of the four corners. The hotel's glass doors and side panels leading out onto the hotel balcony were removed, and Jack skillfully settled the pallet onto the balcony floor.

This was going to be the hard part, and it came with the greatest risk. The Empyrean Towers were built in the late 1800s and had been abandoned for decades. There was nothing up to code, and it had a history of being one of the most dangerous buildings in the city. There was always the possibility of the crane dropping our patient to the street below, but the greatest danger was the floor giving way under our collective weight, bringing the entire building down.

I, along with two firemen, two EMTs, and four police officers I had called in to help, surrounded Earl's bed. Taking a firm grip on the mattress, we lifted Earl slowly, then shuffled, inch by inch toward the balcony. With each movement the floor groaned under our weight, and I'm sure I felt the surface under my feet give way and drop an inch or two.

Carefully, Earl was moved into place on the platform. EMTs covered him with the blankets from his bed, and one remained on the pallet holding an IV bottle. With amazing expertise Jack backed the crane away from the balcony, and lowered Earl down on the surface of a flatbed truck. With an EMT and a fireman at Earl's side, they were off to the hospital with a police escort.

Standing on the balcony, I looked down at a horde of reporters and cameramen gathered around the crane looking up. I waved to Jack and thanked him for his help, knowing that it was going to cost me lunch one day soon.

Suddenly, without warning, the balcony groaned, and the floor dropped by a foot and pulled another three feet away from the building. My heart leapt into my throat as I gripped the only small piece of railing that remained and watched the audience below scatter like roaches in the sunlight.

"We gotcha, let go of the railing," an officer said as he gripped my uniform shirt, pulling me back into the building, just as the remaining parts of the small deck gave way.

"Wow . . . thanks," I said, as I watched the falling debris scatter around the hotel's entrance.

The room was quiet as I got to my feet. "Gentlemen, thank you for all your help. Let's get out of here before this place falls down around our ears."

Looking at the opening we created by removing the doors and side panels, I was wondering when I could get back here to fix it.

Behind me the voice of the man who met and directed me when I arrived said, "Sergeant, I'll put everything back the way it was, if that's okay."

"Sure, thank you. I know Earl will appreciate it too."

"He won't be back, will he?"

"I don't know. I doubt he'll be staying up here if he does."

"Okay. I'll get some boxes and make sure all his stuff gets packed up. He's got some family that comes by almost every day, I'll give it all to them. Earl is a real nice guy. You should meet him when he's not sick. You'd like him."

"I'm sure I would."

On my way home I tried to imagine what it was like for Earl in his world. To be totally dependent on others for literally everything. His very existence rested completely on the care and compassion of others. As I drove, I thought of a world filled with Earls, each disabled by circumstance, condition, or choice, whose hope rested solely in the hands of others. I had often heard A. J. say, "Only by the grace of God go I." How true that is.

Stopping short of the driveway that led to my personal oasis, I watched my legacy at work in the garage as my bride planted a new patch of Douglas Iris in the planter boxes Papa Joe built for her. God had blessed me beyond measure, but He had not done so for my personal pleasure or exclusive benefit. I knew I had been blessed in order to bless others. There was no better example for me to follow than the man standing at Rosie's side digging holes in fresh soil, Papa Joe. He was the definition of a good man.

After a round of compliments on Joe's workmanship and Rosie's choice of flower and greetings from the crew,

I grabbed a bite to eat and slid between a pair of sheets for some well-deserved shut-eye.

* * *

Something tenderly touched my cheek, warm, soft, and familiar. "Wake up, Bobby." Another tender kiss and I decided to stay put and see where this was going to lead.

Unfortunately, I am the father of three human beings who do not see a closed door as a deterrent, nor do they have any regard for my privacy. "Wake up, Dad," Little Joe said, throwing the door open.

"Get up, old man, time to celebrate your existence," Sonny said.

"Happy birthday to you, happy birthday to you," Critter began as the rest chimed in. It may not have made it into the top ten, but it sure resonated with me.

"Open up, Daddy," Rosie said, as she smeared white frosting on my nose, then put a small piece of cake in my mouth. "Happy Birthday, sweetheart. I love you, Bobby, to the moon and back."

"Okay, guys, some alone time with Mom is in order," I said, as I pulled Mom down beside me.

"Good grief, Dad, we'd tell you to get a room, but it looks like you've got that covered already." Within seconds we were alone.

Rosie curled up next to me, put her head on my chest, and said, "I think we just discovered a way to get some privacy."

"Yeah, we got to buy bigger bricks, they keep getting out of the closet."

For my birthday we decided to bundle up nice and warm, take a thermos of Rosie's special hot chocolate blend, and take seats among a group of obsessed parents, as our offspring hit the field to battle the dreaded Coyotes from Coyote Creek High School. I spotted our warrior as he turned and waved at us from the sidelines. Little Joe had been a member of the Bobcats junior varsity football team of Chabot High for the last two years. This was his first varsity game with the big guys. He had shown himself to be a pretty good tight end, and I thought football was his game, but last week he said that when the season was over, he was going out for track. Oh the joy of youth and the endless array of possibilities.

Sonny and Casey, along with their mother, jumped to their feet and began to shout when they saw him, as if he were the only player on the field. I couldn't be prouder of them, great young men in the making, and a woman of wisdom and beauty.

The Bobcats cheerleading team came dancing out onto the field behind the players, dressed in bright red and white, the team colors, and waving large pom-poms over their heads. As they were forming to lead us in a cheer, one of the girls, an attractive young lady with chestnut hair and a big smile, waved in our direction, and Rosie waved back.

"Who is that?" I asked.

"Just a friend," Rosie said with a slight grin.

As the cheers began, an Oakland police officer walked along a narrow sidewalk between the bleachers and the sideline. He was volunteering his time working security. He most likely had a child that attended Chabot who was either on the field or one of the cheerleaders. Almost every cop in the department with kids in school could be found one time or another working the games, dances, or any number of other activities.

Stopping in front of us he looked at me. "Sir, are you Sergeant Richards?"

"Yeah, that's me."

"Dispatch said that if I saw you here, I was to have you call in when you could."

"Okay, did it sound serious? I'd like to catch the kickoff."

"I don't think so, sir. They just said when you can."

"Great, thanks."

At half-time the Bobcats were holding their own, a perfect time to call in.

"Oakland Police Department, is this an emergency?"

"No, this is Sergeant Richards, I was told to call in."

"Yes, Sergeant, please hold."

"Bobby, this is Carol Swenson, Lieutenant Miller wants to speak with you, but I wanted to catch you first and wish you a happy birthday."

Carol was the department's clerical supervisor and had worked for OPD for nearly twenty-five years. She came to work as a dispatcher a year after her husband, Chuck Swenson, a detective with the San Francisco Police Department, was ambushed while eating his lunch at a Doggy Diner.

The killer was a fifteen-year-old boy who was being initiated into the Golden Diablos, also known as the Devils, a street gang in the Mission District of San Francisco. He was given a gun and told that the only way he could show he had the guts to be a member of the Diablos was to kill someone before dawn.

According to his confession, he had snuck out of his house at four in the morning to earn his place in the gang. The streets were empty at that time, so he walked around looking for a homeless victim, someone sleeping on the street or in a doorway. That is when he came upon the all-night Doggy Diner.

The only person around was a man sitting outside by himself at one of the round metal tables. When the boy approached, the man looked up at him, smiled, and asked him why he was out so late. Then he asked if he was hungry and if he wanted a hot dog. That was when Alberto Perez pulled out his gun and shot Detective Chuck Swenson three times, point blank.

Perez was arrested without resistance a block away from his home as he casually walked down the darkened streets. His confession was not made by a child weeping over what he had done, but rather boastfully by a proud member of the Golden Diablos. He will never attend one of their meetings or parties, because he was sentenced as an adult to life without the possibility of parole, but the story doesn't end there.

Carol has visited Alberto in prison every week since he was convicted. I sat on her employment interview and questioned her about her motive for reaching out to him. She said that she hates what Alberto Perez did and has had private fits of rage over it, but she didn't have the right to seek revenge, and she had been commanded to love him. The visits were therapeutic for them both.

With the exception of his lawyer, she was the only visitor he has ever had. His family and the Diablos have totally written him off. It wasn't easy, but over time they bonded, forming a deep relationship, one in which Carol refers to Alberto as her son.

Rosie was instrumental in getting Carol to speak at one of the Christian women's conferences some years back. She was so well received that she has been invited almost every year to come and share her heart and how Alberto was doing. He was now the senior chaplain's assistant at Folsom State Prison and the author of several books and two devotionals.

"Okay, Bobby, I'll connect you to Lieutenant Miller. Have a great birthday."

"Bob, I heard what happened this morning at the Empyrean Towers. I sent Chaplain Burchett to the hospital to check on Earl Quantel and speak to any family that was there. He called me a couple hours ago and told me Earl passed about three hours after arriving at the hospital. His heart just couldn't take it. I thought you would want to know."

"Yeah, thanks." The tone in my voice gave me away. "If we could have moved just a little faster."

"You did a great job, Bobby. You did all that could be done. You know as well as I do, sometimes the dragon wins."

"Yeah, I know, but this time, Lieutenant, he didn't win. That big man is now free, probably for the first time in his life."

CHAPTER EIGHT

Tonight is what we call the "Double Dump." Happens once a year, every year. It's when the clock falls back an hour, letting barflies double down on getting "cork high and bottle deep." Some of the finer establishments close their bars at 1:00 a.m. on this night, rather than 2:00 a.m., putting the first wave of inebriated Mario Andretti's behind the wheel. An hour later, those that remained open to earn an extra buck push their intoxicated piston-heads out onto the street so they can join the race.

Things tend to pick up during the two hours following the bar dump, and thanks to daylight savings time, tonight we will get an extra hour of tanked-up insanity. If by some good fortune the bar's benefactors make it home without running over someone, getting into an accident, or being arrested, that's when the family fun begins. Normally, by 4:00 a.m. things have settled down, and only those without a home, or thrown out of theirs, are found wandering the streets.

I picked up a cup of coffee and a sandwich from an all-night McDonald's and found a quiet spot to park overlooking the city. Before my shift was over, I needed to review some of the arrest reports submitted by my team. Of course, just when I got settled in, the tranquility of the early morning was shattered.

"Xray-10, possible abduction in progress, Empire Place apartments, 1850 Empire Avenue. Apartment A. Unit to cover?"

Xray-10 was Officer Chelsey Defo, Oakland's first woman to work the street and, with the exception of my departed friend A. J., probably the best cop I'd ever known. Grabbing the mic, I spun a donut in the street, "1850 Empire, WC-2 en route."

A block away I shut off the lights and rolled to a stop behind a large, overgrown manzanita tree about thirty yards from the apartment. The complex consisted of four rows of five identical rundown fourplexes with carports in front of each. The ground floor doors faced each other under a set of stairs that led to the apartments above. The second story apartment doors faced each other across a small landing at the top of the stairs. The back of the building was against a small hill that sloped back some fifty yards to an open field.

Empire Place was well known for drug and domestic disturbance calls, and it wasn't uncommon to have a shooting or stabbing at least once a month. It had gotten so bad at one point, OPD had set up a substation in the apartment next to the office. Unfortunately, it was short lived due to budgetary constraints.

"WC-2, go to Tac 2," a channel used to communicate information during critical incidents. It provided a place to speak openly without code, allowing for more detailed instruction.

"Dispatch, this is WC-2, go ahead."

"Bob, I have Susan Kempner on the line. She's at a neighbor's with her boyfriend. Her husband, Lionel Kempner, is in her apartment with her nine-year-old daughter. Lionel is not her father. He showed up unexpectedly and forced his way in. He beat up the boyfriend and threw them both out. Lionel was recently released from Pelican Bay and has been known to be armed and violent."

Taking the mic, I said, "Got it. Do we know if he is armed? Did she see if he had any weapons on him?"

After a moment's silence, she replied, "He wasn't armed when he came into the house, but her boyfriend has a 9mm Smith & Wesson in the nightstand on the left side of the bed."

"Okay. Tell her to come out with her friend and walk straight to the road. She'll see me there."

Our suspect's last known address was Pelican Bay State Prison. This was not good. Pelican Bay housed California's most violent prisoners. The majority were serving life sentences, and all had been transferred there because of violent assaults they committed in other state prisons. That along with Kempner's history, the access to a gun, and the little girl, presented a recipe for disaster.

"Bob, this is Lieutenant Miller. Don't approach, keep it as quiet as possible, let's not wake the neighborhood. I have the SWAT wagon en route. They're bringing with them Sergeant Max Acker, our hostage negotiator. He will assume command unless things go bad, then the tactical team commander takes over. I've called some dayshift officers in early. They'll rally with you for possible crowd control and help keep the media away as much as possible."

"It's pretty quiet at the moment, Lieutenant. I hope to keep it that way."

Even with an extra hour of sleep, Oakland was waking up early. In the distance I could hear a siren, but assumed it was heading for a call somewhere else. Just as I keyed the mic to acknowledge the lieutenant's instructions, an OPD unit with lights on and siren blaring rolled past us and up to the front of the suspected building.

"What was that?" Lieutenant Miller shouted.

"Officer Glasser, sir. He rolled in hot."

Now I'm in the middle of a possible child abduction, by a barricaded and possibly armed suspect with a violent history, and who shows up, that obnoxious LA transfer. Stepping out of his car he stood there, lit up like a Christmas tree in the flashing multicolored lights. A civilian ride-along that was in his car with him slid out the passenger door and moved to the back, looking at us with an expression of fear and stunned amazement.

"Glasser, turn off those lights and get your tail back here," I said.

Turning around he glared at me, then walked casually toward me, refusing to turn the lights off, as apartment windows lit up throughout the complex.

"So, do you need a real cop to take care of this?" Glasser said mockingly.

"Richards, is Glasser near you?" Lieutenant Miller shouted through the radio.

"Yes, sir."

"Glasser, this is Lieutenant Miller, can you hear me?"

"Yes, sir. Loud and clear."

"What the hell's wrong with you? You know better than to roll in hot on a hostage call," Miller growled.

"Well, sir, in LA we moved into situations like this fast and loud. A few flash bangs, a quick entrance, and it's all over before you know it," Glasser said arrogantly.

"Right . . . well, Glasser, we do things differently here in sleepy Oakland. Get your butt behind the building. Don't do anything, just cover the back. Got it?"

"Yes, sir," he said and disappeared between the buildings.

"And turn off those lights," I shouted.

The SWAT wagon arrived, parked, and the tactical team deployed in seconds. Mrs. Kempner and her boyfriend were placed in Officer Defo's car, where they were quickly interviewed by Sergeant Acker. After several minutes he stepped away from Defo's car and took a seat in the SWAT wagon. Calling the Kempner home, he made contact with Lionel by phone and began to negotiate a quick resolution. Getting the little girl out safely was our first and, at the moment, only concern. Doing it before the apartments unloaded a mob on us was running a strong second.

Two SWAT team officers approached the building and evacuated apartments B, C, and D, while Acker kept Kempner busy on the phone. Chelsey and I knocked on the doors of the buildings on either side of the Kempner fourplex, waking up the residents and evacuating them to an open field about a hundred yards from the targeted building.

Returning to the area around the SWAT wagon, we gathered and waited. Fortunately, other than the evacuees, only a few of the Empire Place residents ventured out into the early morning air to see what was happening. Either they were deep sleepers, or our presence was so routine it wasn't worth getting out of bed for.

My portable radio crackled with the voice of Sergeant Acker. "SWAT stand down. The little girl is coming out. I repeat, stand down, the little girl is coming out."

"Come with me, Chelsey," I said, and we approached the building and crouched behind the bullet resistant shields of the two SWAT officers who had cleared the building.

The door to the upper left apartment opened, and a small girl, dressed in pink pajamas and holding a teddy bear, walked out and down the steps, one at a time. Chelsey stepped from behind the shields, opened her arms, scooped up the girl, and ran back to the wagon.

Acker's voice split the air again. "The girl is safe. Kempner will be coming out next. He is unarmed and has been instructed to descend the steps with his hands clasped behind his head."

The two SWAT officers with the shields split up, taking a position on either side of the stairwell. I remained behind the one on the right. Kempner appeared at the door with his hands behind his head. Slowly he moved down the steps and at the bottom dropped to his knees. I patted him down, cuffed him, and stood him to his feet. Walking him back, the two SWAT officers ran up the steps and entered the apartment. Moments later they reappeared and shouted toward the SWAT wagon, "It's all clear."

"We are Code-4, I repeat, we are Code-4. The building is clear, the suspect is in custody," Acker said.

"Attention all units, Empire Place is Code-4," Dispatch repeated to alert all who had been monitoring the situation.

Just as the team gathered, the sound of gunfire sounded from Kempner's building. Everyone immediately resumed their tactical positions. In the apartment on the bottom right of the building, a faint outline of a figure moving through the rooms could be seen, and the sound of someone yelling could be heard. Scanning the perimeter, I could see two snipers, one on a knoll to my left, and the other on the roof of the SWAT wagon. They were fixing their sights on the outlined figure behind the thin curtains.

"Are you sure everyone is out of that building?" I asked the SWAT commander.

"Yes, sir, my men went through each apartment to make sure."

I keyed my portable. "Glasser, do you see any movement back there?"

After a long unanswered pause, I said, "Glasser, this is Sergeant Richards, answer your radio, now."

The lights came on inside the bottom right apartment and the door slowly opened. Officer Glasser stepped out with a grin.

"It's all clear down here," he shouted as he casually walked toward us.

"Explain to me what you were doing in that apartment? You were told to cover the back, and why didn't you answer your radio?" I barked.

"Sorry about that. I forgot to take the radio with me," he said with a smirk. "I waited back there and didn't hear anything for some time. It seemed reasonable to me to get into that apartment as quickly as possible and rescue that little girl."

"The girl's been rescued, Kempner's in custody, and that's the wrong apartment," Lieutenant Miller shouted as he exited his car. "I want you to get in your car, now."

"Hey, Lieutenant, I was only making sure—" Glasser began.

"Not another word, Glasser," Lieutenant Miller said between gritted teeth. "Get in your car and return to the PD. There is a chair in the hall outside my office. I expect to see you in it when I get there. Now move."

I instructed a couple of the dayshift officers who were called in to let the residents know that they could return to their homes, and to be sure to thank them for their cooperation.

Lieutenant Miller accompanied Chelsey and I inside the apartment Glasser had been in to see if there was any damage. We had heard a shot, so there was going to be something broken.

Once inside we found the rear sliding glass door shattered and a bullet hole through the back of the couch. Several things made of glass were broken on the floor, and all but one open door had been kicked in, pulling them nearly off their hinges.

"I truly believe the cheese has slipped off that boy's cracker," I said, assessing the damage. Walking back into the living room we found a heavyset woman in a flowered nightgown and robe standing at the open front door, looking around the room.

"What happened in here?" she asked softly.

"Ma'am, I am deeply sorry for the damage. Your apartment was mistaken as the one where a little girl had been taken hostage," Lieutenant Miller said as he wrote on his business card. Handing it to her, he said, "We will help you clean this all up. Tomorrow, call the number on the back and ask for the Community Services office. They will fix and reimburse you for any damage. I will let them know you will be calling."

"I just got that sofa from Goodwill," she said, looking at the hole in the couch.

"Well, it looks like you will have to go to a real nice, expensive furniture store and get yourself another one," Miller said with a smile. "Now, Officer Defo will help you straighten up here. If there is anything else you need, just let us know. Again, I sincerely apologize for our mistake."

"Is the little girl okay?" she asked.

"Yes, she is just fine."

"Good. That's all that really matters."

Chelsey joined me as we spent the next hour cleaning up glass and trying to rehang the bedroom doors. A guy from the city's corporation yard where public works stores equipment, vehicles, and materials, brought in a couple of sheets of plywood and covered the broken patio door.

As we were about to leave, the lady told us she had nothing to give us, but if we wouldn't mind, she would like to thank us by praying for us. Chelsey was quick to accept, so I stood there silently as the two held hands and prayed. I don't think I could have been so amenable if my home had been ransacked and my belongings busted up, but this sweet lady took it in stride. I guess you could chalk it up to being old, or maybe it was just a grandma gene. I've seen others, even Rosie, smile at adversity. She says that it was a peace that Jesus gave her, not when things were good, but when things went horribly bad. Me, I usually flew off the handle.

I had no idea that Chelsey was the religious type. She sure was getting into the prayer thing.

Following the morning's briefing, Abel Glasser signed out and simply disappeared. Word had it, he was offered a job in a small Southern California town as its sole law enforcement officer. Just one more community of folks we needed to add to our prayer list.

CHAPTER NINE

It's been two years since Rosie's surgery, and as we entered the Christmas season, we were blessed to receive the news that her biannual checkup revealed no sign of the cancer returning. The past twenty-four months hadn't been easy, but it was getting better. I had to wake up and grow up to recognize that the pain she had experienced went far deeper than what the surgery inflicted on her body. She had undergone a dramatic physical change, but that paled to the emotional scarring. It had taken a season, but my sweet Rosie had come to see that I found her more beautiful now than at any time in the past. The boys and I were taking her out for dinner to celebrate the good news at a teppanyaki restaurant. She loved the food, and the boys love the entertaining way it gets cooked.

After dinner we went for a drive through the various neighborhoods that are known for their elaborate Christmas decorations. In one location we parked, got out, and walked through the light show. Midway through we were given a cup of hot cocoa.

As I watched my family stroll through all the glitter, illuminated snowmen, reindeer, and Santas, I was once again overwhelmed with gratitude. I do not deserve the kindness and goodness of God's grace, but He chose nonetheless to give it to me. That was reaffirmed on the next block as we stood before a depiction of the greatest Christmas gift of all, a Lamb, that was born to die, so that all might live.

Filled with dinner, cocoa, and Christmas cheer, I dropped my crew off at home and headed to work. The first couple of hours of my shift were quiet, allowing me to enjoy my coffee, but it was too quiet to last.

"WC-3, I have a full board due to mutual aid at People's Park and we have a medical assist at the Webster Arms Apartments, 1660 Canal Street, building D, apartment 2. It's on the ground floor. This may be an infant. EMTs en route."

"Ten-four, I got it," I said, keying the mic on the dash.

It was 3:00 a.m. on a Monday morning with a chill in the air that had sent most night owls home to the comfort of warm blankets. There was little traffic on the street this early, so I spun the wheel, bounced hard over the center divider, hit the lights and siren, and punched it. Despite the empty streets and my foot driven almost to the firewall of the Ford Interceptor, it still took me over five minutes to get to my destination. To my surprise the EMTs hadn't arrived either.

The complex was one of the oldest multi-family projects in the city. Built in the late 1940s, the multiplex housed the families of employees and soldiers stationed at the Oakland Army Terminal. Little had been done to make improvements over the years, and the only fresh paint those walls had seen was the multiple layers of graffiti. The windows of apartment 2 were covered with tinfoil on the inside, and the wood around the doorknob and deadbolt-lock had been chipped away where someone tried to break in.

Checking the door, I found it unlocked, so I banged on it several times with no response. Pushing the door open, I stepped in.

"Oakland Police, I'm coming in. Police officer."

On an old, tattered couch sat a woman in her early thirties in a floral nightgown, as old and warn as the sofa. The room reeked of the sweet, woody smell of marijuana, and although I burst through the door she didn't react or even look up.

"Where's the baby?" I shouted but got no response. "The baby, where is it?"

In the back of the room was a small kitchen, to my right a short hallway with three doors. The first door led to a bathroom, the second a bedroom that could have been mistaken for the city dump. A lamp without a shade sat on a side table next to several used syringes, a spoon, a lighter, and a large figure sprawled on the bed, but there was no baby.

Behind the next door there was just as big a mess, but it had a cradle, with a little person the size of a loaf of bread lying next to a folded pillow. I scooped up the tiny human, and the blanket next to it, and ran through the apartment out onto the street expecting to see the EMT vehicle, but I was alone.

Laying the child on the passenger seat, I began CPR with one hand, and with the other keyed the mic. "Dispatch, I'm running Code-3 to Montgomery General with a non-responsive infant. Tell them I'm coming and get someone over to Webster Arms and secure the scene."

"Ten-four, WC-3."

Starting the car, I flipped on the lights and siren, put it in gear, and floored it, without stopping the rapid three-finger

depressions on the baby's chest. Out in front of Montgomery General's emergency entrance stood a cluster of white
and blue gowns that converged on my car as I rolled in.
While a medical team cared for the child, a nurse took the
information I had, as sparse as it was. I got the names of the
doctors for my report and told the nurse that I would call
with the parents' info as soon as it was available.

"Dispatch, this is WC-3, drop to Tac 2."

"WC-3, how's the patient?"

"I'm not sure, but it doesn't look good. I'm ten-eight
from Montgomery General, going back to Webster Arms.
Who did you assign the call to?"

"The original call went to you because all units on
my board were active. Although it's outside of her area of
responsibility, I assigned Officer Defo because she was the
first to become available, and she's good at dealing with parents in these situations."

"Good job, thanks. Complete an incident report from
your prospective of the call and the following events. I want
to make sure we cover all the bases on this."

"Done, WC."

Back at the apartment, Officer Defo was sitting at a small
wooden table with the woman, holding her hands. On the
sofa sat a pile of hair in a hoodie with its head in its hands.

"What's your name, sir?" I asked the sofa dweller.

There was no response. That's when this human lint
began to snore. This pile of waste was sleeping while his
baby was being taken to the hospital. I looked up at Defo
who shrugged and shook her head.

"They haven't even asked about the baby. I don't think
it's theirs," she said.

I nudged the shaggy mop hard, and he fell back on the couch, let out a groan, and began to curse. "Hey man, that's police brutality. You can't put your hands on me in my own home."

There was something familiar about him, but I couldn't place it.

"You got some ID?"

"I don't need to show you nothin'. This is my home, get out."

"I don't think so," I said, getting a firm grasp of his collar with my left hand and a clump of greasy hair with the other. Shifting my weight to my right foot, I dropped my shoulder and pulled. He didn't expect that reaction from me and was easily lifted off the cushion and onto his face on the floor.

Putting my knee on his back I cuffed him and said, "You're under arrest for possession of drug paraphernalia and child neglect." That proclamation drew from him a hailstorm of expletives, as I removed a wallet from his pocket, and from it an Oregon driver's license.

"Officer Defo, do you have ID on her?"

"Yes, Sergeant," she said, handing me a California driver's license.

Keying the mic on my portable radio, I said, "Dispatch, wants and warrants on two."

"Go ahead, WC-3."

"First, William Steven Kurkland, D-O-B 8-16-50. Second, Katty Louise Russell, D-O-B 3-10-52."

"Ten-four, WC-3, stand by."

In the kitchen I pulled up a chair and turned the woman's chair to face me. Sitting quietly for a moment I let her see the sincerity on my face.

"Katty, is that baby yours?"

"Yes," she said as tears pooled in her eyes.

"Did you give birth to that baby?"

"Keep your mouth shout!" yelled the hairball on the floor.

She began to shake. "No, but he's mine."

"Katty, listen to me. If that child dies, you and your boyfriend will be charged with murder. Now I want names and how you came into possession of him."

"Don't I have rights?"

"Not yet, not until we know what we're dealing with. Now whose baby is he?"

"Shut your mouth, don't say another word. I'll kill ya!"

"Officer Defo, go put him in my car, and if he gives you any trouble, any trouble at all, put him in the trunk and cover him in mace. That's an order," I said, with as much growl in my voice as I could muster.

"Yes, Sergeant," Defo snapped, "Won't that look bad? That'll be the second one this week."

"Don't worry about it. I forgot about the last guy, but a corp yard mechanic found him when he came in on Monday morning. Nobody cared then, they won't care now."

"Yes, Sergeant," Chelsey said with a wink.

The mouth on the floor went silent. When Chelsey reached for him, he pulled back and got up on his feet without any assistance. As he turned to look at me, I could tell he wanted to say something but clearly thought better of it and went out willingly, without resistance or discussion. Watching her boyfriend being escorted out in handcuffs brought Katty to the point of panic.

"He was abandoned. The baby was just left in the park. Nobody wanted him, so we took him." She began to cry. "He's ours now."

"Calm down, Katty. It's wonderful that you were the ones to find him because you really care. What park was he in when you found him?"

"It was in Concord, where all those little kids' rides are, the spinning cups and stuff."

"You mean the Pixieland Amusement Park?"

"Yeah, that's it, Pixieland. Billy wanted to go there last week."

"Officer Defo, I'll be right back," I said as she came back in. "Did he give you any trouble?"

"Nope. Gentle as a lamb."

Looking around the kitchen and living room, I asked, "Katty, where is your phone? I need to call in."

"I don't have one," she said.

"How did you call the police department for help with the baby?"

"I didn't," she said.

Going into the baby's room, I switched my portable radio to Tac 2 and keyed the mic. "Dispatch, MC-3, come in."

"Go ahead, Sergeant."

"Contact Concord PD and ascertain if an infant has been reported missing from Pixieland Amusement Park within the last two weeks. If so, connect me with the investigating officer."

"Ten-four, WC-3."

Gripping the rail of the crib I closed my eyes and spoke from my heart. "Lord, that little man needs your help. He doesn't have enough time in grade to do anything wrong. He was just at the wrong place at the wrong time. Guide the hands of the doctors and give them a clear eye, and, Lord, help us to reunite him with his family. He's in your hands."

"WC-3, I have info. Are you ready to copy?"

"Go ahead."

"Sergeant, an infant was reported abducted from the Pixieland Amusement Park last Tuesday. Detective George Austin, Concord PD, is working the case. I have him on the line and will connect you when we're done. Is there anything else you need from me."

"No, not at this time. Go ahead and connect us and record our conversation for the report."

"Sergeant Richards, I'm Detective Austin, Concord PD, call me George."

"George, I'm Bob."

"Okay, Bob, I understand you may have some info about a child that was reported missing from Pixieland last week?"

"That's affirmative. We have in custody Billy Kurkland and Katty Russell who were found with a baby that isn't theirs. According to Russell they found the baby abandoned in Pixieland Park and took him home. The child is presently at Montgomery General."

"What's the condition of the child?"

"I don't know, I haven't gotten any word. I'm still at the apartment where the child was found. The subjects we have in custody will be transported to the PD for interview. We need to determine if the little guy is your missing case."

"I'm going to reach out to the family right now. I'll arrange to meet them at the hospital and let you know the result. Thanks for the heads-up. Look forward to working with you."

Back inside, Chelsey said, "Bob, you need to hear this. Katty, tell Sergeant Richards what you just told me."

"That baby was a gift from Billy. He has given me a lot of children, but never a baby. This one was the first," Katty said with a glazed look and a slight smile.

Her words rattled around in my head. There was something inside of me that wanted to reject what she just said. "Where . . . where are they? The other children, where are they?"

"Some have run away, and some are just too weak or noisy, so Billy lets them go."

"Lets them go?" I had to stop and calm myself. I was about to erupt, and I knew that would slam doors shut that needed to remain open.

"Bob, she told me that Billy has given her a lot of little boys, and when they become hard to handle, he lets them go. She doesn't know any more than that, he just lets them go." Chelsey's face went pale.

Oh my God. What are we dealing with? I thought.

"Katty, if you didn't call the police department for help, then who did?"

"Mary came here and said the baby needed help. She called."

"Who is Mary and where can we find her?"

"We call her Mother Mary, and she said we can never talk about her, to anyone."

"It's important that we talk to her because she helped save the baby's life."

"I don't know anything about her, that's the truth." She began to cry.

"Chelsey, after transport gets here, have them take Billy back to the PD, and you accompany Katty. Get Katty something to eat, she looks hungry, and make sure that each have their own lodging." In other word's keep them separate and put them both in lockup.

Leaning over Chelsey's shoulder, I whispered, "I'm going to button up this place for a search warrant. Make sure to keep her away from Billy."

"Okay, Sergeant. Are you hungry, Katty? I know I could sure use something to eat," Chelsey said, walking Katty out to the car.

Going through the apartment I locked all the windows and doors, then walked around the outside of the building, checking to make sure everything was secure. In the back across a small alley were four large storage sheds, one behind each of the four apartment buildings. Each shed consisted of three individual units about the size of a single-car garage, with a roll up metal door.

A deep gravel voice caused me to almost jump out of my skin. "Can I help you with something, Officer?"

Behind me stood a very tall, thin man dressed in red silk pajamas that shimmered under the streetlight. He looked like a stretched-out candy cane with pockets.

"Yes. What are these."

"Storage for the tenants. They're rented separately," he said, stepping under the sodium vapor streetlamp. His long hair and full black beard covered most of his face except for the scar that began just below his left eye and ended at his mouth.

"Do you know if Billy Kurkland rented one of these storage units?"

"Yep, that one right there," he said, pointing to the last shed. "You may be able to see what's in there in the back. Each unit has a window, but most are covered up with junk."

"Thank you," I said, heading for the back of the garage. "My name is Bob Richards, what's yours?"

"Ahab, that's what folks call me. They say I look like Captain Ahab in the movie *Moby Dick*."

I noted the number for the search warrant and went around the back. Shining my flashlight through the window I instantly had a wave of nostalgia. Under my light's narrow beam was a 1950s Volkswagen minibus, painted in wild psychedelic colors with large peace signs covering the side windows. I'd seen this van and the hair ball that owned it before. He was the storyteller, and I may have met Mother Mary before too.

CHAPTER TEN

En route to the PD, I stopped by Montgomery General to check on the little guy. In the Neonatal Intensive Care Unit, the nurse at the desk told me to take a seat and the doctor would speak with me shortly. At the end of the hall a couple was talking with a man in his thirties and wearing a Pendleton smoking jacket with patches on the sleeves. The muffled sounds and distinct odors of the hospital brought back memories of when my boys came into this world. I had sat on this very bench waiting to meet my first born, Joseph Alan, aka Little Joe, the first of the litter. That was when dads weren't allowed in the delivery room. So much had changed, yet so much had remained the same.

"Sergeant Richards?"

Looking up, I saw an extended hand and the exposed butt of an automatic in a shoulder holster, under the Pendleton smoking jacket. "Bob, I'm Detective George Austin, Concord PD."

"Good to meet you, George. Have you spoken with the family?" I asked.

"Yeah," he said, pointing to the couple at the end of the hall. "Come on, I'll introduce you. We're waiting for the doctor so we can see the baby and confirm his identity."

"George, let's hold back for a couple minutes first. I need to bring you up to speed."

"Sure," he said, waiving to the couple and raising two fingers.

Stepping into an empty room, I said, "We may have a much bigger problem. Katty Russell told us that her boyfriend, Billy Kurkland, has given her other little boys, and when they become a burden, he lets them go."

"Lets them go where?"

"All she knows is Billy lets them go. Only God knows where."

"Oh my God," he said, dropping his head. "So, the baby we have could be anybody's child. Do we know if the Bay Area was their only stomping grounds."

"No, but I believe they have been at it for a long time. There's an old hippie van in a storage shed that Billy rents behind his apartment. I know that van. I've seen it before, a long time ago."

Shaking his head, he said, "Oh God, I pray this doesn't get any uglier."

"Prayer is a good place to start," I said. "Let's go see if we can close this case on a positive note."

"Mr. and Mrs. Stevens, this is Sergeant Richards of the Oakland Police Department. He is responsible for recovering the child."

I extended my hand when Mrs. Stevens threw her arms around my neck and hugged me. "Thank you, thank you," she cried.

"You're welcome, ma'am."

I wanted to explain that this child may not be hers, but I didn't have the heart to bring her down to that reality. Not yet anyway.

"Detective, shift is about to change, and I need to get back to the PD. Would you mind giving me a call later?"

"Not at all."

"Thank you. Mr. and Mrs. Stevens, it's nice to meet you. You are in good hands with Detective Austin. One of our detectives will be getting in touch with you as well to follow up on our case."

I turned to leave but was caught in my tracks. "Mr. and Mrs. Stevens, may I ask you a question about the day your child went missing?"

"Sure, anything."

"Did you see an old van, painted with peace signs over the windows, anywhere near the park?"

"No," Mrs. Stevens said.

"Yeah, I did," Mr. Stevens said. "It was one of those old hippie vans. It was all painted up, even had the wooden bumper. I remember it because some of the bigger kids thought it was an ice cream truck."

"Did you get a look at anyone in the van?"

"Not a good look. I think it was a woman driving it."

"Thank you. If you don't mind, I would like to speak with you again."

"No problem. Call anytime."

I drove slowly back to the PD with Chelsey's words repeating over and over in my head. *Bob, she told me that Billy has given her a lot of little boys, and when they become hard to handle, he lets them go.*

Before going into the squad room for briefing, I dropped a note in Lieutenant Miller's in-box, requesting a meeting with him before he went off duty, and marked it *urgent.* Following the briefing, a cadet came in and handed me two notes, one from Detective Austin, with a phone number and a message, and the other from the lieutenant, saying yes for a meeting, but hustle up.

Austin's message read, "Richards, I have positive identification on the baby, five-month-old Jason Stevens. Medical says he's a tough little guy, doing pretty good considering he's dehydrated and suffering from malnutrition. The Stevens family are open to your call any time."

Running out of the squad room and down the hall, I learned two important facts: first, we are not to run in the office, and second, our hardwood floors had just been waxed. All I saw was the lieutenant's wide-eyed stare as he watched me slide past his office into one of the clerical cubicles.

Once on my feet I entered my boss's office slowly, red faced and upright. "Thank you for giving me a few minutes," I said, looking over my shoulder at the hallway. "You have to hand it to the maintenance crew."

"Okay, what do you have, Sergeant?" he said without a smile.

I spent the next fifteen minutes filling him in on the details and my feeling that this was much bigger than it appeared. Policy dictates that cases like this were to be handed over to the detective bureau for investigation. I was asking him to breach protocol and allow me and Officer Defo to do the interview.

"Lieutenant, I have them both in the box. I believe Katty is open to talk. A relationship has been formed between her and Officer Defo. If we don't move on it now, we're going to lose an opportunity that may save the lives of some kids."

"Okay, Richards, you and Defo can run with it, but an OPD detective will be in the wings, following every move. If for any reason there is a hang-up, it goes to the detective bureau. I don't want to let that scumbag back out on the street, got it?"

"Yes, sir. Thank you, LT," I said as I headed out the door.

"Sergeant," Miller shouted, "slow down, you're going to bust your butt."

Grabbing the phone on the closest empty desk I dialed the number. Expecting to hear the voice of a Concord police receptionist, I was surprised when a small boy answered.

"Hello, this is the Austin residence."

"Hello, are you Mr. Austin?" I asked.

"No, that's my daddy."

"Is your daddy there?"

"Yes," he said, and hung up on me.

Once I regained my composure I redialed, and this time his daddy answered.

"I'm sorry about that," George said.

"No problem. I needed something to lighten my day. Listen, I'm going to interview Kurkland and Russell in an hour. I want to strike while the iron's hot and not give them time to get their stories polished. Can you get here by then?"

"Sure, on my way."

Cases like these where multiple agencies worked together were historically complex, disordered, and mismanaged. Personalities got in the way, and egos got bruised, creating a lack of communication and a duplication of efforts. I didn't know where this was going to go, but I wanted to start it right. I found Chelsey in the observation room, watching Katty Russell through a one-way mirror, who was in Interview Room A.

"Chelsey, the child has been identified as a baby missing in Concord. Detective George Austin is covering the Concord case, and he's on his way."

"Okay," she said, without taking her eyes off Katty.

I watched as she studied Katty. She saw something there that I was missing.

"So, what do you think?" I asked.

"I'm scared, Bobby," she said, shaking her head slowly. "Do you remember when that big spider was in the squad room? No one wanted to get near it, so I swatted it with my shoe. Remember?"

"Yeah, I remember. A thousand little spiders came out of her. Freaked us all out."

Focusing her gaze on the woman seated at a flat metal table, in an empty room, she said, "I think we may have just poked the spider."

When George arrived, he was ushered into the observation room of Interview Room A, introduced to Chelsey, and given a seat and a cup of coffee.

"George, I would like Officer Defo and myself to begin the interviews with Katty. Chelsey has developed a rapport with her that I believe is valuable, and she knows me. Do you have any issues with that?"

"No, not at all. I'm a new face. Besides, three of us in the room would only cause undue pressure. She might just lock up."

"Good. Can you give us a brief rundown of your case, witness statements, evidence, and any questions you want us to ask before you come in?"

For the next half hour Detective Austin went over his case as Chelsey took notes, and together we watched Katty sit stoically in her metal chair, hands folded on the table, and her eyes staring at the mirror on her side of the glass.

Entering Interview Room A, I took a seat opposite Katty, as Chelsey pulled a chair up to her right. "Katty, would you like some water or a soda?" Chelsey asked politely.

"Yes, please," she said, not taking her eyes off the mirror. "Am I under arrest?"

"Well, we're not sure what we are dealing with here. Have you done something to be arrested for?" I asked.

"The baby was left in the park. Nobody wanted it," she whimpered.

"Okay, let's start there. Where in the park did you find the baby?"

"Billy found him and gave him to me."

"Were you with Billy when he found the baby?"

"No."

"Katty, let's talk about the others. Where did Billy get the other children he gave you?"

"They're everywhere. Billy's good at finding kids people don't want."

On a top corner of the door frame behind Katy's chair, a small, almost imperceptible red light flashed twice.

"Officer Defo, I need to step out for a moment. Would you mind keeping Katty company? I'll be right back."

"Sure, Katty and I are becoming friends, aren't we, Katty?"

In the observation room Lieutenant Miller said, "Bob, I think it's time to Mirandize her. It appears she isn't grasping the seriousness of this situation, or what's even happening."

"I agree," Detective Austin said. "There isn't much of a case on her, and so far, we've treated her more as a witness than a suspect. If we're going to keep her in custody, she needs to be advised."

"Yep. It's only a matter of time before she says something that implicates her as an accomplice," I said. "Okay, but what if she wants to leave?"

"Let her. I don't think she'll be hard to find. Besides we still have Billy, and she has implicated him as the one who took the baby," Miller said.

Back at the table I reached across and patted Katty on the hand. "Do you know how serious this is, Katty? That baby boy was reported as abducted, stolen, not abandoned. So, I need to read you your rights."

"Me and Billy didn't know that someone stole him. We thought nobody wanted him."

"I know, Katty, but you need to know that you don't have to talk to us, and if you want a lawyer, we'll make sure you get one. I want to read you something, and it's important that you listen very carefully, okay?"

I read the Miranda form slowly, emphasizing each point, and asked if she had any questions at each step. Turning the form to her and handing her a pen, I said, "Do you understand your rights, Katty."

"Yeah, I got it," she said, staring at the form.

"If you understand your rights and are still willing to talk with us, you need to sign this form."

Signing along the dotted line, Katty looked up and smiled.

"You are doing a very good thing right now. Do you know that?"

"What am I doing?" she asked, almost childlike.

"You are helping us find lost and abandoned children."

Her face brightened as a smile slowly formed. "Really?"

"Really. Now were you ever with Billy when he found a child that had been abandoned?"

"No. Billy said I couldn't go with him when he was on the hunt. That's what he called it when he went out to find boys that weren't wanted, the hunt."

"Was it always boys that Billy found?"

"Yeah, he once told me that the Minted only wanted boys."

"The Minted? Who is that?"

"I don't know," she said, shrugging her shoulders.

"Now I'm confused. I thought Billy went on the hunt to find abandoned children for you, but now you're saying he went on the hunt just for boys for someone called Minted."

"Yep, sometimes he would find a boy that Minted didn't want and he would bring them home to me. That's how I got the baby. Minted didn't want babies."

The next hour was spent mapping out where Katty thought Billy had gone to find abandoned little boys. So far, we had been able to identify nine possible locations, all within the Bay Area. Repeated questioning about the whereabouts of the boys Billy let go went unanswered. Katty simply didn't know. Something as small as eating the wrong thing could cause a boy to be let go. In one instance a crying child woke Billy up, and the next day the boy was gone.

The Minted and Mother Mary remained a mystery, but it told us that we might be dealing with a much wider web, like the thousands of little spiders under Chelsey's shoe. Billy might only be one of those tiny spiders.

Katty was placed into protective custody, which meant she was locked in a cage, provided food and water, and given a small portable TV and books for entertainment. Lieutenant Miller arranged for our shifts to be covered, so Chelsey could participate in the serving of the search warrant. At home, Rosie made sure I had an uninterrupted seven hours of sleep by treating the boys to breakfast at Grandpa Joe's.

I awoke to the sound of dishes being washed and the smell of hot coffee. Jumping out of bed, I started for the shower, then had a better idea. Sneaking stealthily down the hall, I crept up behind my bride, wrapped my arms around her, and kissed her neck.

"Good morning, baby," I said.

"Good morning," came a deep baritone response from the family room.

Jumping back, I turned to find my father-in-law sitting on my sofa reading my newspaper.

"Don't let me get in the way," he said with a snicker. "Just remember, she *is* my daughter."

"Good morning, Joe," I said while looking down and realizing I was as naked as a jaybird. "All right, enjoy my coffee and paper. I'm going to hit the shower."

"Love the suit. I heard a story about an emperor who had one like it." Joe chuckled.

CHAPTER ELEVEN

Everyone in the locker room wanted to know what was going on. In less than twenty-four hours the rumor mill had kicked up enough static to bury our investigation in false leads and bogus headlines. Lieutenant Miller made an appearance during the morning briefing and addressed the importance of keeping a lid on the scuttlebutt. Any officer found gleaning his or her fifteen minutes of fame by talking with the press or anyone else outside of OPD, would find themselves writing parking tickets to seagulls along the marina.

"Sergeant Richards," Miller said, waving me forward. "Would you mind filling us all in with what transpired, so we have the facts and not rumor?"

"Yes, sir," I said, stepping to the podium. "During yesterday's early morning shift I responded to a medical assist of an infant at the Webster Arms Apartments. The EMTs had not arrived so I transported the infant to Montgomery General. Upon my return to the scene, it was determined that the child did not belong to the residents but was in fact a child abducted from Pixieland Park in Concord last week. The child is in good condition and has been reunited with his parents. The residents were arrested for child neglect and drug paraphernalia. Sergeant Tillis will be covering my shift so I can complete my part of the investigation. That's pretty much it for now."

In the hall I met Chelsey and Detective Austin, and together we walked silently to Interview Room A. When we entered the observation room, we found Lieutenant Miller standing at the two-way mirror, watching Katty as she sat quietly with that same blank stare.

"Good morning, LT," I said.

The tension in the room was palpable. Without turning around he said, "I read your notes, Bobby. This is bigger than one guy snatching kids for his girlfriend. Our suspect, Billy, goes out for a hunt. He's capable of snatching kids from right in front of their parents, yet he comes home empty-handed. Why? What's he doing with the kids he doesn't bring back to Katty? What is he doing with the kids that are trouble-some, those he *lets go*? Who is Mother Mary, and what is Minted?"

For several minutes we merely stood without a word, looking at Katty and contemplating our next move.

George broke the silence. "I want to book them both on kidnapping, and maybe that will loosen her tongue."

"What if we call the DA and negotiate a deal with Katty?" Chelsey said.

"A deal for what?" I said. "She has already implicated her-self and Billy. There's not much more she can do. Besides, I don't think she knows anything else," I said.

"You're all right," Miller said. "Detective, you have the strongest case at this point, and you need to wrap it up. I agree with you, Bobby, there may not be much more she can give us, and Chelsey, there will be a time to bring in the DA, but not yet."

"Chelsey, I want you to introduce Detective Austin to Katty and remain with him while he interviews her. You've developed a relationship with her that will prove to be valuable. Try to determine who or what Minted is. It seems to play heavily in the scenario."

I stayed in the observation room and watched Chelsey bring George into play. Katty stared at him for a long moment, her eyes sunken, black, and puffy. Then she stood and moved hastily to the corner of the room and vomited in the trash can.

"I guess that tells you what I thought of breakfast," she said, wiping her face off with her sleeve and returning to her seat.

Chelsey got up, took the trash can out, and gave it to a cadet for disposal. She came back in with a couple bottles of water from the clerk's desk and set them on the table in front of Katty. "Feeling any better now?"

"Yeah, yeah. Man," she said, shivering. "You guys keep it cold in here. Can I get a coat or a blanket."

"Sure, we'll get you one in a minute," Chelsey said, knowing that the chills would pass quickly and the hot flashes would start.

Katty stretched and groaned as sweat began to form on her face and neck, and goose bumps rose on her arms.

"Didn't sleep much last night, did you?" George asked.

"No, it was uncomfortable, and I don't like being in a cage. When can I go home?"

"We need you to stay a little while longer. We have more to talk about. Besides you're going through withdrawal,"

George said. "Heroin, right? If I sent you home now, you could get hurt, and I'd never forgive myself."

The interview was proving to be of little value so Katty was returned to the holding cell where she could get something to eat and be overseen by medical staff as she battled the shakes. George went back to Concord with the plan of returning the next morning to speak to Katty one more time, and then interview Billy.

Chelsey and I spent the remainder of the day with a handful of volunteer officers calling police agencies in Alameda, Marin, San Francisco, Contra Costa, Solano, Santa Clara, and Sacramento counties. Each was an area where Katty said she and Billy were living when he brought home a new little boy. So far, we had confirmed four reports of missing boys over the last eighteen months, between the age of six and eight, all from the North Bay. I was about to tell the team to take a break when Chelsey and I were called back to Lieutenant Miller's office.

"Okay, guys, thank you for your help. Defo and I have to roll, so let's close it up for now. Complete your reports, and submit them to Admin for transcription."

Walking into Lieutenant Miller's office we could tell something was up. "Have a seat," he said. "I have some bad news."

Chelsey looked at me inquisitively, and I shrugged my shoulders, expressing my ignorance of what was to come.

"You two have done an outstanding job. Bobby, from what I've been told you saved that baby's life, and Chelsey, you showed unique care and compassion for Katty Russell, and that provided the info needed to reunite that baby with his parents. You make a good team."

"Thank you, LT, you've softened the blow. Now what are you going to hit us with?" Chelsey said.

"Okay, I want you both to complete your reports and provide a thorough narrative, log in any evidence you may have, and submit the case to the detective bureau. This case is going to require a significant amount of follow-up, and quite honestly, being on patrol, you don't have the time. You have done all that you can do, and you've done it well. Now it's time to pass it on."

Chelsey began to squirm in her seat. She was not happy. But the directive the lieutenant was giving was the right one. This wasn't some TV show, where a crime scene tech and a meter maid save the day in sixty minutes. This was real and needed to be dealt with accordingly.

"A search warrant is being drawn up and will be served this afternoon by Detective Austin," Miller said, taking a deep breath. "Concord PD will take the lead on this because they have a kidnapping case. You did a great job, but all we have is a drug paraphernalia charge. Austin said you are welcome to join them if you want. I will make sure you both are covered if you want to be part of the search this afternoon, but then I need you back to work."

I didn't like it, but I understood it. If we were going to reel in Katty's hairball boyfriend, Billy, this was the way it was going to have to get done. Besides, we hadn't gotten to the point of interviewing him. It was the perfect time to hand it off to Concord.

"I'm going to pass, LT. I have some things at home to take care of, and I need to catch some z's before graveyard shift," I said. "Chelsey, if you go, let me know what they find."

"Yeah, I'll go. I want to be there to see it wrap up," Chelsey said.

"Good, I'll get your shift covered," Miller said, standing. "Sergeant, go hook up with the sandman."

As we stood to leave, I touched Chelsey's arm. "Make sure they impound the van that's in the storage unit behind the apartment. There's an APB on it, and it's stolen. I have a feeling it's going to turn up in the investigation again."

It was mid-December, and the sun was setting early. I turned onto our street just in time to see Rosie's Ford Pinto station wagon pull into the driveway, and behind her Grandpa Joe's Chevy pickup. I pulled in behind as the Richards crew hit the pavement, and the boys each grabbed a box or basket. It was the second Friday of the month, the day when Alberta, my mother-in-law, would come to our home and create some new, never-tasted culinary expression of her love. In some households that might sound disgusting, if not outright dangerous, but not in ours. Alberta was an artist in the kitchen, her skill with a skillet, legendary.

The next few hours were tasty and filling. Grandpa Joe brought two new VHS movies that Grandma chose, and following dinner the gang kicked back for a two-hour snooze fest in front of the TV. Alberta went about cleaning up in the kitchen, as usual, refusing any help. Midway through the movie Joe and I went out on the back deck and lit up a couple cigars. Joe swore they were Cuban, but I told him if they were, I would have to arrest him. Sitting quietly, we sipped on a glass of red wine and watched the grass grow.

Slowly a simple conversation began to form, and as always, it got around to my work. If I didn't know better, I would swear Joe was an undercover psychotherapist. He had a way of listening and without formally diagnosing me invariably providing the counsel I needed. I always left our "stogy sessions" feeling better. I even slept better. Joe's non-counsel had proven invaluable to me over the years.

When we received Rosie's diagnosis, I shared with him how importuned his love and support was to us, and how he always knew just what to say. I remember his eyes filling with tears as he said, "None of it's me, son. It's the Holy Spirit speaking to you. If I were not there, God would use someone else." Watching this very special man blow smoke rings, I thanked God for bringing him into my life.

"Bobby, you're wanted on the phone," Rosie said from the serving window in the kitchen. "I think it's Lieutenant Miller."

"I have to catch this, Joe," I said, taking the phone and pulling the extra-long cord through the serving window.

"This is Richards," I said, unraveling the cord and returning to my seat and cigar.

"Bob, this is Lieutenant Miller. I know you were trying to catch some sleep, but I think you would want to hear this."

"What's going on, LT."

"Well, we have a problem. Concord PD went out to serve the search warrant at the Webster Arms Apartments and found it secure, locked tighter than a drum. Even the crime scene tape you put on the doors was intact."

"Okay. But what's the problem? Was there something wrong with the way I left it?"

"No, I wish there were. That would at least answer a few questions."

"So, what's wrong?"

"There's nothing there, Bob. Not a stick of furniture, no dishes, no trash, nothing."

"That place was a mess. It was almost uninhabitable," I said.

"I know. Officer Defo was there when they entered, and she's blown away. Said she could barely move around because of the trash."

"What about the van in the garage out back?"

"There's nothing back there, no van, nothing. Detective Austin thought he had the wrong address, or maybe you secured the wrong apartment."

"No, he has the right place. Besides, Defo can attest to the right location. Well, at least we still have Kurkland and Russell."

"That's a problem too, Bob. They have both lawyered up. Katty has signed a statement that she had asked for legal counsel, and you refused to provide it. She says that she felt threatened and that's why she signed the Miranda form. Everything she said to you and Officer Defo was a lie."

"You know that's not true."

"I was there, Bob, I know it isn't true. Concord PD is hoping to get the DA to file a complaint for kidnapping. Everything rests on the Stevens family and their testimony. It's possible the only thing we will be able to get on them is the drug paraphernalia charge."

"Wow," was all I could say. I just sat there dumbfounded.

"Is everything okay, son?" Joe asked.

"No, no it's not. Joe. Once again, the system has proven to be exactly what it is called, 'criminal justice.'"

When I got back to work, I had one destination in mind, and around three in the morning when the early morning activity was at an ebb, I headed to the Webster Arms Apartments. It was about this time in the morning that I ran into Ahab, and with any luck I would find him again. Parking in front of the apartment, I turned off the engine, got out, and got comfortable sitting on the hood with my back to the wall.

After nearly an hour, it was getting cold, and it looked like Ahab was as gone as everything else that had anything to do with this case. Sliding off the hood I opened the door and was about to climb in when out of the darkness appeared Ahab, this time dressed in dark purple.

"Officer Richards, I presume," he said.

"That's me. How are you doing, Ahab?"

"I'm okay," he said, handing me a small tightly folded piece of paper. "See you around, Officer Bob," and he walked away.

I started the car, drove a couple miles away, and pulled into a 7-Eleven parking lot. Turning on the dash light, I read the note: *Tuesday, 4:00 p.m., Dr. Greenfield 400 29th St. Come alone, no uniform.*

Following the morning briefing I went in and showed the note to Lieutenant Miller. He agreed that I should follow up on it but to be safe. He was going to arrange to have Detective Austin back me up.

On Tuesday at 3:50 p.m., I walked into Dr. Greenfield's clinic in Levis and a hoodie. Seated in a chair in the lobby was George Austin reading a dog-eared magazine. Looking up, he nodded slightly and went back to reading. Unsure of what to do, I approached the receptionist, gave her my name, and said I had a 4:00 p.m. appointment with Dr. Greenfield. After thumbing through a spiral binder, she smiled and told me to have a seat.

At precisely 4:00 p.m. the door opened, and Ahab, hair pulled back in a ponytail and dressed in blue surgical scrubs, called my name.

"Follow me, Mr. Richards," he said, leading me down several narrow hallways to a little room with a small desk, two chairs, and an examination table. "Have a seat, sir. I'll be right back."

Now I was curious. Within about five minutes, he returned with Detective Austin behind him. Closing the door, he motioned for George to take a seat while he sat on the exam table.

"Sorry for the cloak-and-dagger routine, but I don't want to find myself pushing up daisies."

"Let's begin by getting your name. Are you Dr. Greenfield?"

"No. If I was, I wouldn't be living at the Webster Arms. I'm a nurse practitioner in training. My name is Harold Murphy, and someday I'll be moving from the Webster."

"Nice to meet you, Harold. May I see your driver's license, please."

"Sure. Why?"

"It's just procedure," I said, looking it over and handing it to Austin who pulled out a notepad and pen and began to write.

"Why are you concerned for your safety, Harold?"

Looking at Austin, Henry said, "You were there when they came to search the place. I saw you. What did you find? Nothing, right?" Turning to me he said, "They cleaned that place out shortly after you left with Billy and Katty."

"Who came?"

"I don't know but they were ready for a fight. I've never seen that much artillery except in the movies. They were all wearing black with sky masks. They loaded up two trucks in the middle of the night with everything, and even swept it out. They almost spotted me when a tow truck came and got Billy's van."

"Did anyone else see this? The manager, or neighbors?" George asked.

"I don't know. I don't think so. I didn't see anyone else."

"It seems like there would have been a lot of noise," I said.

"They were quiet, man. They knew what they were doing. There were two guys with the big guns that stayed outside and walked around the building. If anyone were to look out and see those guys, they're probably still under their bed."

"Describe for me exactly what they wore and what they drove," Austin asked.

"They were all dressed alike, those outfits that are one piece and zip up the front. You know what's funny? They all wore the same kind of tennis shoes—black with white soles. The trucks were black too. They were big, square rigs, not like pickups, bigger. They were like those trucks you see coming out of the Oakland Army Terminal."

"Okay, I am going to arrange for you to come and make a full statement. I promise it will be just as cloak-and-dagger as this. Give me a number where I can reach you to let you know when and where," Austin said.

"Harold, the case belongs to Concord PD, because that is where the initial crime took place. You will do well with Detective Austin. Thank you for your help in this matter."

CHAPTER TWELVE

George and I left Dr. Greenfield's office separately and met up at Dee's Country Kitchen for coffee and sweet rolls. We discussed what Harold told us, and it seemed a bit over blown, but the evidence was there. That apartment was now the cleanest unit in the complex. It was a professional scrubbing, but why?

The circumstances justified getting a second search warrant and having OPD's crime scene unit go over it again, but this time the search was to see if the cleaning crew left anything behind. Thanks to the close relationship Lieutenant Miller had with Deputy District Attorney KP Cooper, a second search warrant was issued, and CSU was sent back out to see what they could find.

On my way home, I stopped by the Webster Arms to see how CSU was doing. Just outside the apartment a group of curious neighbors had gathered, tossing questions at two uniformed officers stationed at the front door. Stepping around them, I stood at the threshold of the door and watched what looked like large earless bunnies with blue paws crawling along the floor looking for an elusive carrot.

"Sergeant Finch, Sergeant Helen Finch," I said.

One of the bunnies stood up, pulled up the sleeves of her white disposable coveralls, removed her blue rubber gloves, and shuffled over to me in matching blue shoe covers.

Sergeant Helen Finch has been the crime scene unit's senior supervisor for the last four years. She came to us from the U.S. Department of Justice, where she served for ten years with Technical Working Group on Crime Scene Investigation, also known as TWGCSI. With her came a suitcase full of degrees, certifications, and awards.

"Sergeant Richards, welcome," she said, pulling back the white hoodie. "Are you to blame for this?"

"Yes, Sergeant Finch, I am," I said, hoping this wasn't a waste of her time. "Have you found anything?"

"Nothing I would call solid evidence. We've looked at everything in this place, and all we've come up with is this," she said, reaching into her pocket and removing a small clear plastic baggie containing a very small round disk.

"What is it, a button?"

"I don't know. The best I can make out are four numbers, one, nine, two, and nine. It could be something off a child's toy. This thing could have been laying there for years," she said, tossing it back in her pocket. "The cleaning crew that swept this place were pros. I've never worked a scene this clean."

"Are you about to wrap it up?"

"No, we'll be here for a while. I want to go over every-thing one more time and then hit the storage area out back."

"Well, thank you for going the extra mile on this."

"Bob, for someone to go to this extent, they've got to have something to hide, and I'm going to find out what it is."

When I got back to work the next evening, I had a note on my locker from Sergeant Finch. The news wasn't good. Although we gave it our best shot, CSU was only able to collect an assortment of smudged fingerprints, a one-inch piece of black plastic, and a small button.

On the inside of my locker door was a picture of Rosie with a date written in red crayon. Rosie's birthday was just around the corner. It is a time like Christmas, Mother's Day, and our anniversary, when I walk through the mall, befuddled with what to get her that she doesn't already have. The woman is a shopper. Oh, not the kind that maxes out the Visa at some upscale woman's boutique or picks through leftovers in a big box discount store. Oh no, my bride wears the finest designer clothing, carries the most sought-after handbags, and is adorned with some of the most creative and exquisite jewelry. She never wears the same outfit twice and is almost always in high heels.

The fashion stores that this woman shops at are Goodwill, thrift shops, and consignment stores. Yep, there is not a single thing she owns in her extensive wardrobe that cost much more than five dollars. Because she has filled her multiple closets with everything she needs or wants, I am at a loss to find the right gift, or any gift. I learned long ago that perfume is totally, absolutely, and completely out of the question.

There was only one person I knew who could give me the answer I needed. Her father, Grandpa Joe. He was the oracle of wisdom when it came to Rosie. She was his little girl.

Picking up the phone in the squad room, I dialed the new number Joe just had installed in his workshop. He added the line to avoid the incessant calls from Alberta's cribbage club.

"You know there is nothing that can compare to a memory," he said.

"A memory?"

"Yes, a memory. Alberta and I will watch the boys while you take her somewhere. Maybe a romantic getaway to Carmel, or a weekend in LA, letting her peruse the shops along Rodeo Drive. If you want to go all out, take her on a cruise. People say they're worth it."

"Have you ever been on a cruise?" I asked.

"Nope, but I've been thinking seriously about it."

"Carmel. That's a good idea."

"Sergeant Richards, I'm sorry to bother you, but we have a situation," the intercom squawked.

"Okay, I'll be right there. Joe, I'm sorry I have to run. I like the idea of Carmel. We'll talk again."

"No problem, just call," he said.

Keying the intercom, I said, "Go ahead, Dispatch, what do you have?"

"Possible 187 at 667 La Salle. Call came in as a medical assist, but the responding officer said that the victim is deceased, and there are extenuating circumstances."

Driving through the Piedmont, I couldn't help but admire the beautiful homes and classic cars parked in many of the driveways. At the intersection of Hampton Street and La Salle Avenue my heart skipped a beat when a cream colored 1975 Cadillac Coupe DeVille blew through the stop, missing me by inches. I shuttered thinking of the damage that tank would have done to me and my unmarked Chevy Nova, a car I picked up from the Corp Yard while mine was being serviced. If I didn't have more pressing issues I would have gone after that sucker.

A mile farther up the road I pulled onto the cobblestone driveway that led to the home of Leonard Corbitt, CEO of Corbitt Industries. He was the second wealthiest man in the Bay Area and a serious pain in Oakland's butt. Several police cars, with their lights flashing, ringed the circular driveway, and in the distance approaching sirens could be heard, possibly an ambulance. At the top of several stone steps leading to the front door stood Senior Officer Axel Heart, from the Piedmont substation. That young rookie who didn't like bridges and was afraid of heights had done well.

"Axel, what do we have?"

"Let's go in, Sergeant. I'll give you a tour."

The large marble entry opened to a massive great room with a huge stone fireplace in the back wall and works of art on the side walls. Arranged in a semicircle were white leather sofas with glass end tables at the corner of each. On either side of the room rose two curved iron staircases leading to the second floor where the bedrooms were located. To the left of the entry was a sitting room, with similar furniture, and to the right was a formal dining room and kitchen.

Ascending the right staircase, I followed Axel down a carpeted hall, past two rooms and a bathroom. At the end of the hall two officers stood at the opened door to the master bedroom. Just past the threshold lay a woman, face down in a pool of blood.

"Claudia Corbitt, I assume?" I said.

"No. Mrs. Corbitt is in Italy visiting friends. We have a couple of neighbors down in the kitchen who told me it may be Mary Ann Avery, the Corbitt's housekeeper. I found her purse on the dresser," Axel said, pointing toward a large, mirrored dresser in the corner. "I removed only the ID. Nothing else has been touched."

"Is Leonard Corbitt or anyone else here?"

"No. The call came in as a possible medical assist. When we arrived, the front door was standing open, and there was no one around," Axel said, looking down at the still body on the floor. "We entered, checked the rooms, and found the victim. I checked her for a pulse, but there was none, then called for you and an ambulance."

It was clear from the extent of her injuries she couldn't have survived the attack. To the right of her head lay several pieces of thick broken glass. To the left was a larger thick piece of glass that appeared to be the base of a trophy with the inscription, *The Argentine Polo Open – Leonard Corbitt.* Careful not to disturb any of the glass, I leaned down and examined the victim's injuries. She had been beaten so severely she was nearly unrecognizable. This was rage.

The siren's lowering tone announced the arrival of the ambulance, and within moments two EMTs were sprinting up the stairs. Stepping between them and the bedroom doorway I extended my hand.

"Whoa, gentlemen. Our victim is on the floor. It's clear that she is dead, rigor has set in, so enter slowly and cautiously. Confirm she's gone, then step out the way you went in. I don't want to contaminate the scene any more than we have to. Give your ID and agency information to the officer at the door."

"Yes, sir," the older, more experienced one said, while his young partner glared at me, clearly feeling that I was interfering with his job. After several minutes they exited the room and confirmed that the victim was deceased.

"Axel, if you haven't done so already, call out the crime scene unit and get the coroner out here." Turning to the two officers at the door, I said to the largest one, "I want you to secure the room, and unless I clear them, I don't want anyone in there except the coroner and CSU." Then to the other, I said, "Put crime scene tape around the residence, and make sure no one is on the property that doesn't belong here. As soon as the word gets out, we'll have every look-ie-loo and wannabe reporter on the planet here."

Down in the lobby, several officers stood talking. "Gentlemen, comb the grounds, garage, and outbuildings for anyone or anything you see that's out of place, but begin by going through every room where someone could hide, including closets, basement, and attic. Then canvass the neighborhood, knock on every door, get names of anyone who saw or heard anything, and check for security cameras. This area should have plenty of them. If you hit on something good, call Dispatch, and they can reach me."

Going into the kitchen I found it to be all that I expected—spotless white cabinets, marble countertops, multiple stovetops, ovens, and enough shiny pots and pans hanging over a center island to serve an army. Two couples sat around a glass table in a windowed breakfast nook, sipping coffee someone had brewed up, looking somber and chatting quietly.

"Folks, thank you for sticking around. I'm Sergeant Bob Richards, and I have some preliminary questions for you. We will need to talk with you again, but for right now this will be brief. The first forty-eight hours are crucial." I opened my notebook then pulled up a chair, "Okay, which one of you called the police?"

They looked at one another and the younger man said, "We didn't call. We just heard the sirens and came to see if we could be of help."

One of the ladies, who was on the verge of tears, said, "The officer told us there was a lady injured in one of the rooms, and I told him it may be the housekeeper, because Claudia has been in Italy for a month." Taking a deep breath, she asked, "Is she dead?"

Trying to avoid the question I asked, "Do you have any idea where Mr. Corbitt might be?"

"No," one of the gentlemen said. "His car was in the driveway earlier, but it's not there now."

"Do you know where he might have gone?"

"He may have gone to work. He spends more time there than he does at home."

"What kind of car did he drive?"

"His car is a 1975 Cadillac Coupe DeVille. He loves that car," one of the men said. "I've never seen anyone else drive it."

"Is it a tan or cream color?"

"Yes."

"Excuse me a moment," I said.

Grabbing a couple napkins, I went into the sitting room. Placing one of the napkins over the phone I gently lifted the receiver, and with the other napkin I dialed the watch commander's desk.

"OPD Watch Commander, Sergeant Henderson."

"Sergeant, this is Bob Richards. We have a 187 at the Leonard Corbitt residence on La Salle, in Piedmont. I believe I spotted Leonard Corbitt fleeing the scene while I was en route here. He is our prime suspect, so I need you to put out an APB on him. He's driving a cream-colored 1975 Cadillac Coupe DeVille. I don't have a plate, so check with DMV. Also have a couple officers check the Corbitt Industries building downtown. The neighbors think he might be there. Be careful. Our victim was badly beaten, and I don't know if he's armed."

"Got it, anything else?"

"Yeah, check with Dispatch and find out who took the initial call. I'll need to talk with them, and secure the recording for review and evidence."

After a few more minutes with the neighbors who professed that they knew little about the Corbitt family, I sent them home and returned to the master bedroom where I met the CSU techs. Throughout the room they had meticulously placed a myriad of small yellow numbered placards. Confident that they had found every questionable object, mark, dent, and stain, they then began the exhaustive work of identifying, photographing, collecting, bagging, and marking it.

I wanted to go in and rummage around the room, but I was aware of how easy it is to give defense attorneys ammunition when an overly exuberant cop stomps his way through a crime scene. While they went about their work, I patiently explored the remaining seven thousand square feet of the lavish Corbitt home.

"Sergeant Richards?" came the unique accent of Alameda County's British-born coroner, Albert Huntington.

"Hello, Albert. How is it we get the honor of having the coroner himself come out?"

"We're shorthanded, and a homicide in the home of Leonard Corbitt requires a bit of personal attention," he said.

His signature three-piece dark tweed herringbone suit and matching bow tie, along with his heavy English brogue, gave him an ambiance of authority when he entered a room. Over his shoulder was slung a large leather satchel, which said he came prepared and was ready to go to work.

From the head of the steps, the senior tech called down to me. "Sergeant Richards, you might want to witness this."

Stepping to the left side of the victim, I watched as they were about to roll the victim onto her back. Her arms had been underneath her, so when she was turned onto her back, we could see that she clutched several papers in one hand and a gold locket in the other.

Slipping on a pair of latex gloves I asked the tech for an evidence bag. Coroner Huntington removed the locket and handed it to me. Inside was a small photo of a boy of about six, with no further identification. I placed it in the bag, sealed it, and wrote my name, date, and the case number that I had received earlier on the seal.

The papers were more difficult to remove from her grasp. After some work, Huntington retrieved several crumpled pages. Unfolding them, he stood and moved over to the window for better light. After several minutes reading through them, he looked up at me with a mixture of surprise and wonder.

"Our victim, Mary Ann Avery, filed a lawsuit against Leonard Corbitt for child support. It doesn't actually say it, but it appears Leonard may have fathered her son, possibly the boy in the locket," he said, placing the papers in another evidence bag. "So, what do you think, Bobby?"

"Well, now we have motive," I said.

CHAPTER THIRTEEN

Axel shouted from the bottom of the steps, "Bobby, Sergeant Henderson is on the radio. He needs to talk to you right now."

Charlie Henderson was an old-school beat cop, who could have worked his way up the chain of command but chose instead to work a beat. After twenty-eight years and numerous opportunities to be promoted, he finally sewed on a set of sergeant's stripes and stepped into the role of communications supervisor. Some say he realized it was time for a change when he got into a scuffle with an irate husband and spent three days in ICU.

Going out to my vehicle I slipped behind the steering wheel and keyed the mic. "Dispatch, this is WC-3."

"WC-3, we have a situation pertaining to your suspect. Drop down to Tac 2."

"Ten-Four," I said, reaching for the channel knob on the Motorola. Tac 2 could not be monitored by the news media or grandma, so it allowed for open conversation.

"Go head, Charlie."

"Bob, we just received a call from Anthony Woodward, a Corbitt Industries attorney. He says he has Leonard

Corbitt in his office, and he's willing to turn himself in, with conditions."

"What conditions?"

"Woodward wants to talk to you first. He will call you at the Corbitt residence in fifteen minutes."

"Got it. Get Dispatch to look up Woodward's office address and kick it over to Detective Duffield. He should be in his office. Tell him to call me on the horn. I'll remain on Tac 2."

"Done," Sergeant Henderson said.

After several minutes I was getting impatient when the guttural voice of Detective Patrick Duffield filled the car. "Bobby, this is Pat. What do you need?"

"I have a dead housekeeper at the Corbitt residence. Cause appears to be blunt force trauma. Our prime suspect is Leonard Corbitt, who is sitting in his lawyer's office, Anthony Woodward. He's going to be calling me here at the Corbitt house in a few minutes to negotiate a surrender. I need you to get to Woodward's office and make sure we don't lose this guy. I'll keep him on the phone until you get there. Do not take him into custody unless you have to until I have talked to him. This guy has a lot of juice, so we need to make sure we do this by the book."

"No problem," Duffield grumbled. "I was just given the address. It's only a couple blocks away. I'll be there in five."

Jogging back into the house, I sat on a barstool near the phone and waited for the call. At precisely 4:45 the wall phone rang. On the other end, the voice was low and shaky.

"Sergeant Richards, this is Leonard Corbitt. I know what you have found in my home. Mary Ann was a wonderful woman who worked for us for years and became a member of our family. Sergeant, you must know that I had nothing to do with this, nothing."

There was the sound of shuffling then a stronger, controlled voice came on the line. "Sergeant Richards, my name is Anthony Woodward. I am Mr. Corbitt's legal counsel. Against my advice he insisted on talking to you, but from this point forward he will not be speaking with you or answering any more questions."

"Mr. Woodward, we have sufficient cause to arrest your client. Let me suggest that Mr. Corbitt surrender himself. You can accompany him. He is going to be arrested, and if he resists or fails to surrender we will have no choice but to take him into custody by whatever means necessary. Do you understand, sir?"

"Yes, Sergeant, I understand. There will be no resistance, and I expect that my client will be treated with respect."

I wanted to respond with *We will give him the same respect he gave Mary Ann Avery,* but I held my tongue.

"Detective Duffield is at your location, probably standing at your door waiting for my call. My next call will be to the district attorney's office. A deputy DA will be assigned, and an arrest warrant will be issued. Now, give me five minutes and answer your door. The detective is going to handcuff and transport Mr. Corbitt to the police department. I will meet you there."

"Are handcuffs necessary? He is surrendering after all."

"Yes, he is, but he is not being detained for unpaid parking tickets. He's being arrested for murder. Do you understand, Mr. Woodward?"

"Yes, Sergeant, I understand," Woodward said snidely, followed by a click and a dial tone.

Keying my portable radio, I said, "Pat, are you at Woodward's office?"

"That's affirmative, and there's no one here, just a receptionist. She told me that neither Woodward nor Corbitt came into the office today. She's been calling Woodward and leaving messages on his answering machine."

"Okay, thanks, Pat."

During shift change I briefed the oncoming crew of the homicide and instructed them to give the Corbitt residence extra patrol and to keep a lookout for a cream-colored 1975 Cadillac Coupe DeVille.

I was about to dismiss them when Lieutenant Miller stepped into the room. "Sergeant Richards, excuse me, I have an update on the Corbitt case."

Stepping to the podium, he said, "Mr. Corbitt's attorney arranged for him to surrender before Judge Linda Ventler this morning. She directed him to go through the booking process and then she released him on his own recognizance. We were unaware of the arrangement."

"Where is he now?"

"No one knows. This is a murder case, yet Ventler didn't require an ankle monitor or house arrest. She didn't even make him turn over his passport."

"Like I've always said, it isn't victim justice, it's criminal justice."

* * *

Several days after the discovery of Mary Ann's body, I learned that Claudia Corbitt had returned from Italy. I received the news by hearing her outside my office screaming obscenities at poor Mickey Albert, the desk sergeant, about how she was going to sue him, only after impaling him on a spike.

She demanded that the chief of police, and only the chief, come to her home immediately and remove all the yellow crime scene tape, followed by giving a public apology that was to be printed in every newspaper in Northern California.

Stepping cautiously into the hall, I made my way toward the loud vocal descriptions of the coming apocalypse and expletives I had never heard before. I put on as much affability as I could muster, closed my eyes, and asked God to give me wisdom, then bravely stepped into the lobby. When the orator of the prolific profanity saw me, she instantly turned her attention my way, but before she could utter a word, I grinned from ear to ear and extended my hand.

"Mrs. Corbitt, what a pleasure to see you. How was your flight home? Comfortable, I hope. My wife and I are planning an Italian excursion soon and I would love to get your insights and understanding of the culture. Please come into my office."

Her eyes went wide, her mouth opened, but no sound came out as I reached for her tight fist. Slowly it opened and took my hand as I walked her to my office.

Looking over my shoulder I said, "Mickey, get some water for our guest, maybe some coffee or tea. You prefer tea, Mrs. Corbitt?"

I seated her in a chair in front of my desk and stepped around to my chair just as Mickey appeared at the door with a glass of water and a cup of tea. The speed at which he retrieved these simple peace offerings would no doubt break records.

"Let me begin by apologizing for the crime scene tape. It was my responsibility to see to it that it was removed before you returned home. I am so sorry. I just got so busy working on poor Mary Ann's case. What a tragedy. I'm sure you must be heartbroken."

The expression on her face turned hard. It was clear that there was no love lost between them.

"Would you mind if I asked you a few questions, Mrs. Corbitt? I'm trying to put all the pieces together."

"I'm sorry I am not supposed to talk to anyone about it," she said, dropping her head. A tear ran down her cheek. "My beautiful home has been defiled."

"I understand," I said, noting her concern more for her carpet than her housekeeper. "I assure you I will come to your home this afternoon and personally remove all the tape. Will Mr. Corbitt be there?"

"No, he's staying at his office. He has a lot of work to do."

"You will be there, won't you?" I asked a bit flirtatiously.

Looking up at me with a Cheshire cat smile, she said, "Yes, what time should I expect you?"

"Is 4:00 p.m. okay?"

"That would be fine."

"Wonderful. Then let's hold the questions until then." I wanted her calm and open, an attitude more easily reached in her environment than a police station.

I walked her out and the lobby went silent. After she was in her car, I returned and was met by a round of applause. Once again David fought off the lion, protecting the sheep.

As much as I hated doing it, at 3:30 I headed to the Corbitt residence and went about diligently removing the yellow crime scene tape that the overly enthusiastic but well-meaning rookie put on everything short of the house cat. I was wrapping up at the rear of the house by the pool when Mrs. Corbitt came out in tennis shorts and a tank top, carrying a tray with two glasses and a pitcher of iced lemonade.

"I thought I had better make sure that one of Oakland's finest is properly cared for," she said, placing the tray on a small table between two patio chairs. "Come, you look like you could use some refreshment."

Stuffing the last remnants of the yellow tape into a trash bag, I dropped it near the side gate and took a seat. As she filled the glasses, I discreetly examined my host for any injuries, cuts, scratches, or bruises. There appeared to be none.

"Thank you for the lemonade, Mrs. Corbitt," I said, taking a long sip of the ice-cold drink. I noted several pool toys neatly stacked on the far side of the pool. "You have several children, don't you?" I asked.

"Yes, two, a boy and a girl. My son is attending the California Maritime Academy in Vallejo, and my daughter is in her final year at Stanford."

"You must be very proud. They live here with you and Mr. Corbitt?"

"Oh no. Jimmy lives in the barracks and will be graduating soon. Then he will serve the next eight years as a merchant marine officer. We don't know where he will be assigned yet. Julie has an apartment just a few blocks from the campus, and when she graduates and passes the bar, she will be working as a member of Anthony Woodward's law firm."

"Okay. As I understand it you have been in Italy and they were off to school. So none of you have been here in the house for some time, right?"

"That's correct."

"Are your children aware that Mary Ann's son is their half-brother?"

Sometimes I tend to open my mouth and a torrent of stupid gushes forth, and this was one of those times. By her demeanor it was clear I had just poured salt into an open wound.

Stiffened, her eyes burning, she said, "Absolutely not. That child is not a part of our family. Leonard may have had some moments of indiscretion, but he never fathered that child."

"When did you suspect that there might be something going on between Mary Ann and your husband?" I said, tossing fate to the wind.

She sat silently and glared at me with eyes that began to take on the same fire I saw when she was verbally emasculating the poor desk sergeant.

"When did you learn of the lawsuit seeking child support?" I added.

That did it. She placed her glass on the table and stood up. "You are not hearing me, Sergeant. That is not my husband's child. That woman is trying to hurt my family and embarrass us publicly."

As the fire rose so did the level of her voice, followed by a series of expletives describing Mary Ann and her child.

When she took a break I said calmly, "Mary Ann's attorney had blood tests taken and the results indicate Mr. Corbitt and the boy have the same blood type." Along with eighty-thousand other Oakland residents.

The last part I left out as I stood slowly. With fire in her eyes, she picked up the pitcher, letting its contents spill onto the deck. "Were you not aware that your husband has been paying for the boy's care since he was born?"

"This is my home, my castle, my domain," she screamed. "You cannot come here and insult my family and ruin all I have built. We are the Corbitts, the most influential family in this city."

Her voice lowered to a growl as she inched toward me, raising the pitcher over her head. "That piece of scum is not Leonard's child. I'll destroy you like I destroyed her if you say one more word."

"Let's put down the pitcher, Mrs. Corbitt. You don't want to be arrested for assaulting a police officer."

She stopped moving toward me, but the hatred in her eyes remained. Slowly she realized what she was about to do and lowered her weapon of choice. Gradually her countenance softened as tears filled her eyes.

"Are you going to arrest me?"

"No," I said. "Mrs. Corbitt, would you volunteer to being fingerprinted and provide us a blood sample? If you don't wish to, I understand, but you need to know that I will be obtaining an order from the court that will compel you to provide those two things."

"Sergeant, I'm not going to help you destroy my family, my home, or my reputation. You need to leave."

"Yes, thank you, Mrs. Corbitt," I said, tossing my card on the table. "Here is my number, call me anytime."

I stood and hesitated, reluctant to turn my back on her. The fire in her eyes had not diminished in the slightest, and she still had a firm grip on the pitcher. Taking a deep breath, I turned slowly and walked to my car listening for footsteps behind me. Fortunately there were none.

"Dispatch, this is Delta-2."

"Go ahead, Delta-2."

"Check our records for any reports on or made by James or Julie Corbitt. Also check state and local wants and warrants, and put a copy of their driver's licenses on my desk."

"Ten-four, Delta-2."

Within fifteen minutes I was informed that neither James or Julie had any record locally or otherwise, and James did not have a California driver's license. I didn't know what that kid looked like, and that was my fault. The number one piece of evidence even a rookie detective would pick up at a homicide scene that took place in a personal residence was family photos. Family members are usually killed by other family members.

Detective Duffield was able to obtain a search warrant for Leonard and Claudia Corbitt's fingerprints, blood samples, and a body inspection for injuries. The district attorney was reluctant to extend the warrant to the children at this time.

Duffield left me a note on my locker that the warrant was a bust. Nothing matched. We had an abundance of physical and biological evidence, but thus far no witnesses, and nothing significant to link either Claudia or Leonard to the crime. All we really had were suspicions. Granted there was motive, a few rash statements made in anger, and suspicious behavior, but that in itself wasn't enough.

I remember A. J. telling me, *Never trust just what you see. There's always more to the story.* If Mary Ann's child was the motive for her death, then who else would want her dead?

CHAPTER FOURTEEN

Pulling into the parking lot of the California Maritime Academy, I watched as cadets in starched white uniforms moved from one freshly painted building to the next. Catching one who looked like he knew his way around, I asked where I could find James Corbitt and was directed to the office of the commodore.

The reception area characteristically exuded order, conformity, and formality. The administrative assistant's desk was small, uncluttered, and strategically located near the door that led into the commodore's office. The walls were adorned with photos of previous commodores who held command and plaques commemorating various achievements. A large wooden bench sat under an American flag that was encased in glass and framed in dark mahogany. On the coffee table was a mixed assortment of military, navy, and maritime recruitment magazines, brochures, and leaflets. So far I had spent enough time to read everything on the table, count the number of squares in the drop ceiling, and develop an emotional attachment to the bench. This delay wasn't surprising. I had come to realize during my tenure in the army that waiting was one of the primary functions of military service.

While in advanced infantry training (AIT) at Fort Polk's infamous Tiger Land, myself and thirty of my soaked and shivering fellow recruits stood at attention awaiting the arrival of the assistant base commandant. He wanted to inspect and congratulate the graduating class. We had been warned that delays were common in the army, and the higher the rank, the longer the delay. We had fallen out of our comfortable bunks and into formation in the driving rain in February at zero-five-thirty. It was almost seven when he finally arrived.

I had a sneaking suspicion that a navy commodore ran off the same clock as an assistant army commandant, because I had endured forty minutes on a wooden bench that had once been a church pew. It was on this very bench the term *long suffering* was conceived.

Thoughts of assaulting the office ran through my mind when the young female cadet at the front desk came and escorted me into the commodore's office. Behind a large, antique, mahogany desk, which distressed finish matched his complexion, was Navy Captain William Wilbanks. His flattop haircut, broad shoulders, and extensively decorated uniform gave him a commanding presence.

I walked in and stood a couple feet in front of his desk as the cadet closed the door behind me. I almost saluted, then remembered that this was a different day, and I'd come here with my own authority.

Tilting his head back slightly, his light blue eyes glared at me over his reading glasses. After several seconds clearly intended to intimidate, he looked back down to a newspaper spread out across his desk.

"I've read the papers, and the scuttlebutt is all over the base," he said. "It's not fair to James Corbitt. He's a good kid, just promoted to Division Squad Leader. Now you're here to kick up more dust." Sitting back, folding his arms, and tilting his head to one side, he asked, "What can I do for you, Sergeant?"

"I was wondering if you could tell me if James was on the base on February third, and if so, is there is any documentation to that fact? I would also like to speak with him while I'm here."

Pushing back in his overstuffed leather desk chair, Wilbanks looked me over, debating what he was required to do and what he wanted to do. I could read it in his eyes, he had no regard for civilian authority and wanted to protect James Corbitt and the image of his command.

"Yes, he was on base, as Division Squad Leader. He was responsible to see that those in his squad were in their bunks no later than twenty-one hundred."

"Had he gone off base prior to that? That would give him enough time to leave, go home, and get back long before he had to take a headcount."

"We keep accurate records of who comes and goes, and those records will be made available to you. I assure you James Corbitt was on this base on February third. The boy doesn't even have a car, so he couldn't get very far."

Folding his arms, his expression became a tense gaze. "You will not be able to interview him today because he is in training on the T.S. *Golden Bear* and will be unavailable for the next week. Now if there is nothing else, I have work to do."

I could feel what the next words out of his mouth were going to be—"You are dismissed"—but I didn't give him the chance.

"Commodore, a woman was murdered at his home. At the moment, everyone who has access to that residence is a suspect. I appreciate any help you can provide me," I said, stepping closer to his desk. "However, my investigation requires that I speak to James. If I don't have access to see and speak to him here, in your plush offices, then I'll obtain a warrant, and we will chat in jail."

Wilbanks sat back and stared at me with contempt. Patting the military decorations neatly pinned on his chest, he sneered. "You do what you have to do."

One of his medals stood out to me. It was a small circle with an engraved eagle and the date 1929.

"I don't suppose you would provide me with a photo of James?"

"You suppose right," he snarled.

"Commodore, thank you for your time. We'll meet again soon," I said, stepping back and making a sharp military about-face.

In the lobby I described the commodore's medal to the cadet at the front desk and asked what it represented.

Opening the drawer of her desk, she removed a blank sheet of paper and handed it to me. At the top of the sheet was the California Maritime Academy's logo, a circle with an eagle, wings spread, and the date 1929, the year the academy was established. Then she grasped the gold chain around her neck and pulled it up exposing the same medallion as a necklace.

"Is it produced in any other form, like a button?"

"No, no buttons, but we do have a class ring."

"A class ring. How many of the cadets have one? I suppose since 1929, that would probably be thousands."

"Not thousands, probably fifty to a hundred. The class ring was only made available three years ago."

"Can I get one?"

"Yes, sir, I'll look up the phone number of the company we order the rings from and call you with it."

"Thank you," I said, handing her my card. "If you don't mind, would you please keep this to yourself. This is a homicide investigation, and we're just getting started. The less rumor and gossip the better."

"Yes, sir, I understand."

"May I use your phone?"

"Yes," she said, putting the phone on the corner of her desk. "Dial 9 to get an outside line."

After several rings the voice of a young cadet came on the line, "Oakland Police Department, Crime Scene Forensics, can I help you?"

"This is Sergeant Bob Richards. I wish to speak with Helen Finch."

"Please hold," the phone went dead, then the ever-cheery voice of OPD's criminalist came on the line, "Good morning, Bob. What can I do for you?"

"Good morning, Helen, I was wondering if you have cleaned up that button you found in the Webster Arms apartment?"

"Not yet."

"Okay, I think I found out what it is. Clean it up and I'll bet you'll find it to be a medallion from the California

Maritime Academy. Because of its size, it may have come from a class ring."

The drive from Vallejo to Oakland took no more than thirty minutes. Rush hour would add about fifteen more. There's plenty of time to get home, run into the housekeeper, and get back on base. Total time with plenty to spare, at least an hour and a half. James may not have a driver's license, but that doesn't mean he can't drive.

I dropped off the maritime logo at the crime lab and headed home for dinner and a nap, then back to work.

When you work the graveyard shift as long as I have, you learn how to sleep when the rest of the world is hitting the road. However, unlike those who sleep at night, day sleepers have to contend with continuous interruptions. Somewhere outside someone was having something delivered. How did I know this? It's not by my uncanny ability to hear and discern the incessant beep, beep, beep of a delivery truck backing up in the neighborhood. Oh, no. It's the crazed reaction of the beast we have housed in our home that we call Isabella, Izzie for short.

She's a dog with an overprotective disposition, ready to attack the moment she senses danger. Truth is, she goes off the moment a delivery arrives at the door, or when she gets startled, or when someone simply walks by. I suppose I should feel secure, but Isabella isn't a Doberman or German shepherd, although I'm sure she thinks she is. She's a long-haired Doxie with an attitude and a bark that rattles the walls.

"Isabella. Enough," I shouted.

Rolling onto my side, I grabbed the pillow next to me and covered my head, pressing it tightly against my ears.

The sound faded, and that's when my brain kicked in. It wasn't a truck's back-up indicator; it was my pager going off.

Reaching out from under the covers, I blindly searched for that annoying little black box, knocking the alarm clock off onto the floor. From the living room, Isabella was going ballistic, barking her head off at the noise of my now broken clock.

Finding my pager, I drew it under the covers and pressed the button, and the yellow glow of a familiar phone number flashed across its small screen. With the same dexterity I displayed finding the pager, I went after my Princess phone, knocking off my wallet, watch, and last night's coffee cup. This of course kicked Isabella into another defensive frenzy.

"Izzie, knock it off," I yelled, rubbing the sleep from my eyes while fumbling to dial the number. After several tries it began to ring.

"Oakland Police Department, Lieutenant Miller's office, how can I help you?"

"This is Sergeant Richards. I just received a page to call in."

"Yes, Sergeant, Lieutenant Miller would like you to come in and see him around three o'clock this afternoon. Will that be a problem?"

"No, no problem. Can you tell me what it's about?"

"No, sir, I really don't know. I believe it has something to do with a case you had worked on. What I can tell you is that LT was quite insistent."

"Yeah, okay. Thanks," I said, hanging up.

I stood in the shower, letting the water run over my head, going over what I might have dealt with that could have gone bad, and imagining how I was going to explain to Rosie how I'd chosen a new career at Radio Shack.

I scribbled a note on the fridge telling Rosie that I had gotten called in early and wouldn't be home for dinner. Unless, of course, I get fired before dinner time. That part I left out.

Cruising down MacArthur Boulevard to the PD, I watched several disheveled and clearly intoxicated customers stagger out into the afternoon sun from the Cat's Tail bar, an establishment well known for its late-night brawls and all-night poker games. To the right of this spit-and-sawdust saloon was a store that at one time sold some of the finest jewelry in the Bay Area. Today it stands abandoned, windows and doors boarded up, and a dozen tattered strips of yellow crime scene tape blowing in the wind.

The sight of the fragments of bright yellow tape took me back a few weeks when I was called out there. That was when the tape was new. A couple of old army buddies had gotten into an quarrel over who was the most patriotic American, Cassius Clay or Elvis Presley. The debate was literally cut short when one of them pulled out his military Ka-Bar fighting knife, and the conversation moved from heated argument to mortal combat. The Cat's Tail lost a couple of good-paying customers that night. They were both buried, one in the ground and the other behind bars.

When I arrived at the PD, I stopped by the coffee counter, where a cadet took a cup with my name on it off one of the shelves that lined the back wall. He then filled it with a dark watery substance that by the evidence of steam, appeared to be hot. Then with a smile that spread from ear to ear, he assured me that it was coffee, but after a sip, I wasn't so sure.

In Lieutenant Miller's office were Captain Oliver Lewinsky and Deputy Chief Gerald Stiner, sipping coffee that I was confident hadn't come from the coffee counter. I could feel my gut getting tight. The only time this much brass gets together was for a funeral or a firing. What had I done this time?

"Lieutenant Miller, you wanted to see me?"

"Yeah, Sergeant, come on in and have a seat."

The only seat left in the room was against the wall facing them all. On the wall, just over my right shoulder was a paper silhouette target that had been framed. A series of holes in a pattern the size of a teacup was dead center, and the plaque at the bottom read, *Sergeant Steven Miller, 1st Place, California State Marksman Competition, 1974.*

Great, it is a firing, a real one. Well, whatever it is, according to the shot pattern on that target, it would be quick.

"From what we hear so far it appears you and Officer Defo may well have poked a hornet's nest. This baby case is relatively new, and it already feels like it could spin out of control," Deputy Chief Stiner said.

"Sergeant, we want to make sure this thing is handled right, without a lot of hands in the kitchen that don't need to be there. If it looks like it crossed any borders, city, state, or country, we'll have every agency and their house cat jumping in," Captain Lewinsky said.

"Bob, we've talked this through and come to a conclusion," Lieutenant Miller said, leaning across his desk. "We're going to assign you to the detective bureau. You've demonstrated a unique gift for investigation, and we want to put it to use."

"So, are you open, Sergeant?" Deputy Chief Stiner said.

"Yes, sir, of course I am."

"Good, you will be assuming Detective Sergeant Jerry Gallagher's office," Captain Lewinsky said. "Gallagher has been on medical leave for the last month recuperating from giving his wife one of his kidneys. His surgery went well, but unfortunately hers did not, so he's chosen to take an early retirement to be with her."

"Bob, we don't have an exact date when Gallagher will step down, but it will be within the next four to six weeks. Until that time, you'll be covering your patrol shift, but we want you to focus on the baby case and hook up with Detective Austin in Concord."

"We'll give you a heads-up when Jerry is ready to walk you through his case load," LT said. "Have any questions?"

"No, sir."

"Good, go home and buy a couple sports jackets, that's your new uniform. Come to work, eight o'clock Monday morning. Enjoy the weekend."

During dinner at home, I waited for that moment when there's silence because every mouth is full. "I have a couple things to share with the Richards family tonight," I said, looking around the table and stopping at each for their approval. Rosie nodded, then Joe, followed by Sonny. Casey looked down at the brussels sprouts on his plate and said, "Yeah, if I don't have to eat that."

"Sorry, Critter, every member of the Richards family eats what's on their plate," I said.

"So, what's on the agenda?" Rosie asked.

"We have had a regular routine for a very long time. I've worked nights and slept when you are in school and Mom is at work. I've been offered the opportunity to work during the day, with weekends off. I will be on call however, so I can't guarantee I'll always be home. I'd like to know what you think."

"That's cool, Dad," Joe said.

"Yeah, you can still be at our soccer games, right?" Sonny echoed.

"As often as I can, son."

Casey looked up with a grimace, squinting his eyes, his mouth puckered as he chewed on a brussels sprout. "Yeah, okay," he said, swallowing hard.

"How about you, Mom?"

"I think it's great. It's going to take some getting used to though. We haven't slept together regularly since we got married, but I look forward to the experience," Rosie said with a wink.

"You'll still be a policeman, right, Dad? You're not quitting, are you?" Sonny asked.

"No, I'm not quitting. I'll be working as a detective."

"Wow, our dad is a detective, cool," Joe said.

"Like Columbo?" Casey said with a scowl that spoke of his disdain for brussels sprouts.

"Well, I don't plan on dressing like Columbo, but I sure wish I could solve every case in an hour like he does."

After dinner we pitched in to clean up, while Mom dished up warm apple pie a la mode and Sonny tuned in *The Carol Burnett Show*. I loved that show, and the impromptu laugh fests that would erupt when Carol or one of the other characters would get tickled.

Unfortunately, I never got to see the whole program, because midway through I had to get ready and go to work, but that was about to change.

CHAPTER FIFTEEN

"Xray-4, respond to 1880 River Oak Road. The reporting party is frantic, difficult to understand. She said something about lawn furniture. WC-3, you available to cover?"

"That's affirmative, en route," I said, keying the mic.

When Officer Clark and I arrived, we were greeted by a woman on the street screaming hysterically.

"Ma'am, calm down and tell us what's wrong," I said.

Pointing and jumping up and down, she cried, "In the back, in the back."

Opening the side gate, I was about to enter the backyard when I saw why she was so excited. Looking over my shoulder, I said, "Clark, check with the lady and find out if there was anyone in the backyard, and hurry."

I keyed my portable radio and said, "This is WC-3. Any unit in the area of the Riverdale Project respond."

Within seconds officers began to respond.

"Xray-2, about five away." "Xray-1, ten out," "Xray-6 available," "Xray-3, five out."

Choosing the two closest units, I told Xray-2 and 6 to drop to Tac 2, a channel that would allow me to give directions without the use of code.

"Respond to River Oak Road, and make contact with every resident on the south side of the street in the 1800 block. Determine if anyone was in their backyard during the night, and make sure everyone is accounted for in the house." Each of the officers confirmed by keying their mic twice.

The Riverdale Project is a new concept within the city, developed to address the need for affordable housing. The homes along River Oak Road were new two-bedroom homes on zero-lot-line parcels. Each had a fenced-in back-yard and was built on terraced lots cut into the side of a hill, one above the other. The street in front of the homes was steep, and both the front yards and back had not yet been landscaped or seeded.

"Sergeant, the owner of the house is Nancy Albert, and she's the only one there."

The Albert home was the first lot at the bottom of the street. The rear yard was nothing but mud, three and a half feet deep, rising to the window sills. In the mud was an assortment of patio furniture, barbecues, sun umbrellas, and wooden fencing.

Looking up the hill through what had been individual fenced lots, there was nothing but the remnants of a large above-ground pool behind the last house at the top of the street. As the officers awakened the residents, rear porch-lights began coming on, and stunned neighbors came out to discover that an avalanche of sludge swept away their fence and anything else that had once been in their backyard. For-tunately, none of the residents were in their yards during the man-made tsunami, nor did it appear that any of the homes were seriously damaged.

In the front yard I was met by several angry neighbors wanting to know if I was going to arrest the owner of the largest above-ground pool money could buy. They knew it was the largest because the owner of the pool bragged about it the day before at a neighborhood gathering. That was also the day the owners went on a three-day trip to Disneyland, leaving the garden hose running so the pool would be full when they returned.

From inside the house I heard Nancy Albert scream, "Waldo! Where is Waldo?"

"Mrs. Albert, who is Waldo?" I said, clearing the front door.

With a heavy Australian accent, she began to weep, "Waldo is gone, he's gone."

"Who is Waldo and where did you last see him?"

"Out there," she cried and pointed out the sliding glass doors. "He's my puppy."

From outside the fence that remained, at the farthest corner of the lot, I was able to lift myself up high enough to get a clear view of the entire yard. With my flashlight I scanned along the wall of the house and spotted a squirming small lump of mud. Returning to the front of the house, I deposited my Sam Browne belt, gear, jacket, and shirt in the car, and from the trunk I retrieved a spool of rope.

Giving it to Officer Clark, I said, "I'm going to need help to get out of that muck. Oh, God I don't want to do this."

From the side yard closest to where I spotted the Waldo mud bubble, I tied the end of the rope around me and stepped in the sludge. Each movement caused me to sink a little deeper. The mud and water were only up to my knees, but it was becoming difficult to move. I was within arm's reach when Waldo saw me, wiggled, and disappeared.

Driving my hands into the muck, I grabbed what felt like a small pillow and pulled out a fuzzy agitated mud ball. In front of the house, Clark hosed us both down and returned Waldo to Mrs. Albert. I'm going to miss working the street, it's where it all begins, where almost everything we do is ignited. This was my last night.

"Officer, please wait," Mrs. Albert shouted from the front door. "Please wait one moment."

She disappeared back into the house then reappeared with a large plastic baggie, followed by a brown fluffy flea trap called Waldo.

"Here is a dozen of my famous chocolate chip cookies. Everybody says they love them."

"Oh, thank you, Mrs. Albert," I said, handing the bag to Clark.

"You're welcome. I just wish I could do more. If I were minted I would buy you a new uniform."

"Thank you, the cookies are more than enough. Let me suggest that you call your insurance company in the morning, and possibly the city building department as well. Goodbye, Mrs. Albert, and you too, Waldo," I said.

I reached for the car door, and it hit me, "Mrs. Albert, what did you just say to me?"

Her face took on a perplexed look. "You mean about the cookies?"

"No, about my uniform?"

"I wish I could buy you a new one."

"No, no, you said something about *minted*?"

"Yes, I wish I were minted, then I could buy you a new uniform."

"You wish you were minted? What does that mean?"

"I wish I was wealthy. In Australia, minted is what we call rich people, people with power and position."

Suddenly my brain found the on switch to that lightbulb over my head. William Kurkland, better known as Billy, wasn't finding little boys for Katty. He was stealing children for the wealthy, those holding a position of power. Well, now I know what they are, I just don't know who they are.

* * *

Early Monday morning I walked into the police department wearing a Pendleton sports coat with patches on the sleeves, went to my locker, removed its contents, and took the elevator to the second floor. The doors opened to a receptionist desk, and to the right a seating area. Behind and to the left of the receptionist was a large bay separated by a glass partition, this was the "bull pen" containing twelve cluttered desks, six on each side, with filing cabinets lining the walls. There were four small windows situated high along the back wall above the cabinets. Because they hadn't been cleaned since Moses parted the Red Sea, the sunlight they brought in was defeated by the harsh glare of florescent light that bathed the entire area. This is the Detective Bureau, Part I Crimes Division.

Part I crimes are crimes against persons, such as assault, robbery, murder, and so on. Part II Crimes Division is on the third floor. They investigate crimes against property, theft, burglary, arson, and so on.

Brushing through the glass doors I stood with my box of belongings like a lost child. I had been here before, many times, but it felt different this time. I wasn't just stopping by, I was moving in.

"Sergeant Richards?" came a familiar voice from the far end of the room. "Welcome, Sergeant," he said, working his way around the desks and chairs and extending his hand to me. "Welcome to the pit."

"Thank you, Axel. How long have you been assigned to Part I?" I said, shaking his thick callused hand.

"Been little over a year now, and I love it. Let me show you around," he said, leading me through the maze of desks.

"Have you become a carpenter, a mason, or a farmer?" I asked.

Turning, he looked at me and tilted his head. "How did you know that?"

"The calluses on your hands. You don't see a lot of cops with callused hands unless they have something going on, on the side."

"Well, a little bit of all of those. I build homes for people."

"Wow, that's impressive. I could imagine you make good money doing that."

"Oh, I don't make any money. The people I work for don't have any money," he said, opening a large door and flicking on the lights. "This is our logistics room. We meet here on Mondays at ten to brainstorm our active cases. If Sergeant Gallagher isn't able to work today, I'll introduce you this morning if you don't mind."

"That's fine. I'm curious, what did you mean they don't have any money?"

"In my church, I serve as the leader of a group of men known as The Brotherhood. There are designers, plumbers, electricians, and carpenters. Whatever we need, God has or will provide it. Now we're working on a project that will provide housing for over a hundred families. We're refurbishing two abandoned hotels that will be zoned as condos. The church raised enough donations to buy the buildings, and the city is overjoyed to see the area improve. The price of each unit will pay for the permits, materials, and appliances and will allow people to own their home, not just be housed in it. That builds pride."

Pointing across the room to two doors on the opposite wall, he said, "Those are interview rooms. When the little red light above the door is on, they're recording so we need to keep the noise down out here. That can be hard to do sometimes."

Axel then walked me over to two glassed-in offices at the end of the bay. "This is your new home, Sergeant," he said, pointing to the door on the left with the name *Detective Sergeant Gallagher*.

"I'll have that removed," he said.

"No, don't do that. Gallagher is still on the job. Although I'll be carrying his caseload, I intend to only shadow him for now. Two weeks after he officially retires, then make the changes."

"Good call, Sergeant. Welcome aboard."

CHAPTER SIXTEEN

In what would soon be my office, I sat behind the desk and looked out through the glass at the twelve desks and countless cabinets. Slowly as the morning wore on, it began to fill with men dressed in suits and blazers, and several ladies in pantsuits and dresses. Every one of them held a large Styrofoam cup sporting the logo of the coffee shop on the corner.

"Good morning, Detective Sergeant Richards," came the gravelly voice of a very large man with a very broad smile.

"Good morning, Detective Sergeant Gallagher," I said, jumping up from behind the desk. "Sorry, Sergeant, I was just checking to see if my skinny butt could fill your seat. It can't."

"Well, get another chair then. This place needs some young blood, and it's time for a new butt behind this desk." Looking up over my head, he said, "Hope you drink your coffee strong and black."

At that moment a police cadet cleared the door. "Here's your coffee, Sergeant, and one for you, sir," he said, setting down on the desk two tall Styrofoam cups with the corner coffee shop logo.

We spent the next hour and a half going over the case folders that covered Gallagher's desk. Two were new folders, the Mary Ann Avery homicide and the follow-up file on the Stevens baby case.

Cases are dispersed in a number of ways. If a case needs to be assigned, it usually falls on the division's detective sergeant to do so unless a member of the bureau command staff directs the case to a specific individual. That is what happened with the Avery and Stevens cases; they were assigned by the bureau command staff to me.

If a detective is called out to a scene, he or she will be the primary, or lead, detective on the case. If no one has been called out, then the first detective on the scene will be the primary. If they are working on an active case where the suspects or victim are involved with those of another case, then the detective of the existing case will become the lead detective.

At ten minutes after nine, Detective Sergeant Michael Bender, my counterpart in the next office, strolled in and stopped at the door.

"So, this is the new guy," he said, stepping in and extending his hand.

I took his hand and was about to introduce myself when he said, "Bobby Richards. I've heard about you." Not releasing my hand, he looked at Sergeant Gallagher. "That's quite a jump from a relief patrol sergeant to detective sergeant. Usually, Bobby, you would make your bones in the pit before getting an office." Giving a final squeeze to my hand, he turned to walk out and said, "See you later there, Bobby."

Detective Sergeant Michael Bender is the case allotment supervisor for the Detective Bureau, Part I Crimes Division.

He holds the responsibility of distributing cases to the various detectives as they come in. It's not as simple as it sounds. Bender must know the strengths and weaknesses, the experience and abilities of each member of his team. Every one of those seated in the pit is there by appointment. There are no rookies here. They have all demonstrated unique skills and come with extensive experience. Collectively the bad guys don't stand a chance.

"Don't let Sergeant Bender get to you. He can be a jerk, but he's a good cop. If you can get past his arrogance, you'll find him to be an asset," Gallagher said. "It's ten o'clock. Let's go meet the crew."

The logistics room was laid out like the squad room down on the first floor. Thirty chairs faced a small platform with a podium and projector. On either side of the platform hung two large corkboards, covered with mugshots and sticky notes. On each of the side walls hung several maps with colored pins and a web of red string. Each of the pins represented a crime, and the string showed the link between each event.

"Ladies and gentlemen, good morning," Gallagher said as he approached the podium.

"Welcome back, Boss," someone shouted from the back. "Yeah, welcome back," others began to shout as everyone stood and began to applaud.

"Okay, okay, that's enough. Thank you, thank you very much, now please be seated. We have work to do."

"How is Betty?" one of the ladies asked as everyone took their seat.

"There are a few more tests, but if all goes well, she will be home next week."

"That's great. If you need anything, Boss, just ask," came another voice from the back.

"Thank you all. Your thoughts and prayers are deeply appreciated. Now, let me introduce you to your new boss."

Over the next several weeks I invested enough in the corner coffee shop for its owner to buy a beach house. It was a valuable investment because it allowed me to get to know the detectives under my watch, even though I had to inhale enough caffeine to maintain a mild buzz all day. Together we went over the active cases assigned to them, and I listened to their concerns about the lack of resources, equipment, and personnel. At first it felt overwhelming, but each day that went by, ideas began to form in my head on how I might resolve some of their concerns. Those that required command involvement would have to wait until I earned enough respect for command to hear my voice. Detective Sergeant Gallagher came back and helped guide me through some of the protocols and promised to always be available anytime I needed him.

His retirement party was a great success. With his wife, Betty, seated comfortably on the platform next to him, various members of the Part I team began to roast him, telling stories that caused him to blush and sink in his seat with a grin. Betty, on the other hand, laughed until she was nearly sick. It was a wonderful time, and it taught me a valuable lesson that I must never have a retirement party.

I knew better than to try and step into Jerry Gallagher's shoes. Nearly every one of the detectives under his oversight made their bones with him. He was respected, loved, and revered. The best I could do is simply do what I do best, my job, and that proved to work well. Even Detective Sergeant Michael Bender was coming along.

Bender said, standing at the door of my office, holding two Styrofoam cups of coffee, "Bobby, I got something for you I think you're going to like."

"I'm always open to good coffee, Mike. Come on in and have a seat."

"Patrol popped a winnable gangster last night who has woken up to the fact that we're looking at him for felony assault. He snatched the purse of an eighty-year-old grandmother on MacArthur, almost knocking her through a plate-glass window. She's in ICU at Montgomery General."

"What's her condition?"

"Bad, but they think she'll pull through."

"Good, good. So, who caught the case?"

"You did. I'm assigning it to you."

"Okay," I said, waiting for the next shoe to drop.

"Our snatcher is telling us he can provide information on some of our open cases. He may have some info on one of yours."

Bender handed me a folder labeled "Sanchez, 245/261PC." Inside was a report of an assault with a deadly weapon and forcible rape, along with photos of the badly abused victim. Stapled to the inside was a medical statement describing the victim's injuries, the prognosis of her condition, and the result of a rape kit. I didn't open the folder because I knew what was in it. It was a case that Lieutenant Miller and I had discussed at length over dinner the evening it was reported.

Emily Sanchez was an attractive, twenty-three-year-old medical receptionist who was returning home from work when she was brutally attacked. The only description she could give was a rough guess of her attacker's height and weight. He said nothing, so she couldn't tell if he had an accent, or what his approximate age might have been. The only identifying characteristic she could give me was the strong smell of vinegar. Emily didn't see her attacker because she was blind.

From my office door came the voice of Lieutenant Steven Miller. "Good morning, Detective Richards, Detective Bender."

Miller was a transplant from Los Angeles, and after ten years with LAPD, his career took a hit when he and his partner were involved in a shootout. At three in the morning, they pulled over a banged-up brown 1950 Chevy with its lights off cruising slowly through Bel Air, the richest and most exclusive residential area in LA. Miller ran the license plate while his partner got out and approached the right rear of the car. Both the driver and passenger doors abruptly opened and gunfire erupted. The officers returned fire, killing the passenger and wounding the driver.

The passenger was identified as Jack Jackson, or JJ, a high-ranking member of 16th Ave Gangsters, a relatively new street gang in East Hollywood gaining a lot of attention. Within four years they were involved in burglary, fraud, identity theft, robbery, assault, and murder. Its members ranged in age from twelve to twenty-five, and most were recruited as they walked to school, the store, and even church.

What jammed up Lieutenant Miller was he shot the driver. It was a good shoot, and the driver lived, but he was unarmed. He came out of the car with a two-foot-long iron pipe that was later determined to have been used in the robbery and beating of a sixty-five-year-old newspaper delivery driver. An internal affairs investigation cleared Miller based on the simple fact that shots were being fired at the officers, and in the dark Miller couldn't tell the difference between a pipe and a pistol.

The problem was not the shooting, but who got shot. The suspect's vehicle was registered to twenty-one-year-old Jack Jackson, a violent predator recently paroled from the California Youth Authority. He served six years for killing his girlfriend's father when he was fifteen. The driver of the car was sixteen-year-old Jeffery Dillion, a gang member wannabe with no criminal history and the son of Rampart Division Commander Charles Dillion.

Miller remained with LAPD for another year and a half, scoring in the top three for promotion twice but always being passed over. He was informed by a union rep that Dillion was working behind the scenes to stop him from ever being promoted. Miller filed a complaint, but it went nowhere. His future looked bleak, so he put LA behind him and moved to the Bay Area. He was a smart guy, politically savvy, and a good cop, so he moved up the ranks quickly. His present assignment, the investigation division.

"Good morning, Lieutenant. I'm well, thank you," I said.

"I pulled the file on the Sanchez case so I could look it over. You don't have much to work with, and your victim isn't able to help you much, but there may be a way to fill the gaps," he said, as he stepped in and set two manila folders on my desk.

Dropping into one of the well-worn wicker chairs in front of me, he looked down at the folders and said, "I think we have a serial rapist on our hands."

Before I could wrap my head around what he said, and that I now had two new cases, Bender added a little more to clutter my cranium.

"Richards, you need to talk to this guy in lockup."

"Who's in lockup?" Miller asked.

"Oh. I'm sorry, LT," Bender said. "We have a guy in the box that has been spilling his guts about everything from who stole the pencils to who sunk the *Titanic*."

Shaking my head I said, "Come on, Bender, you know how these guys are. They'll say anything to get your attention or improve their street creds."

"You're right, Bobby. A lot of his stuff is smoke, but he's saying some things that no one should know, stuff we held for evidentiary purposes." Bender then leaned over my desk and put his finger on the Sanchez folder. "According to Officer Hicks, the arresting officer, this guy says he knows stuff about this too."

Standing to leave, Miller said, "Go talk to your dime-dropper, then review these two cases and keep me in the loop as you progress. There's a bad guy out there, and we need to get him off the street before he strikes again."

"Okay, Bender, let's go talk to the snatcher," I said.

Entering the interview room, I took a seat at a four-foot square metal table in a ten-by-ten off-white room with a large, mirrored window and a single door. Across from me sat a tall, gaunt man whose long, dirty hair hung down over his face, and his tattered clothes reeked. Bender sat at the end of the table, and Officer Hicks pulled up a chair and handed me a folder containing the arrest report for one Michael Linden Jefferson, charged with 211 and 242 PC, robbery and assault.

"Michael, I understand you've been sharing some information with Officer Hicks and Detective Bender, and you may have some information regarding one of my cases. Now, before you share with me what you have, I need to confirm that you have been advised of your right to a lawyer and that you don't have to speak to me, right?"

"Yeah, yeah, I know all that stuff. I didn't do anything to that lady, so I don't need no lawyer. If I tell you what I know, I'm not going to get charged with anything, right?"

"No, that's not right, Michael. You are being charged with robbery and assault, but we'll include in our report to the DA that you assisted us."

"Robbery and assault! That's bogus, man. That lady gave me her purse. Just ask her."

"We can't. She's in ICU. If she dies Michael, you're going to need every positive stroke you can get. Right now, you got nothing."

Leaning over the table he put his face in his hands. We let him sit there for several minutes, contemplating his options. Then in a shaky voice he said, "I didn't mean to hurt that old lady. I don't hurt nobody. I just wanted her purse. Why wouldn't she let go of her purse?" he said as tears began to run down his cheeks. "I ain't no murderer."

"She's not dead yet, Michael, but if you want to help yourself, now is the time. What do you know about one of my cases?"

I made a point to avoid providing any information that might be construed as leading him in what he had to say. Our conversation was being recorded, so if what he had to say was good, I wanted to make sure the DA could use it.

Wiping away the tears, he said, "Yeah, yeah, okay, man. What do you want to know."

"This is your time, Michael. You're the one with the information. So, what do you have for me?"

"That lady that was raped, the blind lady, I see her sometimes on Saturdays. I used to think she was drunk, but she ain't. She's blind."

"Okay, where do you see her?"

"Coming out of that big Catholic church on Excelsior Avenue. She gets there late and is in there for an hour then she's out and gone. I work that corner because there's a lot of old ladies with big purses that goes into that church. Now I don't mean I snatch their purses, but those old ladies come out of church feeling generous, so I ask for a few bucks. Saturday can be a busy day for me at that church."

"Okay, so why is that important? What's it got to do with my case?"

"Oh yeah, well the day she got raped, I saw the guy who done it. He was following her."

"Do you know him?"

"No."

"Can you describe him? Age, build, hair, facial hair, clothing . . ."

"Sure. He's about your size, with blond hair, and he wears a black suit. He's around thirty or so, and he ain't got no beard."

"I want you to look at some pictures."

"Sure, no problem. I see him all the time."

"What do you mean you see him all the time?"

"He's always in and out of that church, and on Mondays, Wednesdays, and Fridays he serves in the soup kitchen."

"I thought you said you didn't know him?"

"I don't. I just see him around. Besides I have a reputation. I ain't going to be seen hanging out with no priest."

"Priest! Are you telling me you saw a priest rape a woman?"

"No, no. I didn't see no rape. I saw him follow her. He follows all the good-looking women that come out of that church."

"Where did you see this priest go? How far did he follow her?"

"I lost sight of them when they went around the corner, about two blocks down."

"Let me get this straight. You didn't witness a rape or an assault. All you saw was a woman who was later attacked, go into the church on Excelsior Avenue, come out and walk down the street. Right?"

"Right," he said, beginning to fidget nervously.

"Then behind her a priest came out of the church and walked in the same direction. They both disappeared around a corner a couple of blocks away. Do I have that right?"

"Yep, that's correct-a-menudo."

"Is it possible, Michael, that they were just walking in the same direction, going someplace in the same general area?"

"Yeah, that's possible, but all the stuff you hear about them priests, I mean, it must be him. So, you're going to say something good about me in your report?"

I turned and glared at Bender, who looked like he felt naked and just wanted to run. "I'll leave that to Detective Bender. Thank you for your help."

Stepping into the hallway, behind Officer Hicks, I closed the door, put my hand on his shoulder, and said, "That was very informative. Sometimes these guys just frost my cupcake."

"Honestly, Sergeant, he has given me some good leads, and he said he knew who raped the blind girl. I thought it was worth looking into."

"It was, Officer. You did what you were supposed to do. Don't discard this guy. He may become valuable," I said, patting him on the shoulder. "It's a good lead. Maybe the priest saw something. I'll follow up on it."

Back at my desk, I took a sip of mud—commonly referred to as coffee—that didn't come from the corner coffee shop and opened the folders LT left for me. Each contained reports of sexual assaults along with photos of young women who had been badly beaten. Stapled to the back flap was the medical statement describing the attacks, beatings, and sexual assaults.

Each of the attacks took place in different locations within the Bay Area. One in Walnut Creek, last year, and the other in San Francisco, two years ago. Each assault was carried out with a unique modus operandi, with one glaring similarity, all the victims were blind.

CHAPTER SEVENTEEN

Saint Margaret Mary Church wasn't the largest church in the city, and it was the oldest. Built in 1922, it sat on a hill with its towering steeple rising above the community it served. When I was a boy, I thought it was a castle with its white turrets and bell tower. Inside the white walls, stained-glass windows, and ornate altar made you feel like you just stepped into God's living room.

"May I help you?" a young man dressed in black asked.

"Yes, I'm Detective Richards with Oakland Police Department. I'm looking for the parish priest. Would that be you?"

"No, sir, let me take you to his assistant."

While he was leading me to a door on the right side of the altar, I looked up at the huge crucifix suspended from the ceiling and wondered why Jesus was always looking to the right, and what's the point of keeping Him on the cross. He's alive, right?

"Sister Donna, this is Detective Richards from the police department. He's looking for Father Vincent."

"Thank you, Charles. Please check with Sister Elizabeth in the rectory. She needs some help moving some furniture."

"Yes, ma'am."

"Priests are getting younger these days," I said, watching Charles disappear down the hall.

"Charles isn't a priest. He's a volunteer. How may I help you?"

"I would like to speak to the parish priest. I assume that would be Father Vincent."

"Yes, that's correct. Please have a seat and I will see if I can locate him."

Before the hard wooden bench became uncomfortable, Sister Donna and an elderly man in torn work jeans and a sweat-stained T-shirt came through the front door.

"Detective Richards, I presume," the gentlemen said, extending his hand. "How may I be of service to you."

"I would like to ask you a few questions if you wouldn't mind."

"Not at all. Come into my office. Sister Donna, would you please make for Detective Richards and myself some of your wonderful coffee?"

The priest of the oldest church in the city had an office the size of Rosie's closet. One wall was filled with books stacked and stuffed onto shelves in no particular order, and the other covered in Polaroid photos of families and kids tacked to a large corkboard. His desk was an old, ornately carved wooden door resting on two large concrete blocks, and it was covered with folders, notepads, and letters. Behind his chair, the newest thing in the room, was a floor-to-ceiling stained-glass window depicting a shepherd looking out over his sheep.

We spent the next hour sipping some of the best coffee I ever had and discussing the condition of the city of Oakland, particularly the recent assault on one of his parishioners. On the day in question, he had served in the confessional from 9:00 a.m. until 1:00 p.m., followed by a light lunch brought into him by Sister Donna. He remained in his office until 5:30 that evening working on his homily for Sunday, then he retreated to his room. All witnessed by Sister Donna and an assortment of church volunteers. He was a man in his seventies, in good health and sound mind, and was not a rapist.

My attention was drawn to another person of interest when I asked Father Vincent about Charles, the young man who greeted me in the sanctuary.

"Charles is a very special young man," Father Vincent said. "His mother began to attend the church when they moved here from a small farming community in Iowa. The boy had trouble getting used to living in a big city. He didn't make friends easily and was picked on horribly by the local high school boys. His mother came to me on one occasion asking for help because Charles was coming home regularly with bruises, blacked eyes, and a bloody nose.

"He met a girl who lived on his block, and the two became close, but their friendship didn't last. Something happened, and the girl's parents wouldn't allow her to see him. Within a few months she and her whole family moved. That's when I started seeing Charles in church. He has served here for over five years and is now in charge of the volunteer cleaning crew."

"Do all the young men who volunteer here wear black?"

"No," he said with a chuckle, "that's just Charles. He told me that he felt it showed respect for the house of God. Black is what the nuns and priests wore, so he thought he should too."

Father Vincent gave me the address of Charles O'Neal, so I decided to stop by on my way back to the PD and see if he had seen anything. Since he's around the church a lot, he might have seen something that would help me in the investigation.

Charles lived with his mother in the newly built twelve-story west Oakland apartment complex known as City Towers. They had been living in a low-income apartment just a few blocks away from Saint Margaret Mary Church, now they're five miles away, yet every day Charles makes the hour-long trek to serve.

The lobby was an open, airy space with marbled walls, matching floors, and the glaring glow of florescent lights. On the right wall there were two elevators, on the left, three large, framed photos of the city of Oakland, and on the center wall facing the entrance were two-hundred and thirty-one mailboxes each with a call button. I pressed the 1017 button twice, and a woman's voice said, "Come on up."

When the door to apartment 1017 opened, a mid-dle-aged woman in a tattered housecoat stepped back. "Who are you?"

Showing my ID, I said, "I'm Detective Sergeant Bob Richards. Are you Mrs. O'Neal?"

"Yes," she said cautiously. "What do you want?"

"Is this the residence of Charles O'Neal?"

"Why? What did he do? What do you want with him?"

"Mrs. O'Neal, Charles is not in trouble. I just want to ask him a few questions. I just left Father Vincent, who speaks highly of him. I won't take much of your time, just a few minutes."

"Mom, who is it?" came a voice from a back room.

"Okay, come in, but only for a few minutes."

"Thank you, Mrs. O'Neal."

Seated at a small kitchen table, I removed a notepad from my pocket as Charles began to fidget nervously.

"Charles, I'm investigating an assault and I know you were working at the church at that time, and later you were in the area where the assault took place."

I was about to ask him if he saw anything when he blurted out, "Do I need a lawyer?"

"I don't know, do you?" The room went quiet as Charles stared at the floor.

"Is there something you want to tell me, Charles? If there is, now is the time."

"That's enough," Mrs. O'Neal said, stepping up behind her son. "You need to leave, Detective."

"Yes, ma'am. Charles, I will be back to talk with you again. If you have information that you know I need to hear, now is the time to tell me."

I put a couple of my cards on the table. "You can call me anytime."

The sound of the door shutting behind me echoed in the hallway. At the elevator I watched the floor indicator stop at the fifth floor and remain there. After several minutes I headed for the stairwell, when the door to 1017 opened and Charles came out.

"I have something for you, Detective Richards," he said, handing me a large well-used Bible.

"Thank you, Charles, but I can't take this. It would be a gift, or a gratuity, and I'm not allowed to receive them. Please understand that I appreciate the thought, but I also have one of my own at home."

Opening the door to the stairwell, I descended, leaving him there with his Bible. We would be meeting again, because his response to my visit moved him to the top of my list.

"Delta-2."

"This is Delta-2."

"Detective Austin, Concord PD, has asked for a meeting with you in your office at fifteen-thirty. Should I confirm?"

"Yes, and contact Senior Officer Chelsey Defo and see if she's available to join us."

At 3:30 p.m., both Austin and Defo were sipping coffee from the corner coffee shop in my office.

"So, George, what's been going on in your neck of the woods?"

"I'm here about the Billy Kurkland and Katty Russell case. You know that Katty changed her statement, saying that you coerced her into a false confession and refused to provide her an attorney when she asked for it."

"That has been shown to be a lie by witness statements and the recordings," Chelsey said.

"Yes, it has, but it doesn't end there. They were brought before Judge Linda Ventler who granted them bail. The bail was in cash, and significant. We have no idea where it came from, but your note to me about the meaning of the *minted* made sense. Someone with significant resources is backing these two. I got a letter from a high-priced attorney informing me that I was not to communicate with them or their family at any time."

"Who's their attorney?" Chelsey asked.

"Some big legal outfit in your backyard, The Woodward Law Firm."

"Anthony Woodward represents Leonard Corbitt, CEO of Corbitt Industries, a suspect in a homicide case I'm working on."

"Small world, Bobby," Chelsey said.

"Yes, it is, and Leonard Corbitt also went before Judge Ventler and was OR'd on a homicide case." Turning to Detective Austin, I asked, "Do you know where Billy and Katty are now?"

"That's the next thing. We do know where they are," Austin said, dropping his head.

"What's the matter? Are they on the run? Have they left the country?" Chelsey asked.

"Katty's in protective custody. She turned herself in and was given immunity for her testimony. She's been out at the County Farm, an extension of the county jail, for the last month. We received reliable intel of a possible threat. We weren't able to find Billy until yesterday. He had been holding up in a rundown motel in the town of Mojave, a hundred miles east of LA, out in the middle of the desert."

"So, when does he go on trial?" I asked.

"He doesn't."

"What? Does he have immunity too?" Chelsey snarled.

"No, he didn't get immunity. We found him on the floor of his room with a double tap to the back of his head. It was a professional hit."

"Wow. Were drugs involved?"

"No, the coke and grass he had stashed in a jar remained untouched, and the ten grand in cash found under the bed hadn't been touched. According to the tenants in the adjoining rooms, the only thing they heard was someone crying. The tenant above Billy's room said he thought he heard someone begging, but he couldn't be sure."

"Where do you go from here?" I asked.

"There's nobody to prosecute, but we're not closing the case. I think someone is trying to make sure the Stevens baby case doesn't go any further, and I want to know why."

We wrapped up our time and headed home with a great deal to think about.

When I got home, I found the top of the kitchen table covered in brochures, flyers, leaflets, and booklets about Caribbean cruises. The photos of the cruise ships looked more like Las Vegas had collided with a shopping mall. When Grandpa Joe told me about cruising, I was picturing something significantly smaller. Rosie browsed the flyers like a kid getting ready to go to Disneyland for the first time.

"Bobby, they have a Formal Night. It's an elegant soiree where everyone dresses up as if they were attending the Oscars. That would be so much fun. You would look so handsome in a tuxedo, and I'll dress in a gown with so many rhinestones the astronauts will see the moon's reflection from the ship's deck."

"Tuxedo? What if I just stapled some of those rhinestones on my Bermuda shorts?"

"No way, if that ship sinks, we're going down in style."

"When is this floating shopping safari on the pond supposed to happen?"

"Maybe next year after Joe graduates, or the year after when Dad rents the motorhome and takes the boys up to Emigrant Lake."

"You're willing to wait that long?"

"Yeah, I couldn't go on a trip like this now. I have too much to do at work with the new acquisitions, and besides the boys have a lot going on. Joe will be graduating, Sonny has his art exhibits, and Casey will be finishing his freshman year and going to his first prom."

"Okay, this year and maybe next is out."

"Yes, but Bobby, I want you to make me a promise that you will take me to the Bahamas someday soon."

"I promise, baby."

"Good, now let's plan. It's fun to plan," Rosie said with a squeal and a kiss.

"Okay, let's plan." We spent the evening reading all the literature that Joe and Alberta had given us. They had planned their trip and would be cruising the Bahamas in the next few months. When we finally turned in, it was hard to get to sleep. Just as I was about to enter dreamland, Rosie found a brochure on Walt Disney World, and her batteries were recharged. Rolling over, I wrapped the pillow around my head and in a muffled tone said, "I love you baby. Good night."

As I arrived to work the next morning, coming out of the elevator was Liz Baker, the Part I Crimes receptionist. She smiled and offered me a Styrofoam cup with the coffee shop logo.

"Thank you, Liz. What do I owe you for this blessed elixir?"

"Not a thing, and you're welcome. A young man was here waiting for you in the lobby. I don't know how long he was waiting there, but it had to be well before the office opened. He wanted to drop off a gift for you. I put it on your desk."

In the center of my desk was Charles O'Neal's large, well-used leather-bound Bible. Taking a seat, I sipped my coffee and debated if I wanted to get distracted this early in the day by a gift from the young wannabe priest. The files piled on my desk answered the question for me, and Charles's Bible was relegated to the unread books stacked in the corner.

CHAPTER EIGHTEEN

"Sergeant," Liz said, poking her head into my office. "There's a Lieutenant Plaxton with SFPD in the lobby who would like to speak with you."

"Show him in," I said, standing to greet him. "Lieutenant, welcome to the other side of the Bay. What brings you over the bridge?"

"I wanted to bring you up to speed on the child abduction case and run a picture by you of a possible suspect."

From his briefcase he withdrew a manila folder, and from it two photos. One was a mugshot of a large man with long, unkempt, graying hair and salt-and-pepper beard in his late fifties. The other photo was a mugshot of the same man with long, dark hair and trimmed black beard in his early thirties. This man I knew.

"I ran into this guy up in the Headlands a long time ago," I said. "He was with another guy, William Kurkland. They were talking to my sons. At the time, I thought we were going to have trouble, but we didn't. Who is this guy?"

"His name is Chester Scoggins. He has a rap sheet as long as your arm. We picked him up for child neglect. He left his girlfriend's little girl in a hot car for over three hours while he went to score a fix. We got word that Chester had information about the abductions and wanted to negotiate, but by the time we got to him, he had bailed out. We lost track of him for a couple weeks, until yesterday."

"You have him in custody?"

"Nope. Chester was found in a stolen 1951 hippie van at the bottom of the Bay off the Treasure Island Marina. It was reported as an accident until the coroner found two bullet holes in the back of his head."

"We believe Kurkland was involved in stealing kids for someone he calls *Minted*," I said. "He was also out on bail, and we found him in a fleabag motel with a double tap. Someone has gone to great lengths to remove anyone involved with these child abductions."

Detective George Austin, Concord PD, was asked to join us with his file, and together we spent the morning tracking the events. Because of Billy Kurkland's death, the Stevens baby case was closed and there was no reason to keep Katty Russell in protective custody. A call was made to the Contra Costa district attorney's office, requesting to reinstate the charges against her in order to keep her safe, but it couldn't be done because of the binding agreement the DA made with her.

An order was then requested to move Katty from the County Farm to a safe house for six weeks. It didn't require much in the way of convincing once we described what happened to her cohorts. Unfortunately, without a case for her to testify to, her stay was limited to only two weeks.

Arrangements were made to have an interview with her before she was transferred. It would be a roundtable meeting, with all of us in the room, including Office Chelsey

Defo. Katty's attorney would not be present because she had been given complete immunity from anything we discussed.

On the morning of Katty's transfer, we met in Interview Room A on the third floor of OPD's investigation division. Placing a reel-to-reel tape recorder in the center of the table, I plugged it in and pushed the record button.

"I am Detective Sergeant Bob Richards of the Oakland Police Department. It is Tuesday, May sixteenth, 1978. The time is 8:45 a.m. With me in the room are . . ." I gestured to those seated with me to introduce themselves.

"I am Lieutenant Lloyd Plaxton with the San Francisco Police Department."

"I am Detective George Austin with the Concord Police Department."

"I am Senior Officer Chelsey Defo with the Oakland Police Department."

"Now, Katty, would you please state your full name and date of birth."

With a timid smile she looked at me and leaned over toward the tape recorder and said, "I'm Katty Louise Russell, my birthday is March third, 1952."

"Thank you, Katty. Do you understand that this conversation is being recorded?"

"Yes."

"Are you aware that you have been given immunity and that nothing you say can be held against you, and you still have the right to have an attorney present to represent you."

"I understand. I don't want an attorney, but can Officer Chelsey be here?"

"I'm not going anywhere," Chelsey said, patting her on the hand.

Over the next three hours we talked about the children Billy would bring home, their hair, eye, and skin color. Did she see any marks on their bodies like a tattoo, birthmark, scar, or skin discoloration? What was their style of haircut, and did it appear recent? A detailed description of what they wore, how their clothing fit, shoes, and their condition was recorded. Were they wearing hats or socks? Did they have any logos or garment names stitched into their clothes? A detailed description of any jewelry, earrings, bracelets, or necklaces. Did any of the children have an odor or scent that was unusual? During their time with her, did they ask for anyone, like a mother, father, grandparent, or sibling? Did they mention any names, their own or someone else's?

Katty's reflections were a bit scattered, but she was able to provide a plethora of information.

Because police agencies fail to communicate with one another, the next area to explore was researching the timeline. This was essential to define the chronological order of the events, and from that, the general location of where abductions may have taken place. This allowed us to focus on where missing children reports were made.

Where Billy and Katty were living, and when, was crucial. Fortunately, Katty was very certain about where she lived and when Billy would leave the house and when he would return. She was always afraid he would leave her and never come back. She also believed he had a girlfriend.

How long Billy would be away from the house when he went on a hunt gave us a pattern and specific zones we could focus in on. We noticed that the times of his absence were different when he went out to let children go than when he went out on a hunt.

On a map of the Bay, we placed a red pin where a child was reported missing, blue pins where Billy and Katty lived, and yellow pins where they lived when a child was let go. Despite living in San Francisco, Oakland, or Concord, the amount of time Billy was away was consistent, indicating that there was a place close to all three residences where kids were being taken. Running a string to each of the corresponding colored pins, the lines intersected on the small city of Emeryville, wedged between the city limits of Oakland and Berkeley. We found our target, but now what?

It was agreed that we had to go back to our respective agencies and get every detective, cop, meter maid, and janitor to dig up every snitch, rat, mole, and canary and squeeze them for information. There was no way that there wasn't an undercurrent on the street about wealthy people buying children. I would contact Emeryville and bring them into the loop.

Once everyone had cleared out of my office, I ordered a sub from the local deli, spread out the files on my desk, and plugged in my recorder for transcription. The Emily Sanchez assault case lay under my sandwich wrapper, with Charles O'Neal's name staring at me from the top corner. Finishing my lunch, I crumpled up the wrapper and leaned back for a bank shot into the trash can. Instead of dropping into the imaginary net, it bounced off the wall and settled on top of Charles's Bible. Could this be a sign? Yeah, I need to practice more bank shots.

Placing the Bible where my lunch had once been, I thumbed through the pages. Almost every page had been written on, between the lines and along the margins. I stopped to read the napkins, ruled pieces of paper, and index cards that were covered by copious notes and stuffed between the pages. Each one was an accusation of a sin committed by a set of initials, and with each allegation Charles posted a scriptural reference. Most were small things like petty theft, divorce, lust, gossip, greed, and gluttony, but two stood out.

On a pink napkin Charles wrote, "CI is a rapist. 2 Samuel 13, 'Amnon was stronger than she, he raped her, then hated her.'" On a flowered napkin, "JC murders the young. Acts 7, 'He dealt treacherously forcing them to throw out their newborn.'"

On the last page, taped to the inside of the leather cover, was an envelope addressed to Detective Sergeant Bob Richards, with the word *Confession* in bold letters. Below was a scripture verse James 5:16.

Dropping the envelope, I picked up the phone and dialed Detective Axel Heart's desk. "Yeah, Sergeant, what do you need?"

"Axel, would you mind stepping into my office a moment?"

Reaching into my desk, I removed two pairs of rubber surgical gloves and tossed one pair to Axel as he walked in.

"While following up on a lead in the Sanchez assault case, I met a young fella that works at the Saint Margaret Mary Church. He fits the description of someone who was in the area when the assault took place, so I dropped by his apartment to ask him a few questions. The kid is in his early twenties, but he lives with his mother. I began to ask him questions and she got protective and wouldn't let me talk to him, then asked me to leave. The boy tried to give me the Bible, but I rejected it. This morning, I found it on my desk with this letter in it. Because it says it's a confession, I want you to witness me opening and reading the letter, then make a copy for me and log it into evidence. I'll log the Bible in later."

Using a sharp letter opener, I sliced along the fold and asked, "Do you know the Bible verse?"

"Yeah, I do, Sergeant, it's from the book of James, 'Confess your sins to each other and pray for each other so that you may be healed. The prayer of a righteous person is powerful and effective.'"

"Wow, have you memorized the whole Bible?"

"No, just some parts."

The letter was addressed to me, written in very small print and in blue ink.

I am writing to confess, and because what I did is so bad I'm confessing to the police. I know what I did is wrong, and I'm ready to pay the price for my sin. For the last year when Father Vincent is away, and it's after three, I go into the confessional and celebrate the Sacrament of Reconciliation. I hear the confessions of those who come too late.

The first time I did it, I just wanted to see what it was like to sit in Father Vincent's seat. I was about to leave when a woman came in and began telling me her sins. I lowered my voice and whispered her act of penance. I know it was wrong, but it felt really good.

Now I can't sleep very well because of what I have seen. A man came into the confessional and said he had attacked a blind woman in San Francisco a long time ago. He said he had done it before and received absolution for both assaults from his parish priest. Lately he's been having evil thoughts and wanted prayer, expressing contrition and remorse for his sin. I gave him penance for reconciliation, and together we prayed for strength, then he left.

Afterward I spent the next forty-five minutes cleaning up the sanctuary and working around several of the usual ladies that come to light candles and pray. One was a young blind woman. I have seen her in the church often, but on this day, she stood out because of the confession I had just heard. When I finished straightening up Father Vincent's office and the waiting area, I left out through the sanctuary and noted that all the ladies were gone.

I locked the doors and walked up Excelsior Avenue to 13th and cut through the building site of the new Edna Brewer School. I was halfway across when I heard a woman screaming from behind the construction trailer. I'm ashamed to say I peeked around the corner and saw a man hitting a woman with a board. She stopped screaming and I was afraid he would see me, so I ran back to the church and called the police, but I didn't give them my name. I just hung up when they asked for it.

I have kept notes on all the confessions I have heard so maybe Father Vincent can pray over them when I'm in jail.

It was signed *Charles O'Neal.*

Below his name he wrote, *Call me and I'll come in,* and listed his phone number.

Folding up the letter, I slid it back into the envelope and wrote, *Opened and read on May 16, 1978, at 1530 by Detective Sergeant Bob Richards, OPD, and witnessed by Detective Axel Heart, OPD. Case #516237178.*

"We need to get this kid in here. How is your workload?"

"Not bad. Want my help?" Axel asked.

"I do. I have several active with a slew of tentacles. I'll clear it with Bender and let you know when I need ya. What's your call sign?"

"Lema 2."

"Who's Lema 1?"

"Don't know. According to the latrine-a-grams from gossip central, Lema 1 was beaten to death by crazed Oakland Raider fans when he wore his Denver Broncos jersey into the Black Hole."

"Wow, I never heard that one. He wasn't too bright."

"Yeah, but it isn't true. He's still alive. His wife gets a finger or toe every year for Christmas."

"Right . . ."

CHAPTER NINETEEN

I called the number, and on the third ring Father Vincent said, "Hello, Saint Margaret Mary Church."

"Hello, Father, this is Detective Bob Richards with the Oakland Police Department. I thought I was calling Charles. This is the number he gave me."

"Hello, Sergeant. Yes, this is the right number. Yesterday I gave Charles permission to stay a little while in the church rectory. It's not being used, and he seems to be having some trouble with his mother. Would you hold for a moment and I'll retrieve him?"

"Hello."

"Charles, this is Detective Sergeant Richards. I read your letter. Thank you very much for confiding in me," I said gently, because this young man might be in his twenties chronologically, but he's just getting through puberty. "Would you mind coming down to the police department tomorrow, say around ten so we could talk?"

"Okay. Are you going to arrest me?"

"No, Charles, I'm not, because you haven't done anything wrong to be arrested for."

"I didn't help that lady. I ran away," he said, and I could tell he was starting to tear up.

"Charles, you didn't run away. You ran to get help. You're a hero. If you hadn't called the police, that lady could still be lying behind the construction trailer."

"I didn't think about that," he said. "Okay. I'll call a cab in the morning."

"That's fine, Charles. Tell the cab driver that I will pay him when you arrive. If he has any questions, give him the business card that I gave you."

"Okay, I will."

"And Charles, this is an active investigation so please don't say anything to anyone, including Father Vincent and your mother, until after we talk, okay?"

"Okay."

* * *

"Michael, can I interrupt you for a minute? It's worth coffee in the morning," I said, standing at Sergeant Bender's door.

"Coffee . . . it must be serious." Detective Sergeant Michael Bender and I had a rocky start, but I had found that he's a good cop, a good investigator, and a good leader. He was also becoming a good friend.

"I need one of your chicks. I won't keep him, I just want to borrow him for a while on a part-time basis."

"Who?"

"Axel Heart. I have several cases that I feel are about to crest, and I believe he can help me expedite their resolve. I have a meeting in the morning with a witness to the Emily Sanchez assault and rape. I want Axel to be there to meet him. He's just a kid and he's scared. I think Axel can calm him down a bit. So what do you think? Can I share him with you for a little while?"

"Tall black, and a maple bar."

"Wow, you drive a hard bargain. See you in the AM."

Walking into the pit, I was immersed in the clustered clatter of multiple typewriters, the harmony of a choir of voices trying to shout over one another, and the ceaseless whine of the air purification and heating system.

Standing at his desk, Axel had his back to me as he hunched over his IBM Selectric typewriter, pecking feverishly away with both index fingers. I almost felt guilty interrupting him because he seemed to have a rhythm going and seemed intent on getting what was in his head onto a thin sheet of wood pulp. Not wanting to spook him, I walked around his desk and stood in front of him. "Axel."

"Yes, Sergeant," he said, looking up and pushing away from his work.

"I'm sorry to interrupt you. I'll let you get back to it in a minute. Sergeant Bender cleared you to work with me. I have the kid who gave us the Bible coming in, going to be here at ten tomorrow morning. I want you to meet him and get to know him. He needs to be comfortable with you in case we need to reach out to him later."

"No problem, we'll be buddies before he leaves."

"The kid is scared to death that he's going to be arrested because he sinned, and he thinks he was wrong to run away when he saw Sanchez being attacked. I told him that he was a hero because he ran and got help. My take of him is we're not going to be talking to a man in his twenties but a young teenager in a man suit. I'll call you when he gets here."

"Sounds good. Is there anything else I can do for you, Sergeant?"

"Yeah, pick up a tall black coffee and a maple bar for Sergeant Bender when you come in tomorrow."

On my way home, I swung by the Hensley spread and caught Grandpa Joe in his workshop installing a new marine radio in his twenty-two-foot Boston whaler fishing boat. Come spring he planned on spending another season with the boys on Lake Berryessa and Lake Shasta catching mermaids and coming home with whopping fish stories.

"Good evening, Joe," I said, leaning over the side of the boat.

From under the boat's dashboard, Joe waived a hand at me. "How are you doing, son?"

"Doing good, Joe, doing real good. Listen, don't stop what you're doing, I just had a couple questions."

"No problem, shoot," he said, reaching for a wire cutter.

"You're good friends with Father Patrick Fanahan of the Roman Catholic Diocese of Oakland, right?"

"Yes, I've worked with him on a couple projects, and we try to get a golf game every month or so. Are you planning on becoming a Catholic, Bobby?"

"No, but I may need to talk to one, someone who can guide me through Catholic doctrine and California law."

"Well, Fanahan would be your man. He has a law degree and has passed the bar. He counsels the diocese on legal matters. When do you need to talk with him?"

"I don't know. I may not even have to. I'll let you know if I do. Thanks, Joe."

"You're welcome," he shouted as I headed to the car. "If you need him, I'll arrange for a golf game and make sure you're in his cart."

I always know that if I need anything, all I have to do is go to Grandpa Joe and I'll get it. He's not only the best man I've ever known, but he's also the most resourceful.

At home I cleared the front door and called out, "Rosie, you home?" Not getting a response, I went into the bedroom and secured my weapon in the gun cabinet and headed for the kitchen. There I found my bride at the kitchen sink. When I put my arm around her waist, she turned, threw her arms around my neck, and began to sob.

"What's wrong?"

Stepping back, as her eyes filled with tears, she cried, "They're growing up too quickly, Bobby. They're my babies, and they're growing up to quick."

Taking my hand, she led me over to the kitchen table where several photo albums lay open. "I found these in the bottom drawer of the dresser when I was cleaning the guestroom."

We sat and flipped pages of when the boys were little. As she removed a handful of pictures from a tan Kodak developing envelope, the tears morphed into laughter as she laid out the photos.

"Do you remember this?" She chuckled.

It was a picture of two little boys covered in white flour and sitting on the floor of Sonny's bedroom. The only thing that was identifiable on either one was two wide eyes looking out through a cloud of powder.

Little Joe would sneak into Sonny's room early in the morning before the sun rose to play. Sonny was nearly three and Joe had just turned six. To get his little brother out of his crib, Joseph would crawl under the crib and kick the bottom up until Sonny fell through the slats onto the floor.

On this day, little Joseph's parenting instinct would be expressed to the fullest. He had watched as Sonny would be bathed, powdered, and his diaper changed, so he followed suit. Going into the kitchen he got the almost-full bag of flour and powdered Sonny himself, the room, and everything in it. A literal cloud of white flour covered everything so evenly it was hard to define anything in the room. If it moved, it was one of our boys.

Rosie had woken me up and said that there was something I had to see. She opened the door to Sonny's room and all I could make out were four round spots that periodically blinked. It took everything we had to keep from bursting out in laughter as we quickly got them out of the room so they wouldn't suffocate. We couldn't wash them off in the shower or tub because these little human bread rolls would clog the drains, so it was out in the backyard with a garden hose. It took us nearly two weeks to get that room cleaned out. We were afraid that if lightning struck during a rainstorm, we would explode into the biggest biscuit in the state.

We spent the next few hours reflecting, crying, and laughing. Then we prayed and thanked God for the beautiful young lives He had given us.

At precisely 10:00 a.m. the next morning, Liz poked her head in and said that Charles O'Neal was at the front desk for me and that she had seen him in the lobby when she came in around 8:30.

"Send him in, and buzz Axel and let him know Charles is here."

"Good morning, Charles," I said, reaching out and shaking his hand. "I understand you have been here since 8:30."

"I don't like being late. Mom says it's a sign of disrespect."

"Well, you certainly weren't late. What about the cab driver? I need to pay him. I hope he hasn't been sitting out there with the meter running."

"No, I didn't take a cab; I walked. I feel better when I walk in the morning. It's quiet, a good time to pray."

"Pray," Detective Axel said as he entered. "I like praying in the morning too. It starts the day off right."

Stepping over to Charles, he stuck out a callused hand. "I'm Detective Axel Heart. You can just call me Axel. You must be Charles O'Neal, the young man who saved that girl. You should be proud of yourself."

I could see that Axel just made a solid bond, as a smile formed across the young man's face.

"Charles, let's begin by making sure that you understand what we are doing here," I said, placing my reel-to-reel recorder between us and pushing the record button. "Do you mind if I record our conversation?"

"No, that's fine."

"Good. You are not under arrest or even under suspicion of any criminal act. I am investigating an assault of a young woman, and according to the letter you sent me, and our conversation last night, you are a witness to that assault. Is that correct?"

"Yes. I saw what happened to the lady and who did it."

"Do you know who he is? Do you know him personally?"

"I don't know him personally, but I know who he is. His name is Cliff Infield. I heard him talking to Father Vincent in the parking lot when I was sweeping. I thought his name was funny, that's why I remembered it."

"Can you describe him for me, his age, what he looks like, how he dresses, his car . . .?"

I looked over at Axel as he wrote down the incredibly detailed description Charles was providing. Then with a nod, he was out the door checking records and DMV.

"Well done, Charles. You are helping us get a very bad man off the street."

"I'm glad I can help."

"Let's talk about something else for a minute. In one of your notes, you said JC murders the young. Are you talking about Jesus?"

"Oh no. Jesus doesn't hurt anyone."

"Then who is JC, and what does that mean?"

"A girl came in when Father Vincent was gone, and I was in the confessional. She didn't know what to do because she had never gone to confession before. She wasn't Catholic, but she was really upset so I heard her confession anyway. That's okay, right?"

"I don't know, Charles. It's not illegal according to the State of California, but it may not be okay with the Catholics. You'll have to check that out yourself later."

"What she said didn't make sense. She was upset because of where her brother, who she called JC, worked. It was a place where they sold incense. Then she started to cry again and said she thinks her dad works there too. I asked her what was wrong with selling incense? That's when she got really mad at me."

"Why did she get mad? What does selling incense have to do with murdering the young."

"I don't know, she just kept saying she thinks they're stealing and selling little boys. She said it three times."

The air left the room, I stopped breathing, and my brain went into automatic pilot. Oh . . . my . . . God . . . "Charles, do you think she was saying *innocence?*"

"Yeah, yeah, she could have been saying that. She was crying so hard I couldn't understand her sometimes."

"Charles, we're going to stop and take a break. Is that okay with you?"

"Sure," he said as Axel came through the door with a handful of mugshots.

"Axel, we're going to take a short break. Do you have any money on you?"

"Yeah, about five bucks, here," he said, handing it to me.

"Charles, take about twenty minutes and go down to the snack bar in the main lobby and get yourself anything you want. You've earned it," I said, handing him the bill.

CHAPTER TWENTY

With a tall bottle of soda, a bag of chips, and a fist full of M&Ms, my lead witness sat at my desk munching away and ready to continue our conversation.

"Charles, I want to talk more about the girl and what she told you, but first we need to take care of the business at hand, which is what you saw behind the construction trailer. Detective Axel has a group of pictures that I want you to look at, and let me know if anyone looks familiar to you."

Axel spread out the photos on a small table against the far wall and waved Charles over. "Take your time, we're not in a rush. What you are doing is very important, so if you don't see anyone you know, that's okay."

Putting his culinary delights on my desk, Charles stepped over to the table, looked at the pictures, and immediately picked one out. "This is Mr. Cliff Infield, the man I saw hit the lady with a board."

"Very good, now I need you to write me a statement, covering everything that happened, including our time together and our conversation. Are you willing to do that?"

"Yes, I can do that," he said, chewing on a few chips.

"Okay, what you're going to write will be evidence and a part of my report, so it's very important that it be the complete truth and nothing but the truth."

Nodding he said, "I understand, like the oath they say when you're in court. I've seen that in the movies."

"Are you willing to stick around and talk with me about the girl after that? I'll send out for pizza and soda. Are you good with that?"

"Yep."

In Interview Room A, with a handful of pens and a couple of lined legal pads, Charles set to work writing what he had experienced, in as much detail as he could. Axel returned to his IBM and began to type an update to the Sanchez case, while I went through the details and evidence of our case along with that of the Berkeley and San Francisco reports.

I have found that my first reading of a report is usually rapid and superficial, and thus I tend to miss many of the finer details. The first time I'm reading an engaging story, and the next I'm reading an account.

This reading was no different. In cataloging the evidence, all three of the investigating officers noted the location of the victim's garments, purse, cane, and dark glasses in relationship to where she was assaulted. In each case everything was close to the victim except the glasses. They were a considerable distance away from the victim. They hadn't fallen off during the attack; they were thrown.

I contacted the detectives in the other agencies that had been assigned to these cases and inquired if the victims' glasses were held as evidence, and both said no, but they were printed before they were returned to the victim.

Fortunately, it appeared that there was enough to make a required twelve-point match.

My next call was to Sergeant Helen Finch. I gave her the case numbers of all three reports and asked her to requisition the fingerprint evidence from the other agencies and compare it to Mr. Cliff Infield.

"Helen, OPD has busted Cliff Infield for DUI and battery, so we have his prints on file. We have an eyewitness to the attack, but before I can get a warrant, I'll need some physical evidence."

"I'll get on it," she said. "By the way, how is Rosie doing?"

"She's doing well. So far, every examination has proven clear. Thanks for asking."

"Let her know she is in our prayers."

"I will. One more thing, Helen, were you able to positively identify that button?"

"Yes, I have. You were right, it's the crest from a class ring produced by Jostens Custom Rings for the California Maritime Academy. The date identifies it as belonging exclusively to the Vallejo academy. I have ordered one of the rings for comparative use and will submit it into evidence."

My office door opened, and Liz stepped in and quietly closed the door behind her. The expression on her face said something wasn't good.

"What's up?"

"Sergeant, there's a Mrs. O'Neal here to see you and she is very angry. She has used my phone twice calling attorneys while we waited for you to get off yours. She's here for her son, and it could get ugly."

"Okay. I want to buy a little more time for Charles to write his statement. Tell her I'm on another call, but as soon as I'm done, I'll speak with her. Get her some tea or coffee, and don't let her use your phone again. Send her to the phone booth in the lobby."

I called Axel and told him to check on Charles to see where he was with his statement, and to make sure he wasn't missing anything. I could have had the recording of our meeting transcribed, and then have Charles sign it, but a statement written in the witness's own hand, along with a recording, is gold.

This meeting with the mother bear could offset the Sanchez investigation and completely derail exploring the incense/innocence thing. It was time to call in the big guns. Folding my hands in front of me, I closed my eyes and prayed, "Lord, I believe you are orchestrating these events, and I need your guidance and wisdom. Help me to speak to this woman with compassion and grace and assure her that she and her son are safe. Amen."

I dialed Liz and said, "Is Mrs. O'Neal ready?"

"No, sir, she left and said she would be back. I think she went down to the lobby to use the phone."

"Great, show her in when she comes back."

Axel returned with Charles, both with a mouth full of M&Ms. "He's done, and he did a great job."

Dropping a dozen sheets of lined paper on my desk, Charles dropped into a chair with a smile.

"That was fast. Are you sure you didn't leave anything out?" I said, looking over each page.

"I can write real fast and I have a real good memory. Mom says I have good penmanship too," Charles said proudly.

"I would agree with you and your mom," I said, noting the detail as I thumbed through the pages.

"Charles, your mother is here. She's down in the lobby and will be up to see us momentarily. Remember, I asked you not to tell anyone about our meeting?"

"I didn't tell her. I left her a note."

I looked up at Axel who snickered. "He's got you there, boss."

"Okay, you were right to do that," I said as the door opened and in walked Mrs. O'Neal.

I stood and extended my hand to greet her, but she waved me off. "Come on, Charles, we're leaving."

"No. I have work to do here."

"Charles, you will come with me now," commanded Mrs. O'Neal.

"I will not. Mom, you need to sit and listen to what Detective Sergeant Richards has to say. It is important, really important."

She stood stunned, staring at him. Her countenance made me wonder if this was the first time he stood his ground against her.

"Mrs. O'Neal, please have a seat and let me share with you what's going on."

Reluctantly she slid into a seat next to her son, looked at him, and took his hand. The next forty-five minutes were not only informative but anointed. I allowed her to read Charles's statement, and then I fielded her questions. Coffee was served by the bucket and mom saw her son in a new light. Although he had some special concerns, he wasn't a little boy anymore.

I offered her the opportunity to remain through the rest of our interview, but she chose to let him finish on his own, so long as I personally returned him home.

When the door closed behind her, Charles looked up, smiled, and said, "I guess we had what Mom calls *a meeting of the minds.*"

Pizza and drinks were ordered, and Charles was sequestered in Interview Room A with his pens and paper to author another bestseller. On his lined paper pad, I asked him to write what he remembered the girl had said to him, word for word. We were amazed how clear and precise he was. Everything she said was quoted, with spaces between each comment.

On the second sheet the words jumped off the page, *They're selling little boys. My brother and dad are stealing innocent children and selling them.*

The description of the girl was easily recognizable, blond Farrah Fawcett–type hair, five-foot-three, denim bell-bottoms, black T-shirt, and wood platform shoes. This described eighty percent of the young female population within the San Francisco Bay Area.

"Is there anything that stood out about her?" I asked, hoping she had a hunched back or a third eye.

"No, that's it, I'm sorry," he said sorrowfully. "She sure had a cool car though."

"A cool car? What kind of car?"

"I don't know. It was kind of gold, and the top comes down."

"Did it have an emblem, a logo on the hood or trunk?"

"Yeah, a star."

"That would be a Chrysler. Did it look new?"

"Yeah, it was really shiny."

"Okay, so we have a new sort of gold Chrysler convertible with a star like this on the hood," Axel said, dropping his car keychain on the desk in front of Charles.

"That's not the star that was on the car," Charles said, pointing to the logo.

"It's not? What's different about it?" I asked.

"That has five points. The girl's had only three."

"I'll be right back," Axel said, disappearing out the door.

Returning with a new *Car and Driver* magazine, he opened it and put it in front of Charles. "We're not looking for a Chrysler. We're looking for a Mercedes."

"That's the car, but it was kind of gold," Charles said, excitedly pointing to a photo of a tan 1978 Mercedes-Benz 450SL classic.

"Axel, do a DMV run and let's find out who owns a Mercedes convertible in the Bay Area, then complete your report on the Sanchez case. Charles, I need you to write another statement. You up to it?"

"Sure."

"Good. I'll leave you to it."

Stopping at the door, I said, "Charles, you said she was wearing a black T-shirt. Was there a design on it?"

"Yeah, it was a red square with a Christmas tree."

"Okay," I said disappointed. "When you're done, I'll take you home."

Later that evening, sitting at the dinner table, I watched my boys, healthy and strong, filling their faces and arguing over who held supremacy, the Oakland Raiders or the San

Francisco 49ers. They were good boys growing into good men. Although we had experienced some challenges, my boys were never afraid of being stolen, nor did they ever fear being sold to a stranger. What in the name of God was happening in our world?

Rosie reached over and put her hand in mine. "What's going on, Bobby?"

"Work, baby, just work. We'll talk later."

For now, my greatest challenge wasn't eliminating evil from the streets of Oakland, but cleaning up the dishes and getting the right gap on a set of spark plugs for Little Joe's 1960 Ford Falcon. We had made an agreement with Joe to match every dollar he saved for his first car, an agreement that would extend to all the boys when they reached sixteen. From his paper route to cutting apricots in the summer, Joe had saved $210.85. A very good start.

Then last month, while I was working in the garage, he pulled up in this ugly green Falcon and proclaimed, "Look at what I bought, Dad. I got a great deal, only $175."

He opened the driver's door and stepped back and said, "Check it out, Dad. It needs a little attention, but it runs great."

There wasn't a single knob on the dash panel, the steering wheel had enough play you could almost spin it, and there was a gaping hole in the floorboard where a Hurst conversion kit had been poorly installed.

Looking past the torn and worn Naugahyde seats, I wanted to point out our agreement and say a few choice words about this heap of metal blocking my driveway. The joy on his face, however, quelled my tongue. I could only imagine what his mom was going to say when she saw this thing.

Going into the house, I went to the sink to wash up. "Rosie, Little Joe is out front, has something he wants to show you."

"Okay," she said from the hall, then walked out the front door leaving it standing open. I stood by the sink and waited to hear Rosie's opinion that I was sure would be heard around the block. After a couple of minutes, the only sound I heard was Joe's new acquisition starting up. When I went to the door I watched as a putrid green 1960 Ford Falcon faded down the street with Rosie Richards at the wheel.

Over the next six months, Little Joe invested every nickel he earned on auto insurance and turning that ugly green wagon into a gleaming green chariot.

As the evening wore down, I shared with Rosie the cases I'd been working on and that the closest lead I had was a spoiled Farrah Fawcett wannabe who matched the description of every blond girl in the state. Her only distinguishing characteristics were that she drove a cool car and wore outdated Christmas T-shirts.

The next morning, I was about to pull out of the driveway when Rosie stood at the open doorway waving some papers at me. "Bobby, come here," she shouted.

Going back into the house she directed me to sit at the kitchen table where Joe had spread out pamphlets and guides for colleges and universities he was interested in.

"Take a moment and look at these, Bobby."

"I have to get to work, baby. Can't we do this tonight?" I said a bit irritated.

"No, look through them, please."

I picked up a brochure for UC Berkeley and UC Davis and looked them over. "Okay, can I go now?"

"No, keep looking," she said sternly.

"Okay, what am I looking for? The University of San Francisco, Academy of Arts and Sciences, Stanford University . . ." The room stood still, a light came on in my head, and my brain exploded. "Stanford! It's Stanford."

On the cover of Stanford's brochure was a large red box with the university's name along the top and their logo of a pine tree in the center of a circle at the bottom.

"The girl was wearing a Stanford University T-shirt," I said, reaching over and giving my brilliant bride a kiss.

CHAPTER TWENTY-ONE

My target had grown significantly smaller. Instead of having to find my Barbie in the sixteen hundred square miles of the Bay Area, now I just needed to find her on the Stanford campus.

On my way to work, I drove up to the Stanford University parking lot and identified myself to the security guard at the gate.

"Good morning. I would like to drive through the lot. I'm looking for a blond girl, about five-foot-three, driving a Mercedes convertible."

He looked at me in awe, eyebrows raised, and in a sense of fascination said, "You're kidding, right? That's every third car in this parking lot."

"Thanks," I said, putting it in gear. He was right. Among the high-end luxury toys, I came across seven gold, tan, and yellow Mercedes convertibles and a few others that could fall into the general color range. Scribbling notes of the colors and license plates, I began to wonder if this wasn't a huge waste of time. I hadn't even confirmed the T-shirt logo with Charles yet. I was allowing the tentacles that a case can develop to distract me. If I hoped to find out who this girl was and what she knew. I was going to have to reel myself in.

Back at the PD, I set the list of plate numbers on Liz's desk and asked her to check for warrants and registration information. I also gave her Joe's Stanford brochure and asked her to order a girl's black T-shirt with the logo that was on the pamphlet.

"Liz, if I were to tell you someone smelled like vinegar, what would you think it was?"

She sat there for a moment then grinned. "My dad."

"Your dad?"

"Yes, he was an amateur photographer. He would do weddings and stuff for friends, and he was always snapping pictures of family gatherings. He did his own developing in the basement. Mom would have a fit because of the vinegar smell."

"Okay, thanks."

Axel came into my office and set a four-page list of Mercedes convertibles registered in the Bay Area. They were as plentiful as fleas.

On my desk I had laid out the folders of the Sanchez assault and rape case, the Kurkland and Russell kidnapping case, the Avery murder case, and the two assault cases from San Francisco and Walnut Creek. It was time to make some calls.

"Detective Sergeant Finch, CSU, how can I help you?"

"Helen, it's Bob Richards. Do you have anything on the Sanchez assault?"

"Yes, I was going to call you. Those glasses are the key. Each pair was smudged, but there were enough clear latent prints to make more than a twelve-point match on all three cases. All three pair were broken, and two were pulverized. My professional opinion is that the attacker ripped them off the victims' face and compressed them in his hand so hard he crushed them. He was clearly enraged. I'm surprised none of these ladies were killed. Between your eyewitness and the prints, you got your bad guy."

"Great, send your report over. I'll take it to the DA tomorrow. Today, I'm going to find this guy and put him in a box."

Selfishly, I didn't want to share any of the glory with the San Francisco or Walnut Creek detectives, so I elected to let them know of Cliff Infield's arrest after I booked him into jail. It was childish, I agree, but there's a little boy in me that sometimes just wants to be the best at show and tell.

Once again, I stood at Axel's desk as he pecked away at the letters of his IBM. Even without looking up he sensed my presence and said, "What's up, Boss?"

"Prints came back on Infield. Want some A and E?"

"Don't you mean R and R, rest and recuperation?"

"Nope, I've been sitting at my desk too long, resting and recuperating, I need some A and E, action and excitement. Let's go get him."

We had two addresses for Mr. Infield. One came from his arrest for driving under the influence, and the other was the address he put on his California driver's license. The license would probably be more accurate because drunk drivers are quick to give false information.

Cliff's residence at 2700 Derby Street was built in the 1930s, in a well-established neighborhood in southwest Berkeley. The white and blue-trimmed Tudor-style house, with a manicured lawn, blossoming flowers, and trimmed shrubs looked more like the home of Mr. Rogers than that of Charles Manson.

I removed my coat and straightened up my tie, rolled up my sleeves, placed my 9mm in the back of my pants, and tossed my shoulder holster into the trunk. From the backseat I retrieved the Bible I had left there after last Sunday's church service, and I casually walked up to the front door.

I knocked and heard movement inside. On the second knock, a woman's voice called out, "Who is it?"

"Pastor Richards, ma'am, from the Universal Church. Is Mr. Cliff Infield home?"

"No, what do you want with him?"

"Well, a friend of Mr. Infield's asked me to stop by and visit him. Do you know where I might be able to find him?"

"He's at work. He's always at work. You should know that."

"I'm sorry, Mrs. Infield, could you give me the address?"

"I'm not Mrs. Infield. This is my home. I rent it from Cliff. He lives in the converted garage in the back. He's never there because he has an apartment above his office downtown. I don't have the address, but it's on Durant Avenue."

"Okay, thank you. What's the name of his business?"

There came no response. "Ma'am, can you give me the name of his business?"

Still silence, then, "You better leave. I'm calling the police. I don't know who you are."

"Okay, ma'am, we're leaving. I'm sorry to have bothered you. My name is Richards. I'm going to leave my card here at the door. You can call me any time."

I carry two business cards. One is issued by the PD with my name, rank, phone number, and OPD logo. The other is blank with just my name, phone number, and a nondescript logo I found on a discarded chewing tobacco tin. This is the one I left her.

"Dispatch, this is Delta-2."

"Go ahead, Delta-2."

"Check with the city of Berkeley for a business license issued to one Cliff Infield. The business may be on Durant."

"Stand by."

Within five minutes I heard, "Delta-2, Cliff Infield received a business license in 1969 for 'Berkeley Ophthalmology Clinic' located at 2410 Durant Avenue."

"Ten-four, thanks."

"He's a doctor, an MD, specializing in eye and vision issues. He diagnoses them, treats them, then he rapes them," Axel said. "Let's go get this sick SOB."

Pulling up across the street from Berkeley Ophthalmology Clinic, we sat and watched as fifteen people walked into the building that had recently been refurbished. Above the front door hung a black awning with the business name in silver script. Above that was an eight-foot sliding glass door, behind a wrought iron gate. That was Cliff Inland's apartment. I wonder if he stood there looking down on the street, looking for potential victims. Was it from there that he saw Sanchez?

I could tell Axel was getting amped and wanted to jump, but sitting there I was getting a different vibe.

"Hold up, Axel, let's not get him yet," I said.

"Why not?"

"If we show our hand now, he'll be out by morning. And if he hadn't already called someone from the jail, he'll be home cleaning house. Let's go to the DA in the morning and get an arrest and search warrant. That way we can search both the house and business at the same time we take him down."

"Sergeant, I want a piece of that guy's butt today, but you're right. Okay, he takes a fall tomorrow," Axel said.

We stopped by Dee's Country Kitchen and enjoyed lunch while I called Liz, asking her to set up an appointment for us tomorrow morning with Deputy District Attorney KP Cooper, better known as Coop. He was one of the sharpest, most aggressive deputy district attorneys in Alameda County. A transplant from New York, he loved to spend his evenings riding along with the officers on the streets of Oakland. He was handy to have around, particularly when we rolled in on a homicide or some other major crime. Coop had a good reputation of being uncompromising, honest, and trustworthy, and he had a close relationship with nearly all of Alameda County's judicial panel.

The next morning, I prepared the Sanchez report by including CSU's fingerprint examination results and Charles O'Neal's exhaustive written account. I also brought the Stevens baby file. I wanted to discuss how far we could run with the spontaneous utterance by the girl to Charles in the confessional.

Our appointment was set for 8:00 a.m., so we arrived early with three large cups of coffee and found Coop up to his handlebar mustache in case files. It seems every cop in the county wanted him to be the one to prosecute their case.

The usual small talk about family and weather was dispensed with, when he pushed back a pile of paper, opened our file, and said, "Talk to me."

We spent the next forty-five minutes describing the events in their order, the physical evidence, the witness statements, and how each component came together.

"Coop, we have a solid case. We want an arrest warrant for Cliff Infield for assault and rape, and we want a search warrant for his home, business, and apartment."

Twisting the ends of his mustache, he flipped through the report, stopping at Charles's handwritten narrative.

"I think what you're asking for is wrong," he said without looking up.

"Wrong? Sorry to disagree, but this is a slam dunk," I said, feeling my body starting to tense.

"I didn't say it was a bad case. Actually it's too good. A case this tight will be pled out. A deal will be made, the assault will be dropped, and he'll get two years for the rape."

"You really think that's what will happen?" Axel asked.

"I know it. The DA is a political office. All he wants is a high clearance rate. The more convictions and the less time and money spent on trials, the better he looks to the voting public."

"So, what are we going to do?" I grumbled.

"Well, I want to have him arrested for assault with a deadly weapon, aggravated assault, and attempted murder. He beat a blind woman that he just raped, with a board. I'd say he wanted her dead. I want to arrest him for kidnapping and false imprisonment during the commission of a crime. I want to arrest him for first-degree robbery, with aggravating factors, the inflicting of great bodily harm, and there's evidence tampering, intimidation of a witness, and petty theft, when he took her driver's license. And of course, I want to arrest him for the forcible rape of a defenseless blind woman. The search warrant must also include all the vehicles our good doctor owns. You need to make sure they are impounded as evidence so they're available for search whenever we get around to it."

"Wow. Do you think all that's possible?" I asked.

"No, not all, but it's a good start. If there isn't any major news on the local or national front, we might be able to get the press to blow this up. That always lights a fire under the DA."

"Thank you, Coop," I said, choosing not to bring up the Stevens baby case. All I have on it is suspicions based on what could be nothing more than coincidences.

"No problem, you did good work. I'll write up the warrants and take them to Judge Andrews during his usual morning break. You should have them in your hands by noon."

After dropping Axel off at the police department, I swung by the O'Neal home to show Charles the photo of Sanford's red square logo with the pine tree. After coffee and several of Mrs. O'Neal's great chocolate chip cookies, he confirmed that it was the print he saw on the front of the girl's T-shirt.

Next stop, California Maritime Academy, to speak to Jimmy Corbitt who should be back from his offshore training.

Just as I pulled into the visitor parking lot, I heard, "Delta-2."

"This is Delta-2, go ahead, Dispatch."

"Delta-2, you have a special delivery envelope from the District Attorney's office. It says on the cover, 'Important Deliver ASAP.'"

"Thank you, Dispatch. Please get it into Detective Heart's hands and tell him I'm heading back now."

Looking over my shoulder, I began to back out, then hit the brakes as a gold Mercedes convertible drove past into the Command Staff parking lot, stopping under the eave that led to the commodore's entrance. The driver appeared to have difficulty getting out of the car, but once he did, I could see that it was the bulbous form of Commodore William Wilbanks.

Walking around the small car, he opened the door for his passenger and graciously extended his hand to assist a dark-haired lady in a golf hat, dressed in jeans and a black T-shirt, adorned in sequins.

Reaching up, she wrapped her arms around the commodore's neck and kissed him passionately, then turned and walked around the back of the car and sat in the driver's seat.

I knew that woman. That was Claudia Corbitt.

CHAPTER TWENTY-TWO

Parked in front of Cliff Infield's ophthalmology clinic, Axel and I watched as clients came and went. I wanted to go in and get him, but his business included optical surgery, and I wasn't about to disrupt him in the middle of a surgical procedure. We sat for nearly an hour watching people come and go and decided we had waited long enough.

"Dispatch, this is Delta-2, drop to Tac 2," I said, switching the Motorola.

"Go ahead, Sergeant." I recognized the voice as Supervisor Lacy Smith, whose daughter worked with Emily Sanchez at the San Antonio Neighborhood Clinic. Her interest in this case went beyond just being inquisitive.

"Lacy, we're about to make an arrest on the suspect in the Emily Sanchez case. I need you to call the Berkeley Ophthalmology Clinic and ask for Dr. Cliff Infield. If he gets on the phone with you, that means he's not in surgery. Keep him on the phone and have Dispatch clear us."

"Will do."

"Give us five minutes to get in place."

"In five," she responded.

Axel and I split up, walking up the street in different directions then crossing the street and approaching the clinic from different sides. Just before we reached the door, Axel spoke into his portable radio and gave me a thumbs-up.

Clearing the door, we walked past a half dozen patients and a protesting receptionist into Dr. Cliff Infield's office. I took the phone from his hand as Axel bent him over his desk and cuffed him.

"Thank you, Lacy, we're Code-4," and the line went dead.

Strangely, Infield allowed himself to be handcuffed and seated in a chair without resistance or even a question. It was as if he expected us. I stepped into the lobby and told those waiting for their appointment, "Ladies and gentlemen, Dr. Infield will not be seeing any more patients today."

Flustered, an elderly woman said, "Well, when can he see me?"

"In about forty years," I said.

"Wait a minute, who do you think you are?" the receptionist said angrily, reaching for her phone.

I showed her my ID. "I'm Detective Sergeant Bob Richards, and we have a warrant for the arrest of Dr. Cliff Infield and a search warrant for his business and his residence," I said, taking the phone receiver from her hand and hanging it up. "Do you have the keys to his apartment above the clinic?"

With fire in her eyes, she said, "I'm not going to help you do anything if I don't see a warrant."

Unfolding the warrants, I placed them on her desk and turned my attention to those in the waiting room, who had made no sign of leaving.

Jumping to her feet, the receptionist screamed, "Forcible rape, attempted murder, and kidnapping . . . are you serious?" and the waiting room was instantly emptied.

"Mrs. Anderson," I said, reading the nameplate on her desk. "Please calm down. We are going to need your assistance. Will you help us?"

"Yes, yes. My name is Rachell," she said shaking her head. "I just knew something like this would happen."

"Really, why?"

"Whenever an attractive woman is put under monitored anesthesia or conscious sedation, Dr. Infield will clear the room."

"What about the anesthesiologist?"

"Dr. Infield is a certified anesthesia technologist," she said, pointing to a wall filled with framed degrees and certificates.

"I'm going to ask you to remain at your desk. If you have other appointments or drop-ins, you are to tell them that Dr. Infield is unavoidably detained. That is all you are to say, and make no other calls."

In the office I admonished Infield of his rights as Axel began a search for any documentation or physical evidence. Infield remained stoic, refusing to acknowledge his Miranda rights, sitting silently staring at the floor. The only movement he made was to look up when Axel opened one of the drawers on a large wooden filling cabinet that contained patient records.

The files were alphabetically listed with the patient's name, address, and phone number handwritten on the raised tab at the top right of each folder. I ran my hand over at least a hundred files in the drawer and began to wonder what it was I was looking for. Then I felt it.

On twelve of the folders a small piece from the left corner of the raised tab was cut off, and on five of those a piece of the right corner had also been cut off. If you were only looking for patient names, you wouldn't notice the difference. When I began to remove the files with the clipped tabs, Dr. Cliff Infield woke up and began to shout.

"You can't touch those. They are patients' personal files. You have no right to look at them."

"Dr. Infield, do you want to talk to me about these?" I said, before I opened any of them.

"No, I have nothing to say. I want to call my lawyer."

"Okay, Dr. Infield, you have said the magic words. Axel, call for a wagon, and let's get the good doctor to County for booking. That way we can take our time here and at his hideaway on 2700 Derby Street."

The mention of Derby Street lit a fire of emotions as Cliff Inland's calm, cool demeanor liquefied into a whimpering puddle of tears. Sitting at the doctor's desk, I opened one of the files. Stapled to the inside of the cover was a black-and-white Polaroid photo of a young woman, along with medical records. This was true for all twelve folders, but one was familiar. It was the medical file for Emily Sanchez. Her file folder, along with four others, had the tab cut twice, and each file contained a patient who was blind.

The receptionist, Rachell Anderson, wrote a thorough statement of what she knew and what she suspected, while fielding calls and canceling appointments. Except for the twelve files, nothing of any evidentiary value was found either in the clinic or in his apartment. Next stop, Derby

Street. Once we convinced the little lady in the house that I wasn't coming to steal Cliff's stuff, we entered the converted garage with the keys his receptionist provided us.

Inside, the strong smell of vinegar filled the air. A long, well-worn blue sofa sat in the center of the room. Photos of partially dressed women, appearing to be asleep, were tacked on the walls, and several photo albums lay open on a coffee table. The photos in them were of woman who had been badly beaten, and one photo was of Emily Sanchez as she was found the night she was attacked.

The small garage had been divided in half by a wall with a heavy canvas curtain covering the entrance to the other side. In there we found a complete photo lab, with dozens of photos of woman of all ages hanging from a string line that crisscrossed the room. All were partially clothed, but completely exposed, and unconscious.

Rather than risking contamination of a crime scene, we stepped back out and called CSU to respond.

From our investigation it was determined that Dr. Cliff Infield was a solo act, a prolific serial rapist and molester, who was quickly becoming psychopathic. Once the CSU completed their work, and the reports were completed, the Emily Sanchez case would be brought to DA Cooper for prosecution, and a copy sent to SF and Walnut Creek PDs to aid them in their prosecution. The case, however, would not be quickly closed. With as many photos he had taken, there was little doubt that an avalanche of victims would soon be appearing on the horizon.

I stuck my head into Michael Bender's office and waved the Sanchez case folder. "Permission to enter, Detective Sergeant."

"Permission granted," Bender responded.

"Michael, we have Cliff Infield in custody," I said, placing the file folder on his desk. "The DA has the case, and it's a slam dunk, but we're not going to be able to close it yet."

"What do you have in mind?"

"Axel has worked closely with me and is familiar with every facet of the investigation. The evidence shows that there are more victims, a lot more, so I'm requesting that Axel assume the lead on the case. I'll assist, but I need to focus on the Avery and Stevens cases. The San Francisco and Walnut Creek rape and assault cases that were given to me have been returned and will be prosecuted by their respective DAs."

"Okay, we'll give Axel the lead, but you're still on board."

"You bet, thanks," I said heading out the door.

It was getting late, but I couldn't shake the feeling I was missing something big, something just out beyond my reach. My dear friend A. J. called it a divine itch. He once told me that it was a cop's sixth sense, the ability to know when something is wrong or danger was at hand. It's information we feel without using sight, hearing, touch, smell, or taste, and I was feeling it.

After four rings, Little Joe's slightly breathless voice came on the line. "Hello, Sherry?"

"Ah, no, sorry, son, it's Dad."

"Oh, hi, Dad."

"So, who's Sherry?"

"Just a friend. You want to talk to Mom?"

"Sure, but first tell me about Sherry."

"Mom, Dad's on the phone for you," he shouted. "Love ya, Dad. Talk to ya later."

"Hi sweetheart, what's up?" Rosie chimed in.

"Sounds like there's a new lady in Little Joe's life?"

"You mean Sherry? She's such a sweet girl. We met her at one of Joe's football games."

"The cheerleader? The one with chestnut hair and a big smile?"

"That's the one. Will you be home for dinner?"

"Would you mind if I hung around here a little while? The office is quiet, and I'm struggling with what my next move is. I need to go over what's in front of me and see what I'm missing, because I'm missing something, and I just don't know what it is."

"Sure, stay as long as you need to. Bobby, we know who knows what's missing. Why not ask Him?"

"You're right," I said, bowing my head. "Lord, you know all things, and all things are in your hand. I come before you . . . no, we come before You and seek Your guidance and Your wisdom. Show me, Lord, what I'm missing, and direct my steps, so that I might protect those that I serve. Amen."

It felt good to sit in the still silence, without the shouts and clatter that usually existed just outside my door. I walked over and turned off the fluorescent lights, allowing only my desk lamp to fill the room with a yellow glow. Sitting behind my desk, I stared at the Stevens baby case file to my left and the Avery homicide file to my right. Closing my eyes, I waited for some supernatural impetus that would enlighten me to my next move. There was nothing but a quiet hush and the faint sound of a vacuum cleaner down the hall.

"Sergeant Richards, are you there? Detective Sergeant Richards, are you in your office?"

Startled, I jumped up, jamming my knee into the underside of my desk drawer. My left hand grabbed my knee as pain shot through me like a bullet, and with my right I keyed the intercom. "Yeah, I'm here," I groaned.

"Sorry to bother you, Sergeant. We saw your car in the parking lot and there's a Charles O'Neal on the phone demanding to talk with you. Should I put it through?"

"Yes, put him through," I said, noting that I had nodded out for nearly an hour.

"Charles, are you okay?"

"Sergeant Bob, she's here. The girl I told you about. She's here."

"The girl that told you about her father and brother?"

"Yes, she came in to go to confession with Father Vincent, but because she isn't Catholic, Father Vincent couldn't hear her confession. He sat and talked with her in the church for a while, and now she's sitting by herself."

"Okay, Charles, I want you to go outside into the parking lot and write down the license numbers of every car in the lot. I will be there in a little bit. Do not talk with her. Go back into the rectory and wait for me there."

I arrived within thirty minutes, but she was gone. In the sanctuary Father Vincent and Charles sat in the front row. Stepping in front of them, I could see tears in Charles's eyes and anger in the priest's eyes.

"We have a real problem, Sergeant, a real problem. The Sacramental Seal of the Confessional has been violated. Anything that is heard during the Sacrament of Penance is to be held in absolute confidence and must never be disclosed," Father Vincent said.

"I understand, but Charles isn't a priest, so does that also apply to him?"

"Yes, it does. You will find the utterances shared in confidence with a priest, a pastor, or a religious leader have the expectation of privacy and are considered sacrosanct."

"Okay, what about Charles? Is he in any kind of trouble? He was only doing what he thought was right."

"He's a good boy, with a good heart. I know he didn't mean to do anything wrong, but he did, and we are going to have to deal with it," Father Vincent said.

Turning on the dash light, I sat in the church parking lot looking over the list of three license numbers Charles gave me when he shook my hand. He had drawn a star next to one of the numbers, so I started with that one.

"Dispatch, this is Delta-2."

"Go ahead, Delta-2."

"Registration on personalized California plate, Mike Yankee Golf Romeo Lima."

"Stand by."

Within a couple minutes, I received a shock.

"Delta-2, your plate MYGRL is for a 1978 Mercedes-Benz, registered to Leonard Corbitt."

CHAPTER TWENTY-THREE

The smell of hot coffee and bacon wafted across my senses as an angel pressed her lips softly on my cheek then whispered in my ear, "Wake up, Bobby, time for breakfast."

Rubbing the sandman's work from my eyes, I followed the smoky fragrance of fresh coffee to the nightstand, where next to a steaming mug, Rosie had put a single strip of crisp bacon.

"Baby, just one piece of bacon?" I shouted.

"The balance of your breakfast is out here with the rest of the Richards tribe," Rosie shouted back. "Your bacon is being looked at by three hungry men, so you better hustle."

Around the table the boys brought me up to speed on the football and soccer scene, and Rosie filled us in on the financial workings of Walsh, Harper & Smith in terms only she understood.

I shared some of the details about the Cliff Infield case, because they had already heard about it from channel 7 news anchor, Van Amburg, the Bay Area's king of TV news, and read about it in the *Oakland Tribune*. That is when I noticed it, something I had failed to see until now. Little Joe was growing a mustache, and a healthy one at that.

"What's on your lip? Looks like a scrawny caterpillar's trying to crawl up your nose."

"Come on, Dad," Joe said.

I remember standing in the bathroom with him at my side when he was just five years old. I would lather my beard up with Gillette shaving cream and put some in his hand. He would look up at me with those innocent blue eyes and cover 90 percent of his face with foam. Then for every stroke I made with my razor, Joe made a stroke of his own. Rosie came in the first time Joe and I had a father-son shearing party and almost fainted when she saw her baby boy criss-crossing his face with the new Schick razor I had bought for him. His, of course, didn't have a razor blade.

I just sat there at the table and watched my little boy and his caterpillar lip. He had grown up. He was becoming a man. Lord, where had the time gone?

"Bobby, I have my annual exam next week. Will you be able to get some time off?"

"Sure, baby, you know I never miss an opportunity to sort through the stack of five-year-old magazines in Dr. Chamberlan's lobby. Who knows, there just might be a new *Good Housekeeping* there this time," I said, noting the concern in her voice.

Standing behind me, she leaned over and hugged me. "Thank you, Bobby. When you're there, I feel safe."

Rosie could not have said anything more important to my heart because there is no greater responsibility a man has than assuring that their wife and family feel safe, especially when they're together.

"Is there something wrong? Are you okay?" I asked.

"Yeah, I'm fine. The oncologist Dr. Chamberlin referred me to wants me to get what he called a PET scan as part of my long-term care plan."

I turned and looked at her and could see she wasn't joking. "A pet scan? Except for the boys, we don't have any pets. Besides, what do pets have to do with it?"

The fear in her eyes was replaced by the twinkle I love, as a broad smile wiped away her frown. Slapping the top of my head, she leaned over and kissed my cheek.

"It's not scanning a pet, silly. It's a P-E-T scan. It's a new technology that scans and takes pictures to diagnose cancer and assess what kind of cancer treatment is required. They're not scanning pets."

"Well, that's a relief. I thought we were going to have to snag a stray cat or put a set of rabbit ears on Critter."

It was good to hear her laugh. We can always tell when the follow-up exams were approaching because she would gradually become melancholy.

"So does the oncologist have one of those scanners in his office?"

"No, there's not very many of them anywhere in the country. The nearest to us is in Los Angeles at the UCLA Medical Center."

I stood, grasped her hand, and said, "Okay, let's go."

Over the years, as my bride battled this dreaded disease, I watched and learned from her. Although fear is part of life, there is no benefit living each day within it. To do so merely erodes our hope, leaving us exhausted and spent, incapable of embracing the moments of joy we have together.

Following her radical mastectomy, I watched as slowly she shed the shroud of fear that enfolded her and grasped the good news that there were resources available. She didn't allow herself to be consumed by the *what-ifs*, but instead participated in and soon led others in prayer groups, support groups, survivor programs, exercise programs, even wig- and bra-fitting services. Refusing to be stopped by the circumstances she faced, she helped herself and others heal emotionally and encouraged them to recognize that they were not alone in their journey.

Wrapping my arms around her, I said softly, "Baby, the four men of your Richards clan are ready to be at your side wherever you need to go. When do we leave?"

"Dr. Chamberlan will let us know one week before the scan. Now get dressed and go to work."

Taking her hands, we looked into each other's eyes. I said, "You know I pray for you every day, don't you?"

"I know you do, and I feel it," she said. "And I pray for you."

"God has a plan for us, baby," I said, pulling her to me. "I have watched as your love and compassion for those dealing with cancer has brought encouragement and peace in the middle of their battle. You have shown me that whatever we face, we face it together, and how we walk through our struggles can bring hope to others. I love you, Rosie Richards, and I am so proud of you."

After a long and passionate embrace, Rosie said, "I love you, and am proud of you too, Bobby Richards. And as much as I would like to keep this going, now it's time to stop flirting with procrastination and start dating some productivity. You've got to get to work, Bobby."

One of the perks of being a detective sergeant is the use of an unmarked steel blue 1978 Dodge Monaco, equipped with a radio, a first aid kit, a semi-automatic .30 caliber M1 carbine, and a 12-gauge shotgun in the trunk. These unmarked units are laughingly referred to as "undercover cars." Some of the older cars even have black spotlights mounted by the driver's side door. The only way to make my gifted transportation unidentifiable would be to put it in a garage, cover it with canvas tarps, then close and lock the door. Even then most street hustlers would spot it a mile away.

Today I felt charitable and decided to enhance my relationship with the detectives in the pit by stopping by Dee's Country Kitchen and picking up a couple dozen sweet rolls. There isn't a cop in the department who doesn't love those sweet morsels of sugar and dough.

"Delta-2, drop down to Tac 2."

"Go ahead, Dispatch, this is Delta-2."

"I have Detective George Austin from Concord PD on the line. He wants to meet you in the ER at the John Muir Medical Center. He says it pertains to the Stevens baby case."

"Tell him I'll be there in thirty," I said as I drove past Dee's depository of delectable delights and headed toward Concord. "Maybe another day," I muttered to myself.

Parking just outside of the emergency room entrance, I spotted George standing by an older Buick Invicta station wagon talking to an elderly couple. Getting out, I waited beside the car so as not to interrupt his conversation.

"Bob, I want to introduce you to these folks," he said, waving me over.

"Mr. and Mrs. Russell, this is Detective Sergeant Richards with the Oakland Police Department. Bob, this is David and Jan Russell, Katty's mother and father," George said softly. It was apparent from the streaked tear stains on their faces that this was not a cordial meeting.

"I will keep you informed of our progress. For now I need to meet with Detective Richards, so go home and get some rest. I'll be in touch."

Inside the emergency room things were chaotic as George walked me through to a waiting room with a coffee dispenser and vending machine. Reaching into his pocket he pulled out a handful of quarters and asked, "Can I buy you breakfast?"

Looking at the assortment of dubious delights entombed in plastic, I chose to pass and get down to business. "What's going on, George?"

"I tried to keep Katty in a safe house, but without a case I couldn't make it happen. When she was released, she told me that she was going home to stay with her parents. She was in a program and seemed to be doing well with it. Then yesterday Mr. Russell called me and said that Katty had gotten a phone call that made her very agitated. She went into her room and refused to come out. When her father went in to see her the next morning, she was gone."

"So why are we here, in the ER waiting room?"

"Early this morning a large black truck drove up in front of the Russell home and tossed Katty out onto the yard. According to a neighbor, before the truck drove away, a figure dressed in black with a knit cap got out and shot her twice."

"Oh my God," I said.

"She's in surgery, but it doesn't look good."

"She's alive?"

"Yes, but in bad shape. She was beaten badly, raped, and shot twice in the back of the head. Amazingly, the shooter used .22-caliber shorts, and although they're deadly, they don't have the impact a larger round would. He didn't put the gun against her head but stood back near the truck. It appears that the length and thickness of her hair helped mask the location of her skull in the dark, so what could have been kill shots grazed her deeply."

"The description sounds like the cleanup crew Abe saw at Katty's apartment the night she and Billy were arrested. What do you have on the Billy Kurkland murder?"

"Not much. The Mohave County Sheriff Office turns their homicide cases over to the Major Crimes Division of the Maricopa County Sheriff's Office, who themselves are backed up with their own growing caseload. The lead detective told me that they're in the middle of a turf war between factions of the Sureños, the Mexican Mafia, and local gangs. He said they're responding to several drive-by shootings every day. The sad part is most of the victims are innocent bystanders and children."

"So, Billy's murder is on the bottom of the heap," I said.

"Unfortunately, it is, but I may be able to get it off the heap. Our crime scene guys found the two spent cartridges used to shoot Katty. They're .22-caliber shorts, the same as those used to take out Billy."

George handed me a cup of dark, hot mud that choked its way out of the coffee machine. "I've asked Maricopa County for a copy of their ballistics report. Depending on the condition of the bullets the doctors retrieve during Katty's surgery, and what the Mohave County coroner retrieved from

Billy's postmortem, we may be able to get a good comparison, and possibly some partial prints off the casings."

A short, stocky nurse, with the gait of a drill sergeant, marched up to us and said, "Gentlemen, I'm Head Nurse Cody. Are you officers Austin and Richards?"

"Yes, ma'am, that's us. What can we do for you?"

"Katty Russell is out of surgery. Her injuries are quite severe. She has been taken to ICU and has asked to talk with you. Gentlemen, other than being shot, Katty can barely speak. Her jaw and right cheekbone were broken, along with four ribs, her right arm, and the fingers of her left hand. She is in a great deal of pain, needs to rest, and shouldn't be disturbed." Shaking her head, she added, "I don't believe she will get any rest until she talks with you, so be gentle and quick, and none of that good cop, bad cop crap."

"Yes, ma'am, we'll be good . . . promise," I said as we headed toward the ICU.

At the entrance of room A16, we stood stunned by the sight of a human being lying motionless, mummified in bandages, gauze, and plaster casts and surrounded by a web of tubes, wires, and gadgets hooked to pharmacy bags and medical monitoring equipment.

As we stepped to either side of Katty's bed, she slowly opened her eyes and looked back and forth at us both. She tried to speak, but her lips were swollen and her broken jaw had been wired shut. The sounds that came from her were indiscernible, unsettling, and painful.

Leaning down, Austin spoke softly into her ear, "Katty, you're safe now and we'll make sure you will stay that way. We'll have an officer posted at your door."

"You don't need to talk with us right now. You need your rest," I said. "We can come back, and I'll bring Officer Chelsey with me. I know she would like to see you."

My hand was on the bedrail when she took hold of my fingers and pulled them gently. I leaned closer as she turned her head slightly. In a low, guttural, garbled voice, she said, "They . . . they killed . . . they killed her."

"Katty, just relax, take a breath. Okay, now who was killed?"

"Mother . . . they killed Mother Mary."

"Okay, who killed Mother Mary?"

"The minted, they kill everybody," Katty said as she closed her eyes, and her voice began to fade, "and the little ones," she whispered and went to sleep.

"Katty, who is the minted? Katty . . . Katty who are the little ones?"

Head Nurse Cody wedged herself between me and the side of the bed. "That's enough, Officer. She needs her rest."

CHAPTER TWENTY-FOUR

As I entered the Stanford University campus along tree-lined Palm Drive, the grand sandstone archway of the Memorial Arch came into view. The red-tiled roofs and beige sandstone buildings were each encircled by meticulously landscaped gardens and expansive lawns. The biking and walking paths that crisscrossed the campus, connecting the various academic, residential, and recreational areas, created a vibrant and beautiful atmosphere.

It all brought me back to my days on the University of San Francisco campus. The closest I got to the fraternity lifestyle and campus parties was sleeping in the chapel and attending boring lectures. I was a full-time police officer, working the graveyard shift, and a full-time husband and father, heading home on evenings and weekends. As a full-time student, I worked diligently to arrange my classes around work, home, and sleep.

Fortunately, youth and good health prevailed, and I was able to get comfortable on the hard wooden church pews of Saint Ignatius Church, which happened to be used as the campus chapel. In those days I could sleep on a rock. My first class would begin around 11:00 a.m., giving me nearly three hours to crash on the fourth row of pews from the back.

My alarm clock was the children's choir from Jefferson Elementary. They would come into the chapel to practice each day at precisely 10:40 a.m. and tune up. The chapel's acoustics allowed their young voices to resonate magnificently off the tall spires, beautiful stained-glass windows, and intricate woodwork. Although in those days I had not yet come to the saving knowledge of Christ, and the wonder of God's grace, I was nonetheless inspired by the feeling of awe and reverence whenever I entered the chapel's hallowed atmosphere.

Parking near the administration building, I watched as students—loaded down with books, briefcases, and large multi-colored shoulder bags—jogged, walked, and roller-skated to their next lecture. Inside the foyer a communal buzz filled the air with conversations, mingled with laughter and footsteps.

I approached a long-haired brunette girl who had her back to me, looking at a corkboard display on the wall, and asked, "Miss, I'm looking for a particular student. Can you tell me where I should start?"

The student turned toward me and said, "It's Jerry, not Miss, Officer," the dark-haired young man said, stroking his full beard. Pointing to a door with a sign *Student Services*, he said, "Go through that door. They can help ya."

"Sorry about that. Thanks. Hey, how did you know I was a cop?"

"Lucky guess." He shrugged, turned, walked away, and then over his shoulder shouted, "It was the smell of bacon."

Behind a large oval desk sat a man in his sixties. His full gray beard, bald head, and multi-colored bowtie seemed to fit the campus atmosphere. "Can I help you?"

"Yes, I'm looking for a student. I was wondering if you could tell me where—"

"No," he said, glaring at me. "We do not give out personal information about our students, nor do we give out their location."

"The girl I'm looking for is not in trouble. I just want to ask her a few questions."

"If you are her father, call her. If you are her boyfriend, wait until she calls you. And if you're a cop, look for her someplace other than our campus. Good day."

"The girl may be in danger. I'm not here to hassle her. I just want to make sure she's okay."

"Officer, it's the school's policy and mine. Good day, sir."

I drove through the campus with Julie Corbitt's driver's license photo attached to my visor, hoping to spot her along the way. Her mother said she had an apartment nearby, so I spent the next hour cruising the streets around the campus and was about to call it quits when I spotted Julie's car in the driveway of the Alpha Chi Omega Sorority House.

It was a stately, old building with a large ornately carved front door that stood partially open. I rang the doorbell, knocked, then shouted, "Hello, is anyone at home?"

"Yes, I'll be right there," came a woman's voice.

An attractive lady in her late thirties came to the door. "How can I help you?"

"I'm looking for Julie Corbitt. Is she available?"

Reaching out she shook my hand. "I am Samantha Smith, the House Mother. May I ask who you are?"

"I'm Detective Sergeant Richards with the Oakland Police Department," I said, showing her my ID.

"May I ask what business you have with her?"

"I just wish to ask her a couple of questions. She's not in any trouble. I just have a few questions, just routine."

"Just a moment," she said and closed the door tightly, locking it behind her.

After several minutes she returned. "I'm sorry, Julie doesn't wish to speak with you. I don't wish to be rude, but I need to ask you to leave."

"Okay, Ms. Smith. If she changes her mind, have her give me a call," I said, handing her my card. "Thank you."

Before going back to the PD, I swung by the John Muir Medical Center to see how Katty was doing. Head Nurse Cody met me in the ICU and told me that both Detective Austin and Officer Defo had also stopped by.

Katty's condition was worsening. She was very agitated and in a great deal of pain. She was showing signs of brain swelling, so it was decided by her doctors to place her into a medically induced coma and monitor her closely.

"Katty must be quite a girl. She sure is popular."

"What do you mean?" I asked.

"Well, after the detective from Concord and Officer Defo left, there were two other detectives here to see her."

"Two other detectives? Did you see their identification?"

"No, but you could tell they were. They looked just like you guys, sports coats, ties, and one had a gun. I saw it when his coat fell open. They wanted to go up and see her, but I wouldn't allow it in her present condition. I told them that they could visit her in a day or two and assured them that she was safe because she had a police officer with her."

"What time were they here?"

"Oh, just a few minutes ago. I'm surprised you didn't see them."

"Could you identify these men if you saw them again?"

"Sure."

"Great, I'll be right back," I said and ran to the stairwell, almost falling down several flights of steps.

Clearing the bottom flight, I went out through the emergency room entrance and stood on the elevated landing looking across the parking lot. In the distance I could see a black sedan leaving the farthest exit, but it was too far to get any details.

As I returned to the nurses' station, a young lady in scrubs set a telephone on the counter and said, "Are you Sergeant Richards?"

"Yes."

"Someone from the police department wants to talk to you," she said, pushing a lit button on the phone.

"Hello."

"Sergeant, this is Lacy Smith, Dispatch Supervisor. I just fielded a call that came in for you from a young girl. She was in a state of panic, saying she knew who committed a murder and she knew that you were looking for her. She wouldn't give me her name, and it sounded like she was calling from a bar or a party. I heard a girl call out the name *Jules* and she responded by saying that she would be right there."

"The name *Jules* doesn't register. Could it be Julie?"

"That's possible. Jules is a common nickname for Julie or Julia."

"Did she say how she knew I was looking for her?"

"No, but before she hung up, she said she would call again after harmony."

"Harmony?"

"I don't have a clue, Sergeant."

"Thank you, Lacy."

Back at the PD, I walked through and asked every cop, clerk, and cadet if they knew what *harmony* meant, and all I got were shrugs. Stepping into the pit, I looked across the room and shouted, "Anyone know what *harmony* means when used like *I'll call you after harmony*." More shrugs.

I was about to close my office door when a soft voice came from a small desk in between two large filing cabinets in the far corner of the room. "It could mean House Harmony. It's a bell or chime that notifies the girls in a sorority that it's either time to hit the books or lights out. At least that's what they called it when I was there."

"Well, Detective, that's the best answer I've gotten so far. What time would you think *after harmony* would be?"

"They'll be studying for mid-terms now, so I would say around 7:00 p.m., right after dinner. If it were lights out that was usually 10:00 p.m."

I called Rosie and let her know what I was doing and that I wouldn't be home for dinner. Then I set to work completing my reports on what had recently transpired.

"Hey, boss, are you okay?"

"What?" I said, opening one eye, noting that I was no longer on a beach, but facedown on my desk.

"Sorry to wake you, Sergeant. You were cutting some serious z's, but there's a young lady on the phone for you."

"Yeah, got it, thanks," I said, peeling off a paperclip that had embedded itself into my right cheek.

"This is Detective Sergeant Richards. Can I help you."

"Are you going to arrest me?"

"No, I just want to talk with you."

I spent the next ten minutes answering questions about myself and reassuring her that I wasn't going to arrest her so long as she had done nothing wrong. Then she began to cry, and that's when I began to lose her.

"Are you in danger?" I asked.

"I don't know. I could be. I just don't know."

Although I was sure who I was talking to, she never gave me her name or said anything about herself that identified who she was. She was trying to be as anonymous as possible, which told me this girl was scared to death.

From the sound of traffic in the background, it was clear that she was calling from a phone booth. I didn't want to lose her, but I wasn't getting anywhere and needed to get down to who she was and the murder she told Lacy about. I closed my eyes and silently asked God to guide my words.

"Julie, or should I call you Jules? I know you are staying in your sorority, and that's a safe place to be, but you said you knew of someone who had committed a murder. I need to know who that is and who you believe they murdered. If you are afraid, I promise I will do everything I can to protect you."

Nothing was said. The only sound was the traffic in the background and her breathing. Then the phone went dead. I had blown it.

Sitting there staring at the clock on the wall, I held the phone to my ear as the dial tone played a melody only fools could dance to. If only I hadn't pushed so hard, if I had just let her ask her questions and stay nameless in the shadows, maybe we could have formed some level of trust.

Since my phone was in my hand I might as well make good use of it. "Hi baby, looks like my appointment won't be as late as I thought. Is there any of your ricotta and mozzarella lasagna left, or did the troop grub it out of existence?"

"Yours is in the refrigerator, and I warned the gang that they'll be eating liver and brussels sprouts for a month if they touch it," Rosie said.

"Wow, I hope they can sleep after a threat like that. I should be home in about an hour. Love ya."

I put a few sticky notes on a couple of files along with a cassette to be transcribed and dropped them off on Liz Baker's desk. Because the elevator was too slow, I hit the stairwell, almost tasting Rosie's lasagna as I went.

Crossing the main lobby, I passed by Desk Sergeant Hilbert's perch. He was engrossed in a recent issue of *Field & Stream*.

"Have a great evening, Sergeant," I said, tapping the top of his desk.

Looking up, he said, "Hey, Richards, wait a minute," he said, looking around the lobby. "Where did she go? Jonesy, where did that girl go that was here for Richards?"

"I don't know, Sergeant," Cadet Jones said.

"Well, Richards, I'm sorry. There was a young lady here to see you. Guess she didn't want to wait."

"Did she give you a name?"

"Nope, just wanted to confirm that this was where you worked."

Instead of walking out the side door to the employee parking lot, I went out the front. Sitting on the steps was Julie Corbitt.

"Julie, I'm Detective Sergeant Richards. You can call me Bobby."

CHAPTER TWENTY-FIVE

In Interview Room A sat Julie Corbitt as Senior Officer Chelsey Defo entered the room with two cans of soda and a small portable tape recorder. I watched through the one-way mirror as the two casually conversed about the recorder, school, and the weather while sipping their drinks.

I chose not to enter right away to give them some time to develop a line of trust. I knew Chelsey would connect with this girl because she was not an interrogator. She wasn't just after information. She honestly cared about people, particularly young girls in trouble. After about fifteen minutes, Chelsey slid over next to Julie, reached over, and took her hand. They both closed their eyes and Chelsey began to pray. That was also my cue.

I waited until they were done then entered and took the seat Chelsey had been in across from Julie.

"I want to begin by thanking you for talking with us. It is a very brave thing to do. I want to emphasize that you are not in any trouble, and at this point you are merely a witness. Do you understand?"

"Yes," she said as her voice began to quiver.

"I understand that you are a law student at Stanford, so I presume you know your rights."

"I know I don't have to say anything, and I have the right to a lawyer, but I don't need one, because I haven't done anything wrong, and this needs to stop," she said.

"What needs to stop?"

Dropping her face into her hands, she began to sob. "The boys, and Mother Mary."

The hair on my arms began to stand up, and a chill ran down my spine. I asked, "Who is Mother Mary?"

"She was our housekeeper. I loved her. She has taken care of me since I was a baby, and now she's dead."

"Do you know who might be responsible for her death?"

She buried her face into Chelsey's shoulder. "I think it was my father," she wept.

"Why do you believe your father is the one who killed her?"

"My mother told me. She said she saw him do it."

"Did she tell you why he killed your housekeeper?"

"Mom said that she was threatening to tell people that my father and her were having an affair, and that she had a child that was his," she said. "My daddy wouldn't hurt anyone."

"Now, let me get this straight. Your mother, Claudia Corbitt, told you that she saw your father, Leonard Corbitt, kill Mary Ann Avery, your family's housekeeper, a woman you know as Mother Mary. Do I have that correct?"

"Yes."

"Have you talked to your father recently?"

"No, Mom said he was staying at Uncle Tony's for a while, until the investigation was over."

"Would Uncle Tony be Attorney Anthony Woodward?"

"Yes, he's been my father's best friend for years."

"Wasn't your mother in Italy recently?"

"Yes, she was visiting friends. That's all I know. We don't talk much."

"Okay, what about the boys? You said it had to stop, all the boys, and Mother Mary. What did you mean?"

She pulled away from Chelsey, and the expression on her face went cold. "I think I don't want to talk about that."

"Julie, there may be small children in danger. I believe what you are talking about is child abduction and trafficking. I know you don't want to see anyone hurt, especially children," I said. "Okay, let's take a break."

I took a seat in the viewing room and watched as Chelsey talked to Julie gently and on two occasions held her in her arms. After half an hour, Chelsey looked up at the mirror and winked, signaling for me to return. Rather than beginning on the subject of the boys, I chose to stick with the murder of Mary Ann Avery. There were a few loopholes that needed mending.

"Julie, according to the information we have, your mother returned to California after Mother Mary's murder by several days. How could she have witnessed your father killing her?"

She began rummaging through her large colorful hobo bag. "I don't know what information you have, but she was home before Mother Mary was killed. She travels a lot, but when she gets home, she always lets me know."

Frustrated, she turned the bag upside down and emptied it onto the table. Sorting through an assortment of papers, makeup, pictures, and junk, she pulled up a yellow sticky pad note. "Here," she said handing it to me.

It read, "Jules, I'm home. Mom." The date at the top of the note was two days prior to the Avery murder. At the bottom were the initials *SS*, for Samantha Smith, the House Mother.

"She always leaves me a message when she gets home. I don't know why, that's about the total of our conversations. She didn't even tell me about Mother Mary. It was actually Uncle Tony who told me."

Scooping up the debris, she dumped it back in her bag, sat back, and rolled her eyes to the ceiling. "Mom called me two days after the only woman I really knew as a mother was killed and asked me to meet her."

Her eyes filled with tears. "We didn't meet at home or some quiet place. We met at a coffeehouse, a coffeehouse . . ." She began to cry. "My mother told me that my father was a murderer and that the most important woman in my life was dead in a coffeehouse."

Jumping to her feet, she grabbed her bag and headed for the door. "I can't do this right now, I just can't. Give me some time. I will call you and we can meet again. I have to go," and she was gone.

"Do you think she's in any danger?"

"I don't know. She could be," Chelsey said.

"I want you to follow up with her this evening. Keep in touch because it's clear she doesn't have a woman in her life to guide her."

"I had already planned on that. I have some serious suspicions about her mother."

I gave all the information I had on Julie to Chelsey along with a copy of the Avery murder case, what had transpired with the Stevens baby abduction, and the assault on Katty Russell and murder of Billy Kurkland. We then set a time the next afternoon for her to join me at the John Muir Medical Center and hopefully interview Katty if she was up to it.

It was nearly midnight before I got home. As quietly as I could, I slinked into the kitchen and opened the fridge, and there sat a plate covered with tinfoil—Rosie's ricotta and mozzarella lasagna. Picking it up, I could tell something wasn't right.

Peeling back the foil, I gazed upon an empty plate with a note that read, "Dad, sorry but we weighed out the cost and came to the conclusion that a month of liver and brussels sprouts was worth Mom's lasagna." Below, each of my boys signed it.

Slipping into bed, I rolled over onto my side away from Rosie so I wouldn't wake her. Once I was settled, she rolled over and snuggled up behind me, kissed my neck, and whispered, "Did you check on your lasagna?"

"Yep, if we had girls instead of boys, I might still have some."

"You were late. Did you do something good tonight?"

"I hope so."

"Then I'll make another for you tomorrow. I love you, Bobby."

* * *

The following morning, I arrived at the John Muir Medical Center and parked under a cluster of eucalyptus trees on the south side. I reread my report on the Stevens baby case and waited for Chelsey to join me. At 2:00 p.m., a 1957 Chevy Impala rolled into the parking lot. This was the prize position of Chelsey's husband, Mark. The only person he ever allowed to drive it was Chelsey, and that was only on the rarest of occasions. He kept the car in pristine condition, believing it would one day become a classic.

"How did you get Mark to give up his favorite toy?"

"I had a flat on my car, and I didn't want to be late for our meeting."

On the way into the hospital, Chelsey told me that she had called on Julie this morning and was assured that she was okay and would let us know when she was ready to talk. She knew something about her brother that concerned her but wouldn't reveal it over the phone.

In the hallway we ran into Head Nurse Cody and the dayshift officer assigned to watch over Katty. I checked my watch and saw it was 2:10 p.m.

"Officer, I'm Detective Sergeant Richards. What is your name?"

"Garcia, Sergeant. Albert Garcia."

"Why are you down here and not sitting at Katty Russell's door?"

"I've been relieved, Sergeant."

"By who?"

"I didn't catch his name, but he's a Concord officer, in full uniform."

"Officer, you take the stairs," I ordered, pushing past them and running toward the elevator. Pushing the button, I shouted, "Chelsey, cover the lobby, and call Concord PD and determine if they sent someone to relieve Garcia early. If not, we need cover."

When the elevator door opened on the ICU floor, there was no one seated in the hallway. Peeking around the corner into Katty's room, I saw a uniformed police officer standing next to her bed with his back to me. He wasn't carrying a gun. To conceal myself I stepped into the doorway of the next room over and said, "Officer, may I speak to you a moment?"

He spun around, dropping what was in his hand. "Yeah, sure," he said, walking slowly toward the door. I didn't want to risk hurting Katty, so I waited until he was outside her room. Then stepping out, I raised my Browning 9mm and politely said, "Down on your knees."

He was about to follow my command when the elevator doors opened, and a crowd of nurses and medical interns filled the hallway. One of the nurses spotted me and screamed, "He has a gun!" and that started a stampede. Two rather large orderlies, who clearly played on the varsity team, tackled me and pinned me to the floor.

"I'm a cop. You're letting a murderer get away," I shouted.

Rolling me over so I was facedown, they pulled my hands up behind me, while a nurse pulled my ID from of my pocket.

"He is a cop," she said, holding my badge in the air. "Let him up."

"Sorry, man, you looked like a bad guy," one orderly said while another handed me my gun.

"No problem, you did good," I said, as I pushed my way through to the stairwell. "I'd like to have you on my team,"

Coming out on the first floor, I saw Officers Garcia and Defo standing by the nurses' station with our suspect cuffed and seated on the floor.

"Well done," I said.

Raising his hands, Officer Garcia said, "It wasn't me. This joker came flying down those steps so fast I didn't see him until it was too late. I almost went down two flights of steps with him. When I finally got to my feet and got down here, Officer Defo had him on his face. I'm sorry. I should have known better. Is the lady in the room okay?"

"She's fine. Go back up there and secure the room. Don't stomp around in there, and only let the doctors in who are working on her. Something was broken on the floor, I think it was a syringe so don't touch it, we'll let the evidence techs deal with it."

Bending down to look the young man in the eye, I asked, "What's your name?"

No response.

I stood him up and patted him down, pulling out his pant and shirt pockets—nothing. "Well, Mr. Doe, you must be some kind of hitter, no ID, nothing."

Sweat began to form on his face as he squirmed around trying to avoid looking me in the eye.

Grabbing his shoulders, I pressed him up against the wall. "You're either a very bad man or a very stupid one. Sent out to commit a crime punishable by death without any form of identification. No name tags, not even labels in your clothing. You, my young friend, are disposable. I bet whoever is pulling your strings never expected you to make it out of here alive."

Reaching over the counter at the nurses' station, I dialed the PD and asked for a transport wagon and then called Concord PD. When the wagon arrived, I instructed the transport team to put Mr. Doe in solitary confinement and to make sure no one talked to him.

When Detective Austin arrived, we all went up to Katty's room for a short visit. It was good to see her sitting up, with a small grin and her left eye open. She was still hooked up to a cluster of tubes and wires, but she didn't appear to be in as much pain as she was earlier. Although her jaw had been wired shut, and her lips and face were swollen horribly, she was eager to talk.

"Who beat you, Katty?" I asked.

"I don't know, there were four of them. One said he was sorry, and another said I knew too much. I told them I didn't know anything, but it didn't matter. The big guy said, 'She's got to go, kill her.' The one who said he was sorry wouldn't hit me. I think he even started to cry. The others just laughed and kept hitting and kicking me. The big guy was really enjoying it."

"Could you identify them if you saw them again?"

"Yes, I won't ever forget them."

"Tell us about Mother Mary."

Pushing a button that raised her head, Katty told us the story of a woman she deeply cared for, Mary Ann Avery, also known as Mother Mary. She was the caretaker of the boys whom Billy would bring home. She would wash them and make sure they were well fed and healthy before they were passed on to the Minted to be sold. She was proud of what she did and would often say that she was providing the boys with wonderful opportunities to be raised in a nice home where they would be educated, well fed, clothed, and cared for. As for the boys who just went away, Katty didn't know what had happened to them.

Minted was the name Billy and the others who collected children used to identify those who knew people who wanted a little boy and had the resources to buy one. The name *Minted* came from Europe, meaning wealthy or powerful people. Katty didn't know who they were but knew that they were dangerous. Billy had hoped of becoming one of them. Of course that was before they killed him.

CHAPTER TWENTY-SIX

Mr. John Doe, who did not appear to be much older than twenty, sat quietly in Interview Room A behind the metal desk, his hands folded on his lap, staring at his reflection on the mirrored one-way glass. On the other side of that glass sat Lieutenant Steven Miller, Detective George Austin, Officer Chelsey Defo, and me, those I have dubbed "the crew." We spent a half an hour discussing our approach and decided that George and I would do the initial interview.

I walked in and sat across from him, putting my files on the table. George followed me, put a glass of water in front of Dr. Doe, and took a position standing against the wall to my left.

"Sir, I need your name."

He said nothing, just stared at the one-way mirror.

"Failure to identify yourself is only going to make things more difficult for you. You'll be held in solitary confinement until we can figure out who you are. It will take the FBI at least six weeks to research your fingerprints, and that's assuming they don't have bigger fish to fry."

Still no response.

"Do you know what was in that syringe? It was arsenic. It would have killed her in minutes, and it would have been horrible. I don't think you wanted to do that. You took your time in that room because I think you've never done anything like that before."

A slight twitch of his right cheek told me that I was on the right track. "It would have been ugly, the pain unimaginable, spewing up blood, and convulsing. You would have taken the life of an innocent woman, a woman who did nothing to you, a woman you probably didn't even know."

The boy was right on the edge, and I had to be careful not to push too far, but it was time he came to an understanding of just how serious this situation was.

"Mr. Doe, you are under arrest for attempted murder in the first degree. From this day forward you will never be free again, and those who sent you on that murderous quest have written you off."

Tears began to form in his eyes, and he pressed his lips tightly together so they wouldn't quiver. Lifting his handcuffed hands from his lap, he put his face in his palms, and that's when the reminiscent chill down my spine returned.

Reaching across the table, I grabbed his hands and pulled them violently to me, jerking him halfway across the table. He raised up, face contorted in despair, eyes in shock, just inches from mine as I growled, "I know who you are."

Slamming his left hand down, pinning it to the table, I removed a ring from his finger. It was a class ring from the California Maritime Academy, with a small hole in the center of the stone where an insignia should have been.

"You're Jimmy Corbitt," I said, releasing his hand.

Looking at me with eyes as big as saucers, he curled up and buried his face in his sleeves. I nodded to George, and we left to meet with those in the viewing room, leaving Jimmy Corbitt to stew alone.

"Okay guys, it's time to get the DA in on this," Lieutenant Miller said. "I think this kid is a puppet, and if we work it right, he can open this can of worms for us."

"I agree, LT, but we need to curb any news of his arrest from the papers. Can Deputy Chief Stiner pull some strings for us?"

"I'll see what he can do. Until then, put him back in solitary, get him some food, a few magazines, and don't let anyone talk to him."

Out in the hall, Chelsey caught my arm and pulled me back into the viewing room. "Bobby, I know you are a believer, and you know the power of prayer. I believe we're about to meet families that are experiencing indescribable grief and feeling suffocated due to the loss of a child. I cannot imagine the profound heartache and sorrow they must be going through. There are babies out there who have been stolen and their innocence sold, so we need more than guns, attack plans, and search warrants. We need God's intervention. We may be able to do something about it, or at least keep it from happening in our small part of the world. Bobby, when you go home tonight, pray over your children and for those who have been stolen."

"Of course I will." I knew Chelsey was a woman of faith, but the level of her faith was refreshing and uplifting.

Bowing my head, I waited for Chelsey to begin, and she waited for me, then the door opened. "Oh, sorry to interrupt," Lieutenant Miller said. "Deputy District Attorney KP Cooper is here. Stay put, I'll be right back."

The moment the door closed, I began to pray, then Chelsey, then me again. I was about to say *Amen*, when the door opened and in walked Lieutenant Miller, Deputy DA Cooper, Deputy Chief Stiner, and Detective Austin.

"Bobby, Chelsey, we would like to join you if you wouldn't mind. We need God's hand to guide us in this," Lieutenant Miller said.

"By all means," I said.

Then Deputy Chief Stiner stepped out into the hall and with a firm, authoritative, yet gentle tone said, "Ladies and gentlemen, we have a very serious battle that we are about to wage. We need God's help and guidance. If you wish to join us in prayer, we are gathering now near Interview Room A." Turning to me, he asked, "Would you mind if we wait a minute?"

"Yes, sir," I said.

Dropping my head, I could hear a few people at the door, and a wave of thankfulness settled over me as Chelsey took my hand, and Lieutenant Miller the other. After a couple minutes I opened my eyes to see the entire investigative staff had filled the hall holding each other's hands. I didn't know whether to cry or pray, but God had something else in mind. From the center of the crowd, Detective Axel Heart, my Christian carpenter, raised his voice and began to sing "Amazing Grace," and his voice was majestic. Soon the entire detective division was singing, and others from the floor above and below were joining in.

After a full chorus, sung twice, Axel began to pray, asking for wisdom, guidance, safety, and power, not only for what we were about to face, but for the entire department. His words flowed like a cool breeze on a warm day, touching everyone on the floor. Sniffles could be heard throughout the hall and a unique sense of peace settled over everyone.

It took nearly an hour to clear the hall and get everyone back to work. Deputy Chief Stiner could have gotten them to disperse sooner, but he was so moved by the unity and comradery, he just didn't want to see it disbanded too quickly.

I watched Jimmy as he was being brought into the interview room handcuffed and shackled. He had exchanged the police uniform he had been wearing for orange jail coveralls. The look on his face was fear and dejection. Once he was seated, I entered with George and Coop, putting a soda near his hands. A portable Webcor reel-to-reel recorder was plugged in, placed at the end of the table, and turned on and microphones were placed in front of me and of our suspect.

We sat in silence for several minutes as I watched James Corbitt slowly begin to boil. Sensing that he was about to blow, I spoke into the microphone and gave the date, time, location, those in the room, and who we were interviewing.

"Jimmy, this is Detective George Austin from the Concord Police Department. He is here because he is investigating the kidnapping of a child and the murder of Billy Kurkland, the man responsible for the kidnapping."

"As I told you yesterday, you are under arrest for the attempted murder of Katty Russell. You were literally caught with a smoking gun, in this case a syringe filled with arsenic. Katty, the lady you were going to kill, happens to be the girlfriend of the recently murdered Billy Kurkland, and the insignia from your class ring was found on the floor of their apartment when they were arrested for kidnapping a child. Now if that were not enough, a woman known for her involvement with child trafficking was also recently murdered in your home."

Jimmy was starting to squirm, and he was becoming very pale. He rested his hands on the table and looked around as they began to shake. Looking up at Coop, he uttered his first words since being arrested. "Who is he?"

"He is Deputy District Attorney KP Cooper. He is going to advise you of your Miranda rights and explain how you might be able to help yourself."

I stood up and moved over to the corner. Coop took my place, removed a Miranda rights sheet, read it slowly, and then slid it in front of Jimmy.

"James Corbitt, you have the right to remain silent and have an attorney present. If you choose to do either, you will be returned to your cell to await trial. If you wish to corporate and answer our questions, and assist us in this investigation, I will seek to help you in whatever way I can. This does not mean you will be released, but it does mean you may not be looking at a first-degree murder charge that carries the death penalty. This is not an idle threat, Jimmy. It's the law. Do you understand?"

"Yes, I understand," he said, taking a deep breath as tears ran down his cheeks. "I know what I did was wrong. I couldn't kill that lady. I just couldn't."

"I don't believe you could, Jimmy, but it's time to make a decision. We need your help to save any other children that have been taken and to keep innocent people from being murdered. So, what is it, join us, or go back to your cell?"

The room went silent, even the air stilled. "I'll help you any way I can, but you have to understand, I love my family, I really do," he said, sobbing as he signed the form.

Over the next three hours Jimmy told us of his involvement with transporting several little boys to Ensenada, Mexico. He was part of a crew in training on the T.S. *Golden Bear* and thought the children were members of some of the civilians who were on board. When they returned to base, he along with another trainee who had been on board were called into the office of Commodore William Wilbanks. He told them that the boys were being returned to their parents who were in the witness protection program and that he and the other trainee had proven themselves to be worthy of being a part of a special top secret program. Jimmy knew of eleven boys who had been taken to Ensenada over the last two years.

He knew something was very wrong when he and the other trainee, Martin Sherlie, were assigned to the cleanup crew. Their jobs were very specific. They weren't just cleaning, but sterilizing, and it was done at night under guard. There were offices, homes, and stores that were stripped of every piece of equipment, product, furniture, and clothing. Even personal property, like pictures, prescription drugs, cosmetics, and letters, literally everything.

"Martin had told me and a few others that he was going to Commodore Wilbanks and ask what was going on," James said. "The next day a couple members of the cleanup crew came into the billets and cleaned out his locker and took everything but his bunk. He hasn't been seen since."

"Jimmy, do you know where Martin has gone to?" I asked.

He got quiet and stared at the floor. "I can't say, I promised. He's afraid they'll kill him, like they did the guy in the van."

"You know about the guy in the van? Do you know who killed him?" Detective Austin asked.

"Martin said that he was told to drive an old hippie van over to the Treasure Island Marina and park it there, and then use the payphone to call for a cab. The next day he saw on the news that the van was found in the Bay with a dead guy in it."

"Tell us where we can find Martin and we'll bring him in for his own protection. We also need him to confirm what you're telling us," Coop said.

"Can you protect my family too?" Jimmy said.

"Is your family in danger?" I asked.

Jimmy took a drink from his soda and told us why he had gone to the John Muir Medical Center to kill Katty Russell.

He had been given the use of a pickup truck, known as a M880, on numerous occasions, even though he had no driver's license. He was ordered to meet Commodore Wilbanks in a parking lot of a rundown bar in the city of Richmond, and when he arrived Wilbanks was in the backseat of his car and told Jimmy to get into the front passenger seat and not turn around.

"I was so scared he was going to kill me."

Wilbanks told him that the children being sent to Mexico were actually stolen and being sold to wealthy Americans and Mexicans on the other side of the border. He convinced Jimmy that because of his involvement he was personally responsible and faced life in prison if he failed to follow Wilbanks's instructions. Then Wilbanks showed him a chrome .22-caliber automatic pistol and handed him a syringe wrapped in a white handkerchief.

"He gave me a piece of paper with the room number at John Muir and said that if the job wasn't done, my family would be killed. And if I survived, I'd be in prison for the rest of my life." The tears again began to flow. "I didn't know what to do."

"Jimmy, I need to know, is your father involved with this?" I said.

"No, my father doesn't even know about this. It's my mother."

"What . . . your mother? Claudia Corbitt?"

"Yes, I learned two weeks ago that she and Commodore Wilbanks have been having an affair for a very long time, almost as long as my father has been having an affair with our housekeeper, Mary Ann Avery. Poor Mary Ann, she was such a nice lady."

"Do you know who killed her? Was it your father?"

"No. I told you my father couldn't hurt anyone. Wilbanks told me that he didn't trust me. He would say I was a coward and call me names. When we were going to do a cleaning on an apartment, he made me ride with him so he could tell me in the car that it was my mother who killed Mary Ann. He also said my mother was the one who arranged the transportation and sale of the boys to people she knew. That was probably why she was traveling all the time."

"If Mary Ann, or Mother Mary, was part of this baby-stealing racket, and worked for your mother, why would she kill her?" Coop asked.

"Because she threatened to sue for child support. She wasn't really after anything from my father. She was using the suit as a threat to get money for her son's education from my mother. It was leverage. If it got out that the Corbitt family had a rat in the basement and it became news, then it would only be a matter of time before the whole truth would soon follow. They didn't want any attention put on them."

"Didn't they think killing her would draw attention?" Coop said.

"That wasn't supposed to happen. Wilbanks was going to take care of it, but Mary Ann went to the house before he could do anything and ran into Mother. My mother has anger issues."

"I know, I've met her," I said.

We took a break because we all needed it. Jimmy had been hung out to dry, and we were so overwhelmed by everything we heard, we needed time to sort through it and determine our next move. Dinner was ordered from a local restaurant, and all of us, including Jimmy, got comfortable in the staff conference room.

CHAPTER TWENTY-SEVEN

The recording of Jimmy's interview was passed on to two of the department's transcribers who agreed to work overtime, while Lieutenant Miller made calls to the FBI and the Department of Justice to get them on board. Because we were dealing with an organization that works closely with the US Navy, which could make our case a federal issue, and because our prime suspect was a navel captain who now commands the base, Coop contacted Superior Court Judge Samuel K. Andrews to sign our "no knock" warrants. Judge Andrews had once served as a judicial clerk for the US Court of Appeals, so we also asked if he would connect us with a federal magistrate that he felt would be sympathetic to our cause. A search warrant issued by a federal magistrate authorizes law enforcement to search for evidence in homes, businesses, offices, storage facilities, and vehicles on federal property.

Although it is extremely rare to get federal approval for civilians to search military quarters, buildings, offices, and autos, not to mention arrest a base commodore, the sweet spot is worth the effort. Any military member accused of a crime that violates both military and civilian law may be tried by both a military court and a state court. It's a doubleheader. Now, whether the base is recognized as a military institution or not will have to get worked out by someone above my paygrade.

When the clock struck five, I got on the phone and called the "commodore" of the Richards Rangers and once again apologized for missing dinner. After telling Rosie what the day had brought, she all but crawled through the phone line to get here and become a part of rescuing the boys. Hanging up, I saw Chelsey standing just outside my window with a tall, thin, disheveled man of about twenty-five with a two-week-old beard, clothed in a soiled work shirt, matching pants, and a sweat-stained baseball hat. Seeing that I was off the phone, she tapped on the glass and I waved her in.

"Detective Sergeant Richards, let me introduce you to Mr. Martin Sherlie, who would like to speak to you about your case."

Dropping a tattered duffel bag, he extended a grimy hand, shaking mine vigorously.

"Welcome, Martin, I'm glad to see you here and safe," I said, turning to Chelsey. "Where did you find him?"

"On Mare Island, across the inlet from where the maritime academy docks the T.S. *Golden Bear*. He's been hiding in some of the abandoned buildings left when the navy moved out. He's not only watching what's going on over there, but he's also photographing everything. He says he has pictures of kids being brought onto the *Golden Bear* at night, and they should be clear enough to identify them."

Martin gave me four rolls of undeveloped 35-millimeter film and the camera with a telephoto lens the size of a cannon that took the pictures up close and personal. Putting my initials and the date on each roll, I placed them in a plastic bag, sealed it, dated it, signed the bag, and gave it all to Chelsey to log into evidence and get developed ASAP.

Grabbing a reserve officer who was securing the hall, I gave him ten bucks and asked him to get a couple burgers and fries for Martin. In Interview Room B, I placed a notepad in front of Martin with a couple pens and asked that he write out everything that happened from the time he became a cadet at the academy.

That evening, I explained to Martin that we were about to move on Wilbanks and the academy, and we needed to be sure that he remained safe, so we were placing him into protective custody. I expected some significant pushback, but instead I got a hug.

"Thank you, Sergeant. I can't tell you what that means to me, and thanks for the burgers. I have been dreaming about a hamburger. Is it okay if I took a shower? I don't have any other clothes, but I could wash these in the shower too."

Finding the reserve officer, I gave him my department credit card and told him to get the sizes from the guy in protective custody and go to K-Mart and get him some clothes, a razor, a comb, and deodorant, and put the card and receipt on my desk.

The staff conference room where birthday parties, retirement celebrations, and baby showers took place had been transformed into a War Room, where a combat strategy was being laid out to take down a center with all the trappings of a US military base.

At the table with me were Deputy Chief Stiner, DA Cooper, Detective Austin, Lieutenant Miller, the OPD SWAT commander, and a FBI tactical team leader. Chelsey was staking out the academy from a thirty-five-foot unmarked but well-armed Coast Guard Boston whaler about two hundred yards offshore, sitting silently under a pitch-black, moonless night.

In an unmarked police van, equipped with one-way glass windows, Axel sat in the dark with James Corbitt and Martin Sherlie, parked just off Maritime Academy Drive. He would wait for a signal to bring his passengers to the sports field where they would identify those suspected of participating in or having knowledge of the murders, kidnappings, assaults, and evidence tampering.

"There are several buildings that house personnel, most of whom were totally unaware of any misconduct taking place around them. You must keep in mind, however, that they are trained military personnel, capable of putting up a fight. You must be extremely careful. We don't want anyone getting hurt or killed by friendly fire," I said.

Laying out the aerial map of the campus, FBI Special Agent Cindy Gilroy pointed out the different building locations where personnel would be housed and assigned responsibilities.

"DOJ, you will take the staff buildings facing the sports field. FBI, you will take the cluster of apartments by the entrance facing the residence hall. Oakland SWAT will take the administration building, then clear the remaining buildings in the quad. Everyone is to be brought to the sports field for identification and arrest or release. University police will not be on campus. They will return when we call them in.

"In the assault phase, the strike will be signaled by my announcement over the campus PA system. When you hear my voice, it's time to dance."

Taking a few paces back, she looked around the room. "Are there any questions?"

"Yes, how much time do we have to set up illumination and be in place?" Special Agent Sill asked.

"Considering the distance and set up, I would say six minutes. Let me add that no one is allowed to carry a firearm, load their training weapons, or even have ammunition at any time on the university grounds. If someone shoots at you, they are most likely a bad guy."

Lieutenant Miller thanked everyone and added, "Get some rest. The holding cells have been emptied and cleaned, and extra cots have been added. There are air mattresses laid out in the foyer and in the gym. We've opened the snack bar for you. Just show your ID, it's on the house. Be back here by zero-two-hundred, we hit the road at zero-two-fifteen, and we enter the objective at zero-three-hundred."

At 2:00 a.m. every member of the multi-agency assault team was geared up and ready to rock. Deputy Chief Stiner's booming voice called for everyone's attention. Drawing together in the open foyer, it was a sea of different badges, uniforms, color of gear and skin, weapons, and haircuts. He expressed his appreciation, then turned to me.

"Detective Sergeant Richards, step forward. You are the one that kicked up the dust on this, so I believe it's fitting you call upon God to guide us on this little adventure."

"Heavenly Father, we come before You with a humble heart and ask for Your help. Be our power and shield. Clear our path and put our adversary into our hands. Lord, put fear into hearts of those we are about to confront, and a hedge of protection around the blameless. Innocence has been sold, so we ask you to help us find and return them to their families." Looking up, I saw that each one standing before me had their head bowed, eyes closed, and their right hand on the shoulder of the one in front of them.

"We thank You for Your grace and mercy, and we are prepared to be Your vessel of indignation if You choose to rain down your fury upon those who have stolen or harmed any of those little ones. Thank You, Lord, for what You are about to do. Amen."

Lieutenant Miller stepped up. "Thank you. Be safe. Now let's go save some kids and kick some butt."

At zero-three-ten, everyone was in place. Special Agent Cindy Gilroy, two members of OPD SWAT, and I were at the front door of the administration building, while Austin and two more members of OPD SWAT covered the back. We were given keys and maps of the facility, along with individual floor plans of each of the buildings. On the plan of the administration building, a square had been drawn, pointing out where an additional twelve-hundred-square-foot building existed that was not shown on any of the plans. It was an unapproved structure that Commodore Wilbanks had built. He called it his guest quarters. It had two entrances, one at the back of the building leading out to the parking lot about thirty feet away, and the other with direct access to Wilbanks's office. According to Martin and Jimmy, the guest room never housed a guest but was actually the commodore's quarters.

Below the dim glow of an old streetlight, the tension began to rise. I could feel my heart begin to pound as Agent Gilroy slid the key into the door and slowly opened it. Stepping back, the two SWAT team members entered and stealthily cleared the reception area and Wilbanks's private office. Inside, Gilroy went to a microphone and switch panel on a shelf behind Wilbanks's desk, while I tested the door-knob that led into the guest quarters. It was unlocked.

Looking over her shoulder, Gilroy gave me a thumbs-up and switched on the mic. Her voice resonated throughout the campus as floodlights came on illuminating the buildings and filling the entire area with brilliant intense light.

"Attention, attention, this is Special Agent Gilroy of the FBI. This is not a drill, I repeat, this is not a drill. Step out of your quarters, billets, or apartments, with your hands raised. Do not have anything in your hands. I repeat, exit your dwelling with your hands raised and empty. Do not have anything in your hands. You are surrounded by armed tactical law enforcement personnel. Follow their instructions. This is not a drill."

In the middle of her discourse, I threw the door open, and SWAT went in like a viper to its prey. On a large water-bed partially covered in sheets, lay a massive naked walrus. It strongly resembled the nude body of Commodore William Wilbanks, eyes and mouth wide open in stunned disbelief.

Leaning back against the headboard he began to rant, "You have no authority here. You don't know who you're messing with. This is a military facility. I'm going to have you arrested."

On the nightstand next to him was a chrome Beretta Model 950BS Minx with a pearl handle, capable of shooting .22-caliber short rounds. His left shoulder dropped slightly as his head turned in the direction of the gun.

Stepping to the side of the bed, I pressed my Browning 9mm to his forehead as thoughts of those who had been killed, the families devastated, and the innocence sold ran through my mind.

"Go for it," I said as a slight smile crossed my face. I suddenly had a desperate, almost uncontrollable urge to say, some memorable line from *Starsky & Hutch*, but I repressed it and will probably never have the opportunity again.

The arrogant expression that began to form on his face turned to dread when Special Agent Cindy Gilroy walked into the room. Stepping to the foot of the bed, she showed her badge and announced, "Captain William Wilbanks, you are under arrest for the attempted murder of Katty Russell. Now get your butt out of bed."

Gripping the sheet, he pulled it up over his tonnage. Agent Gilroy moved around to the opposite side of the bed and pulled the sheets back, revealing a naked middle-aged woman lying in the fetal position.

"Well, hello, Mrs. Corbitt, welcome to the party," I said.

* * *

In the sports field under glaring lights and surrounded by thirty heavily armed members of several special weapons and tactical assault teams, sat eighty-seven very quiet and terrified maritime cadets and a handful of university staff members.

I was about to address the crowd when I heard my name called from the pier on the other side of the bleachers. A small, unmarked coast guard vessel docked, and Senior Officer Chelsey Defo stepped off with two wet, handcuffed men who looked like they had clearly gone out for a late-night swim.

"We caught these two bobbing around in the dark, said their boat sank." Chelsey grinned. "They were packing, and when we got them on board, they tried to boat-jack us. It didn't work out because they came face-to-face with Petty Officer Second Class Skip Franklin and his .60-caliber machine gun. Recognizing they were out gunned, they cordially surrendered."

Turning to a sea of people dressed only in their underwear, I was struck by the surreal visual that was worth recording. Thankfully the ever-ready SWAT commander had brought several cameras and recorded every movement. I hoped that a crowd this large stripped down to their boxers would be intimidated enough to respond to my questions and not unite in silence. Fortunately, sitting in the early morning air in nothing but their skivvies proved to be the elixir required to loosen the tongue and encourage corporation.

"Gentlemen and ladies, I am Detective Sergeant Bob Richards from the Oakland Police Department. I have with me FBI Special Agent Cindy Gilroy, DOJ Special Agent Charles Sill, Deputy District Attorney KP Cooper, and my own personal army. I have in my possession both search and arrest warrants signed by a local magistrate and a federal justice. We are now going to determine who's going to jail and who goes back to bed."

CHAPTER TWENTY-EIGHT

As the sun began to rise over the San Pablo Bay, we had identified those who were part of the cleanup crew, those who had sailed on the T.S. *Golden Bear,* and a large group open and willing to provide information about what they think they heard and thought they saw.

Wilbanks, Claudia Corbitt, and eight others were taken into custody, segregated, and placed into solitary in Oakland's lockup and Alameda County jail. The remaining were allowed to retrieve clothing and personal items under the watch of security and were provided lodging for two days at the Holiday Inn in Vallejo. This would allow time for the evidence techs to go over their quarters.

OPD's supervising criminalist was as excited as a kid at Christmas when she showed up with her troop of evidence bloodhounds and was told the whole campus was hers to explore. Her estimated time of completion, with the help from a forensic team from the FBI, was between two days and a week.

It was close to noon when I closed the door to my office and headed to my car. I reached for the door handle when a cadet flew out of the back door. "Sergeant Richards, wait . . ." he yelled. I was tempted to jump in and head home. If

I put my foot to the floor, I'd be halfway there by the time that kid got back inside the building. Then again, I could say I didn't see him, but that would mean I would have to run over him. Well, he was a cadet. We had more . . .

"What?" I said, resting my head on the roof. "What do you need?"

"The dispatch supervisor told me to catch you. She has a lawyer on the phone named Woodward who wants to talk to you."

"Okay, tell her to run the call through to the locker room. I'll take it there."

Clearing the locker room door, the phone on the wall began to ring. "Hello, this is Detective Sergeant Richards."

The familiar, strong, controlled voice of Anthony Woodward, also known as Uncle Tony, came on the line. "Congratulations on your promotion, Detective Sergeant."

"Thank you, Mr. Woodward. What is it that I can do for you?"

"I hear you have had quite an exciting night. It seems your little episode was very well planned and executed."

"How do you know what happened last night?"

"I'm not without resources, Sergeant. I hear things."

"Okay, so like I said, what can I do for you?"

"It's not what you can do for me; it's what we can do for you. How would you like an eyewitness to the Mary Ann Avery murder?"

"Go on," I said.

"We can provide you with names, dates, and addresses of people who purchased young boys, wealthy people, powerful people, people in high places all over the world."

"You have my attention, Mr. Woodward."

"I want complete immunity from prosecution for myself and my client Leonard Corbitt. We are not to be held liable for any violation of the law, whether civil or criminal."

"We're talking about some very serious crimes, Mr. Woodward, crimes that carry the death penalty. I don't see the DA or my bosses being willing to give you a get-out-of-jail-free card."

"I fully understand. I'm more concerned about the civil liability issues than the criminal. What we have to offer far outweighs the value of imposing liability on us for a few small infractions that we may have committed . . ." His voice trailed off.

"You still there, Mr. Woodward?"

"Yes. I'm here. There are children that need to be rescued, and up to now my client has remained silent because he feared for his life. After seeing how far you have gotten with your investigation, he's been encouraged and believes it's time he step up. Would you call the DA and arrange a meeting?"

"Okay, I'll see what I can do, but if you're pulling something and using those kids to do it, I'll make it my life's mission to put you and your client away."

"I understand," he said, and the phone went dead.

Withdrawing DA Cooper's card from my wallet, I called his home number and was told by his wife that he had just fallen asleep and she didn't want to bother him. I told her I understood but asked her to whisper a few words in his ear: "We have an eyewitness and names of baby buyers."

She set the phone down, and in seconds Coop was on the phone. "What do you have?"

I filled him in on Anthony Woodward's call and suggested we wait a day or two before following up on it. If it was some kind of scam, I didn't want to rush into it and risk screwing things up with our case. Besides, we had a plethora of suspects in custody and witnesses to interview.

"Woodward is a shadow with a pulse, always just out of sight and one step ahead. If it's legit, he and Corbitt will be anxious to hear from us, so they'll set aside their caution and step out. This sounds like it could be big, so we need to make sure we're the ones who are in control of the narrative."

"I agree," Coop said. "I'll have my assistant call Woodward and arrange a meeting in a few days. In the meantime, let the commodore and Mrs. Corbitt stew in solitary overnight. The Feds want in on the interview so they're sending over a special agent from San Francisco. Let's pull Claudia out of the box first around noon. I want to interview them in a holding cell at the county jail. They need to see that they aren't in control anymore."

"I think it would be a good idea to interview some of the lightweights we have in confinement first thing in the morning. They may give up something new we could use when we get around to the big fish," I said.

"See you at eight," Coop said, and hung up.

The following morning, I arrived early and arranged to have the two interview rooms available to us for the day. In each, I placed a reel-to-reel recorder on the left side of the metal table with three microphones, one for the suspect who would be seated facing the one-way mirrored window and one for each of the interrogators.

When I returned to my office, I found Lieutenant Miller and the rest of the crew waiting a bit impatiently to get to work.

I said, "Our interviews today should help us string together a series of events that range from burglary, kidnapping, child trafficking, conspiracy, and murder. Our efforts today are going to extend to other cases throughout the state and nationally and internationally. The cases we have to date have been consolidated into a single investigative effort we've titled 'Innocence Sold.'

"Each of the various agencies involved will be provided a complete account of everything that has happened to date, access to all existing evidence and forensic reports, as well as the resulting interviews from those we have in custody. They will prosecute their cases within their respective judicial districts as they see fit, with full cooperation from OPD. There's no grandstanding here. We have children to find. Because of the extent to which this case appears to reach, the FBI, DOJ, and Interpol will ultimately assume responsibility for the investigation."

Picking up a stack of manila envelopes, I continued, "We have eight people in custody that need to be interviewed and two primaries. I have assigned each of you an interview room on this floor. Cooper and I will take Wilbanks and Corbitt in Interview Room A on the second floor."

Handing each an envelope with their name and room assignment on it, I said, "You are not on the clock. If you are making headway, then keep going. We are looking for information on the child abductions, their involvement, the involvement of others, and most importantly the location where the children are being held.

"Each of you come with unique experience from different agencies that have different protocols. Today you must work as a team. Children's lives are at stake."

It was 9:00 a.m. before the first interview began, and it didn't take long to strike gold.

Three of the men who either manned the *Golden Bear* or served on the cleanup crew demanded a lawyer and refused to speak. That was expected from these specific cadets because they had graduated years earlier and should be serving somewhere in the US, not at the academy they graduated from. The parking lot contained evidence that these gentlemen must be doing well with some side job because each had an expensive luxury or sports car registered to them.

There were also two inexperienced kids fresh out of high school. They entered the interview room with youthful swagger and attitude, but that melted away faster than an ice cube in Phoenix when they were told what they could be charged with. Sweat began to form and fear filled their eyes as they dissolved into a puddle when photos of the homicide victims were shown, and the names of missing children were read to them. Several reported seeing children being brought onto the *Golden Bear* at night, just before setting sail for Ensenada. They had been told that they were the children of some of the crew.

A female cadet said she and her cadet boyfriend snuck out of their quarters late one night and met in his car to talk (right . . .). They saw a group of older cadets and some staff members get into black cars and two trucks and leave the base around two in the morning. What was odd was the vehicles were painted black, they were dressed in black clothing, they wore head and face scarves, and several were armed with M-16 rifles. When they brought it to Commodore Wilbanks's attention, he told them they were members of the tactical strike force team out of Travis Air Force Base, practicing night maneuvers.

Two of the staff confessed to participating in transporting small boys to Mexico and being a part of the cleanup crew but denied any involvement with any killing. However, they did say they could identify the one who was in charge.

Liz Baker, the receptionist, stuck her head in my office and said, "Bobby, that attorney, Anthony Woodward, has been calling all morning. He insists on talking with you. Said he will come down here if he can't get you on the phone. What do you want me to say to him?"

"Put him through. We have enough going on around here, and we don't need to add him to the mix."

Picking up the receiver, I took a deep breath and pushed the flashing button. "Hello, Mr. Woodward. I apologize for not being able to speak with you right now, but we are in the midst of a major investigation. I understand we have a meeting in a couple days with the DA."

"Yes, we do, but that may be too late."

"What do you mean, too late?"

"Leonard Corbitt is threating to leave the country. He is frightened that the information he has is going to get him killed."

"Okay, tell him to sit tight. We can put him in protective custody and set him up in a safe house. He's been keeping out of sight pretty well so far, so tell him to hang in there."

"Sergeant, that isn't good enough. If you want what he has to offer, we need the immunity from prosecution for myself and Leonard now."

"Sir, you know better than that. This isn't something that just gets typed up and stamped. The investigation isn't complete, and we haven't heard what Mr. Corbitt has to say. Now, I don't wish to be rude, but I have to go. I will see you in a couple of days."

I could hear him yelling as I hung up. Pressing the intercom button, I said to Liz, "If Mr. Woodward calls again or comes by, I have left my office, which is what I'm about to do. I truly don't have time to deal with him right now."

CHAPTER TWENTY-NINE

I retrieved a copy of the mugshots of all those booked from the maritime academy, along with the photos of James Corbitt and Martin Sherlie. Then I added a dozen more of various bad guys and ladies from the past just for good measure.

The two staffers willing to cooperate were placed in separate temporary holding cells on the first floor. Spreading the photos out across the metal table, I asked each one independently to identify who was involved in the crimes and who gave the orders.

Sorting through the photos, they both chose mugshots of Commodore William Wilbanks and Claudia Corbitt, and made a stack of eight additional mugshots.

"Wilbanks would give the orders to hurt people who needed straightening out," one of the staffers said. "I heard him say that some woman who was in the hospital needed to be removed. I knew what he meant."

Picking up the photo of Claudia, I asked, "What about this woman? Who is she?"

"I don't know, but she was always around. She would be in the room when the commodore told the squad what needed to be cleaned up and who needed hurting or removing." The staffers' statements collaborated with one major addition: Claudia Corbitt gave the orders and made the arrangements to transport the little boys that were taken to Ensenada.

What was most disturbing was discovering that there was yet another layer behind this criminal enterprise. It was the business end of developing a buying market, acquiring just the right child to meet the buyer's desire, and then completing the transaction. This person was seen only once when one of the junior cadets, Craig Smitty, was cleaning up garbage along the roadway. A black limo drove by leaving the academy, and a gray-headed man in the backseat rolled down the car's tinted rear window and tossed a handful of trash out at the cadet's feet. He wasn't about to forget that face.

While the two staffers in their holding cells completed writing their witness statements, and the interviewing team took a break for lunch, I headed to John Muir Hospital with Officer Defo to show Katty a few pictures.

Katty was lying in her bed tilted up in a seated position and reading a leather-bound Bible. She looked up as we entered her room, and a big toothy smile crossed her face. "Hi, Chelsey," she said, opening her arms, arms that still supported a number of tubes and wires. After a lengthy hug, I cleared the lunch trays from the rolling table and replaced them with stacks of mugshots.

"Katty, I need you to look through these and see if you recognize anyone," I said.

Looking at the pictures, she stopped and handed me the photo of James Corbitt. "This is the one who cried. I don't think he wanted to hurt me."

A few more photos down she handed me another, of Claudia Corbitt. "This woman came to our apartment with Mother Mary. She met Billy out in front and yelled at him . . . a lot." Her lower lip began to quiver. "The next day Billy brought me the baby, my baby."

Spreading the remaining images across her table, she shuffled them around and stopped cold while staring at a mugshot in the center of the pile. Her breath became rapid as she gripped the sides of the table.

"Katty, what's wrong? Katty . . ."

"That's him; that's the man. He did things to me." She began to cry.

Chelsey reached out and embraced her, pointing at a photo. "Is this the man who hurt you?"

Sniffling, she nodded. "He kicked me. He told the others to kick me . . ." Now sobbing, she said, "He dragged me out of the car and beat me. He got in the car. I thought he was leaving, but he went to get a gun . . ." She was trying to breathe, her words mixed with tears were difficult to understand. "He pushed me down and I heard a loud noise then I was in the hospital . . . Why? I didn't do anything. I don't know anything."

"Okay, that's enough, take a breath," I said, picking up the picture that started Katty's emotional tsunami. It was Commodore William Wilbanks's mugshot.

Chelsey was about to pick up the photos, but Katty began to sort what was left, removing two more pictures, identifying them as the other two who assaulted her.

Back at the PD, Coop caught me in the hall. "Bobby, what's with that lawyer, Woodward? He's been calling my office all morning demanding to talk with me. Says you've dropped the ball, that he has everything we need to wrap up the child abduction case and believes he can tell us where they are. If he really has information where those kids are and isn't telling us, I'm inclined to have him arrested on obstruction. Problem with that is we'd have to work through the issue of attorney-client privilege."

"He's been calling me too. Says Corbitt is about to grow wings."

"Well, if he's got good intel, maybe we need to see what he's got," Coop said.

We elected to let our primaries, Wilbanks and Corbitt, stew a bit longer, while we saw what Leonard Corbitt and his friend and attorney Anthony Woodward wanted to provide us.

Standing to stretch my legs I heard Liz say, "Sergeant, the crime lab is on the phone for you. Says there is some good news."

"Great, thanks," I said, reaching for the phone.

"Sergeant, we have another issue out here. It's that lawyer that's been hounding us all day. He's in the waiting room, says that he won't leave until he talks with you," Liz said with a tone of frustration.

"Okay, tell him that the DA is here with me and to have a seat. We're dealing with another matter and will be with him in about twenty minutes."

Pushing the button for the speakerphone, I said, "Finch, this is Sergeant Richards. I understand you have good news. Before you begin, please be advised that I have DA Cooper sitting here with me."

"Good afternoon to you both. I have good news. We conducted a gunshot residue, or GSR, test on Wilbanks and it came back positive."

"That's great," Coop said. "But how did you get gunshot residue off of him after a week?"

"Soap, hot water, and vigorous washing can get rid of about ninety percent of gunshot residue, but the good commodore doesn't think his malodorous carcass needs to hit the shower but once a week, and that has worked well for us.

"The expended cartridges from the Katty Russell shooting matched test rounds fired from Wilbanks's gun that he had on the nightstand. The ballistics tests and casings are being sent to San Francisco County to match the casings with the killing of Chester Scoggins, the man found in the hippie van off the Treasure Island pier, and to the little city of Mojave for the murder of Billy Kurkland."

Finch continued, "One more thing. The photos the cadet took with his telephoto lens, Mr. Martin Sherlie, are exceptional. You can make out the faces of the children clearly and all those on board the *Golden Bear*. I even recognized Claudia Corbitt. I've seen her at a few local fundraisers. He even took pictures of several people who came to talk with the commodore."

"We impounded several military style vehicles. Did you find any evidence in—" A loud knock on my door interrupted me, and Detective Axel Heart walked in with Junior Cadet Smitty in tow.

"We have something you need to hear," Axel said.

"Dr. Finch, I'll have to call you back. I'll stop by tomorrow if you're available."

"That would be fine. Have a good evening," she said and hung up.

"Okay, what's up?"

"You got the big boss, the Minted. Wow! Cool, man, way to go," Cadet Smitty gushed.

"What are you talking about?" I asked.

"The man, you got the man," he repeated.

I looked at Axel. "What's he talking about, the man?"

"I was returning him to solitary when we walked past the mirrored windows that look out into the lobby, and he saw this old guy sitting there. He pulled away from me and ran down the hall, trying to hide in the recess of one of the office doors. What he saw scared him bad."

Smitty sat in one of my wicker chairs and rocked back and forth. "You got the Minted, the one who calls all the shots. Man, if he knows I'm in here, I'm dead. You got to protect me."

"Okay, calm down. Let's go see who you're talking about."

"No way, man. I'm not about to be seen by him."

"He can't see you. Let's go."

Going down the stairwell to the hall outside the first-floor lobby, we stood behind the one-way mirror as Smitty stood behind Coop's large frame, peeking over his shoulder.

On a plastic molded chair, in the brightly lit surroundings of the police lobby, sat a balding older man in an expensive, tailored charcoal gray suit, spit-shined shoes, and a hand painted tie. His head shined under the fluorescent lights, with only a few silver strands combed meticulously across the top. He fidgeted, glancing repeatedly at his gold watch and the closed door across from him. His discomfort with his disheveled, intoxicated companions in the lobby was clear. His face was pale and lined with stress, and his eyes darted around, trying to avoid contact with the uniformed officers that passed by. He was definitely out of his element, especially when two of Oakland's ladies of the night came in and sat on either side of him.

"That's the Minted; that's the big boss."

"How do you know that?" I asked.

Stepping back away from the window, he started, "On the first Tuesday of every month, we got our pay, in cash. Coincidentally, the commodore had poker games in the guest quarters on the first Tuesday of each month, and if you were invited to play, you played and you didn't have a choice. Well, I got invited, and as expected I lost everything. As I was leaving, I saw Wilbanks put his winnings into a paper bag and stash it under his mattress."

"Okay, Smitty, this is all interesting, but what's it got to do with you and the guy in the lobby?" Coop said.

"I'm getting to that," Smitty said, nervously peeking at the lobby.

"Later that night, I was outside having a smoke, and in pulls this big black sedan, and the old man who threw garbage at me got out. Wilbanks came running out to meet him, and they both walked over to the canteen, to get a drink I guess."

Taking another peek at the window, he said, "I saw it as my moment. So I ran over to the back door of the guest quarters, slipped the lock, and went in. I was about to snag that bag of cash when Wilbanks and the old guy walked into the office."

Taking yet another peek, he asked, "Will I have to say this stuff in court?"

"Most likely," I said.

Dropping his head, Smitty just stood there for a long moment. After taking a deep breath, he continued, "Okay, okay. I heard them talking about taking little boys to Mexico on the *Golden Bear* and selling them. The old man was angry because one of the boys on the last trip tried to escape and jumped overboard. From what he said no effort was made to rescue the kid, they just kept going. The old guy was mad because of the money he lost. He was spitting threats and orders, and I could hear that the commodore was scared, his voice was trembling. 'Yes, sir,' and 'no, sir,' he would say. I hid in the closet and prayed they didn't come back there. When the old man left, Wilbanks walked him out and I headed out the back."

"Can you remember enough of what they said to write out a statement?" Coop asked.

"Sure, I remember a lot of it," Smitty said. "I was scared but what they were saying blew my mind. I'll never forget it. They didn't care anything about those kids. It was all about the money."

Axel took Smitty back to lockup and got him started on his statement. Then he retrieved Wilbanks, placed him in Interview Room B, and handcuffed him to the table, while Coop and I went to meet with Anthony Woodward, also known as the Minted.

"You know, Bobby, you and I will never have another case this convoluted," Coop said.

"You never know, Coop. It's a big, goofy world out there."

Walking into the lobby, Woodward looked up, saw us, and almost jumped to his feet. "Mr. Woodward, it is a pleasure to finally meet you. I am Detective Sergeant Bob Richards, and this is Deputy District Attorney KP Cooper," I said. "Please, let's retire to my office. It's much more comfortable there," I said, patting him on the shoulder. "Would you care for some coffee or water?"

"No, no, thank you . . . Ah, Mr. Cooper, was it?"

"Yes, you can just call me Coop."

"Okay, well, Coop, am I to assume that you are the one with the authority to provide immunity to myself and my client Leonard Corbitt?"

"That is correct," Coop said with a smile.

"Wonderful, then you will like what I have to show you," Woodward said, patting his leather briefcase.

"I'm sure we will," Coop said with a slight glance my way.

CHAPTER THIRTY

We placed Attorney Woodward in Interview Room A with his back to the wall and facing the one-way mirror. In front of him I placed a water bottle, a soda can, a couple bags of chips, and a coffee cup, and then I apologized for having to step out, leaving Uncle Tony alone. I inadvertently, with full intent, left the door to Interview Room A's observation room open to anyone who walked by in the hallway.

In Interview Room B, Coop and I sat with Wilbanks and politely asked him a few questions, getting no response.

"Why are we wasting our time with this guy? We've got more than enough to put him away," I said.

"I told you, I want to find those kids and get them back to their parents, and whether you like it or not, he's a navy captain. I was navy, so he deserves some respect," Coop said.

Turning to Wilbanks, I said, "If you want to help yourself, you need to start talking now. We already know everything."

Shaking his head and rolling his eyes, he chuckled. "You don't know anything."

"We have a witness. In fact, he's making a deal with the DA right now. He knows where those kids are, who has them, and he's having a great time burying you, Commodore. If you talk to us, it could keep you off death row."

"Not a chance, you've got nothing," Wilbanks growled.

"Okay, we tried. Sorry about that navy," Coop said.

We walked Wilbanks out into the hall and were almost past the observation room of Interview Room A, when Liz called out, "DA Cooper, sir, you're wanted on the phone. They said it's very important."

"Go ahead and get it; we'll wait for you right here."

"You sure?"

"Yeah, no problem. Go ahead."

"Okay, Liz," Coop said, letting go of Wilbanks's right arm and retreating down the hall. "I'll take it at your desk."

We stood for a few minutes as Wilbanks looked around at the receptionists, the offices, the receptionists, the furnishings in the hallway, and the receptionists again. Then he looked through the open door of the first observation room as obscenities filled the hall. Stiffing up, he tried to pull away, but I held tight. Wilbanks asked, "What's he doing here? What's he saying?"

"A lot," I said as he stared at the Minted with his jailhouse luxuries spread out in front of him and no handcuffs. "We had hoped on getting your side of all this, but I guess not. With everything he's given us, I'll bet he'll be sleeping soon on a beach somewhere in witness protection."

It suddenly struck me that I might have overstepped. This guy was big, and I really didn't want to find out if I could keep up with him on the dance floor. "Commodore, let's go back and sit down. If you want to talk to me, I'm all ears."

When Coop and Axel came in, I excused myself and went to the reception area. "Lizzy, my dear, your timing was perfect. We need to do it one more time with Claudia Corbitt. See if you can find Chelsey and have her meet me in solitary."

While I was walking Mrs. Corbitt to an interview room, Liz called me to the phone and Officer Defo held her in the hall until my return, and coincidently, it was in front of the open door to the observation room. Her response to seeing Uncle Tony sitting comfortably in the interview room led to the same response as that of Wilbanks. They instantly became a willing source of information. Their stories lined up with each other, with one exception: she said it was Wilbanks who killed Mary Ann Avery, and he said it was her. What I found interesting was neither of them implicated Leonard Corbitt.

When Coop and I entered Interview Room A, we expected Woodward to boil over because we left him for nearly two hours in an empty room with an assortment of vending machine snacks that tasted like cardboard drizzled with regret. What we found, however, was an attorney going over his notes and a stack of folders, each with a photograph of a child stapled to the cover. Once we were seated, Woodward began to talk.

"Gentlemen, I am here as a witness to a ghastly series of events. It is imperative that my client Leonard Corbitt and I be immediately exonerated of any possible charges so we might share the information we have with you without fear of reprisal. I assure you, we have done nothing wrong, and that will be proven out as we proceed."

"Mr. Woodward, what is the rush? I'm sure you are aware of the process and our requirement to fully investigate this matter," Coop said.

"The rush is these children need to be saved, and my client has threatened to flee, and right now he is unaccounted for. I want to help, but I must have immunity because I'm about to violate the attorney-client privilege. I will be disbarred."

Coop sat back in his seat and stared at Woodward. "Sir, you need to be made aware that we have a number of witnesses, even photographs, of what has been transpiring on that base, and your involvement."

"Mr. Cooper, I will not be treated in this way. I have come to you as a cooperating witness to assist you, not—"

Coop interrupted him, "Sir, you may have come as a witness, but now you are a suspect. I want you to listen to this very carefully, you have the right to remain silent . . ."

After Woodward was admonished of his rights, I placed him under arrest, and he refused to speak any further. He was searched and placed in a holding cell across from the commodore's cell. To say the conversation between those two was heated would be a colossal understatement, and it took a whole reel of recording tape to capture the number of expletives these two were able to dig up.

It had been a challenging week, and today was exceedingly long. There was a mountain of paperwork, dictation, and evidence submission, but finally our guests had been checked into their new lodging. It's Friday, and thanks to Abraham Lincoln having a birthday, the courts were closed on Monday, so they wouldn't be arraigned until Tuesday afternoon. Thus, I had plenty of time to go home, reintroduce my boys to their father, and the queen of the realm to her dashing troubadour of love—me.

That evening we gathered around the fire pit in the backyard with Joe, Alberta, the boys, and two new additions—Sherry, the cheerleader with the chestnut hair and Little Joe's favorite squeeze, and Aubrey, who is just a friend according to Sonny, but that wouldn't last, not the way she was looking at him.

Joe did the barbecuing because after I turned four expensive prime cuts of beef into briquettes, I was no longer allowed to do the cooking. This was fine by me because Joe was a great cook, and I had the eating thing down to an art.

Along with a great meal and much needed family time, I also gathered some unexpected intel concerning the department when Aubrey asked about the investigation that OPD was conducting at the maritime academy on Mare Island in Vallejo. I asked how she knew of the investigation, and she said, "My uncle—well, he's really my dad's best friend—is an Oakland police officer. We hear about everything."

"So, you have a connection with part of the OPD family?" I asked with a smile.

"Yep, we know what's happening before it's in the papers," she said with pride. "My dad knew what was going to happen at the academy before it happened."

"Wow, that's cool. What's your uncle's name? Maybe I know him."

She sat for a long moment, then said, "Uncle Nick is all I've ever known him by. Actually, my brother and I used to call him Uncle Nickel, and he would give us a nickel. That's funny, because I've known him all my life and I never knew any more than that. I guess I didn't need any more than that."

"Well, I'll try to look him up some day," I said, storing Uncle Nick in my head for later. What I was certain of, we had a leak somewhere in the department.

As we were preparing to wrap the evening up, Rosie said, "Can I have everyone's attention for a moment?" She stood with a backdrop of stars and a beautiful glow from the fire on her face and figure.

"I wish to share something with the family. Sherry and Aubrey, you are included because you have been adopted," Rosie said warmly.

"Yes, more girls for the Randall clan," Grandpa Joe shouted as Alberta poked him.

"Guys, I have an appointment in two weeks for a PET scan. Dr. Chamberlan and my oncologist are concerned with a few things and want to get a better look. I would like to ask you for your prayers. I know I am in God's hands, and although I could not be more blessed by the family God has given me, it's still a burden that's hard to carry. I love you, each of you."

It was as though the night got just a little darker and a bit quieter. Alberta sat next to her little girl, Rosie, putting her arm around her and cradling her. Joe, the boys, and I sat in the still of the night allowing God to speak to us and through us. The girls, without saying a word, went about picking up the dishes, then one washed and the other dried all in silence. Before they left, they sat on either side of their boyfriend's mom and held her hands, and Sherry prayed. This was followed by a long and emotional tear-filled embrace.

The three-day weekend made for a long-awaited break, and an opportunity for some serious family time. Saturday morning, Little Joe called our favorite place to hit the slopes—Rainbow Sky Lodge at Truckee—to check on the condition of the snowpack. With a good response the Richards hit the road and spent the day strapping sticks to our feet and flinging ourselves down a mountain, all while making every effort to look cool. It was, nonetheless, time well spent. After several harrowing rides on a dangling park bench suspended on a zip line, looking down over the trees, and pondering the softness of the snow, Rosie and I retreated to the bar. Within moments we were seated on the back deck of the lodge, bundled up in thick blankets, nursing a hot mocha, and watching our boys zigzag effortlessly down the slopes. The entire day worked its magic and brought a smile to my dear Rosie amid her trepidation.

After returning home and grabbing a quick shower, I called and left a message for the HR department to pull the files on any active OPD officer with the first name of *Nick* or *Nicholas*, and to calendar me for several days of personal time when Rosie was to have her PET scan.

Sunday morning the whole family, including Joe and Alberta, sat comfortably in our usual spot—third row from the back on the left—while Pastor Gallagher imparted a message from the Book of James, my personal favorite. Just as he was about to share the part about my faith having to be seen, my pager went off, drawing the attention of those around me.

The message that flashed across the screen was "NOW," and the number was DA Cooper's. Leaning over to Rosie, I whispered into her ear, "Sorry, baby, I have to take this." Retreating through the sanctuary doors into the lobby, I met the head usher who led me into the office to use the phone.

"What's up, Coop?"

"I have a search warrant for Woodward's home and office. I've been informed that he was allowed a phone call, so evidence could be getting tossed as we speak. We need to serve it now."

"Got it. Do you have any surgical gloves and baggies?"

"Of course, what self-respecting DA would ever venture out into this world without protection?"

"Okay, pick me up in front of Calvary Chapel Church on Twenty-sixth."

Taking my seat next to Rosie, I whispered, "I have to go. Coop is picking me up. Sorry. I love you."

"You be safe," she said, squeezing my hand.

I went back to the church office and called Dispatch, telling them to send an officer to both Woodward's office and his home, and stop anyone from entering either. If there was someone there, they were to be detained until we arrived. I recruited Axel and Chelsey to assist us, and assigned them to Woodward's office, while Coop and I went to his home. There we hoped to find Leonard Corbitt.

Anthony Woodward was a single man living a lavish lifestyle. His home sat on a hillside overlooking the Bay, with large floor-to-ceiling windows, a jagged stone fireplace, thick shag carpet, and stained wood paneling, but no Leonard Corbitt.

We spent the entire afternoon going through everything and found nothing, which was also true for Axel and Chelsey. Woodward's life and home were spotless. Exhausted, we dropped down on the massive cushions that lined the sunken conversation pit that opened out onto an infinity pool. I could see the frustration in Coop's eyes.

"Well, we have witnesses," I said.

"Yeah, but without physical evidence, we don't have anything to collaborate their testimony. We can bake Wilbanks, and some of the others, but Claudia will be difficult, and Uncle Tony almost impossible."

"You want some coffee? I'm sure he has coffee somewhere around here," I said, heading for the kitchen.

Coop pulled a barstool up to a serving island in the kitchen, and I poured two cups of java that I brewed from one of the fanciest coffee makers I had ever seen. We sipped in silence for several minutes considering our next move and wondering what we had left out.

"Bobby, what do you think happened to Leonard? No one has seen or heard from him since Mary Ann Avery was killed."

"All I know is Woodward said he was holing up here and that he threatened to run if he didn't get immunity."

"We've got to find those kids," Coop said angrily. "I'm not letting that piece of crap get away with this, and I'm not giving him immunity!" he shouted, slamming his fist into the countertop. He hit it with such force the island shifted slightly, toppling cups and spilling coffee everywhere.

Under the sink I located the paper towels, took a few, tossed the roll over to Coop, and began to clean up the mess. Pushing the island back into place, I realized that it wasn't the island that moved but the countertop. Then I saw it, everything in the kitchen was granite, except the laminated top of the island that matched the granite pattern. Putting the cups in the sink and wiping away the spilt coffee, I told Coop to move back from the island as I gripped the sides of the top and pushed. With little effort the top slid back, revealing an open cavity with steps leading down into the darkness.

Glancing up, I saw Coop looking at me with eyes as big as the ceiling fan spinning overhead. A Cheshire cat grin formed just under his nose. "Let's go, Bobby," he said, putting on a new set of gloves.

CHAPTER THIRTY-ONE

I searched through the drawers for a flashlight and then headed for the garage when Coop shouted from the bottom of the steps, "We're got lights, Bobby."

Basements were unusual in California because our end of the world tended to rock and roll. This basement was the size of a large bedroom with eight-foot ceilings and was lit up like noonday from neon lights. On one wall there were two filing cabinets, one on each side of a metal desk that sported a large computer screen. On another there were four large chest freezers, each padlocked. On the wall that faced the stairs hung a series of small, framed pictures of smiling families. Each photo consisted of one man, one woman, and a small boy. On the bottom of each frame was a strip of white masking tape with a date imprinted on it.

The filing cabinets contained folders with a series of numbers and letters written on the tab. The file folders were in ordered groups that had the same first three digits. Inside were pictures of boys ranging in age from three to eight.

"Bobby, we need to get Finch and her team out here. After she goes through the place, we can go through the files. I understand Woodward is a shark in court, and I don't want to risk losing something because we got in a rush."

"You're right, Coop. Let's get out of here," I said. "I'll give her a call and get a couple uniforms out here to secure the scene. The Feds have a team that specializes in crimes against children who may be able to identify them with what we have here."

Back in my office I had pizza and sodas brought in for the crew while we waited to hear from Finch, and it didn't take long. I was into my second bite of a pizza that could only be described as a warm hug from the universe with extra cheese, when my phone began to ring. Pressing the com button, I said, "This is Sergeant Richards."

"Bobby, this is Finch. You may want to come back out here."

"Why, what's up?"

"It's Leonard Corbitt . . ." she said, and I excitedly cut her off.

"Great, don't let him get away. I'll be right there," I said jumping to my feet.

"No rush, Bobby. We have him on ice for you."

"What?"

"We popped the padlock on the first freezer on the left by the steps and found Leonard Corbitt inside."

What she said stunned me. Then my soul shivered when a question rose up in my throat that I didn't have the heart to ask.

"Have you opened the other freezers?" Coop asked, relieving me of the question.

"Not yet. I wanted to talk to you first."

"We'll be right there. Don't do anything until we get there," and with that we were out the door.

* * *

Coop, Axel, and I stood with Finch, who had already removed the remaining padlocks. "Okay, Axel, open that freezer." At the top of the steps, I could hear Chelsey groan. She couldn't bring herself to come down.

After a long tense moment, he grasped the handle and apprehensively lifted the lid. Stepping forward we all looked in at nothing, absolutely nothing. This was also the case with the other two, which gave us some sense of assurance. What did he need with all the freezers?

"Alright, close everything up. We need to call the coroner and I need to keep Leonard in his present condition until I can do a proper postmortem," Finch said, pushing down the lid to secure it. "Gentlemen and lady, this is my crime scene, so I need to ask you to leave. I will have a briefing by midday tomorrow and a full report in a couple days."

"When can we go through those filing cabinets and get those pictures?" Coop asked.

"You can have them after my briefing tomorrow."

There was nothing else we could do in Woodward's lair than stomp all over it and contaminate the evidence, so it was a good time to leave and talk to our primary suspect back at the PD. Ascending the steps, I could hear Axel and Chelsey praying in the kitchen. I knew that God had ordained this union of men and women who recognized the need to seek guidance from more than merely their training and experience.

From the observation room of Interview Room A, I watched Anthony Woodward write feverishly on a legal-size notepad. What was Uncle Tony writing? What was the Minted up to?

I was soon joined by Lieutenant Miller and KP Cooper. Together we stood in silence watching our heartless nemesis, the one who orchestrated what had become known as Innocence Sold, a case that went way beyond the borders of the city of Oakland.

"Mr. Woodward, I believe you know Deputy DA Cooper and Lieutenant Miller," I said, taking a seat across from him.

He looked at each of us with contempt and said, "You have no right to hold me. You have no evidence that I have done anything wrong. I demand that my attorney be present."

"You have invoked your right to remain silent and to have your attorney present, but we're not here to question or interrogate you. No, on the contrary, we are here to simply inform you, to fill you in on what we are going to do, so you can tell your attorney what to expect."

Reaching into my briefcase, I removed six folders, each with numbers and letters handwritten on the tabs. The expression on his face told me what I had hoped to see, which was stark terror.

"What we have here are just a few of the folders we took from the filing cabinets within your hideaway. These folders, like the others, have your fingerprints all over them, and they contain photos of children reported missing from within the Bay Area.

"The number on the tab was easy to decrypt. It is a date and a location given in terms of latitude and longitude. It's only a matter of time before we have located all the boys you have sold. Our graphology expert has confirmed that you are the one who wrote the numbers on the tabs, which provides us with an interesting twist. What are we going to find that took place on that date and at that location? That's not a question, just an observation."

Sitting back, I let the news filter its way into Uncle Tony's gray matter. I could tell it was hitting home because he looked as if he regretted every life choice he'd ever made that led to this moment. Good time to stop dribbling and take the shot.

"Mr. Woodward, we are going to prosecute you for child abduction and trafficking, resulting in the death of at least one child and possibly more. We are going to prosecute you for the premeditated murder of Leonard Corbitt and first-degree murder-for-hire of Mary Ann Avery, Billy Kurkland, and Chester Scoggins. We are going to prosecute you for the rape and attempted murder of Katty Louise Russell. We will seek the death penalty, and we will get it. We will lock you in a five-by-eight concrete block until the day comes when we will take you out and kill you."

Picking up the folders, putting them back in my briefcase, I stood and headed for the door.

"Wait a minute, just wait . . ." Woodward said. "What about the immunity you promised? You said I could get immunity."

"That's when you were a witness. Now you're the prime suspect. Judas Iscariot has a better chance at getting immunity than you do, Anthony," Coop said.

Back in my office, I found five folders from HR on my desk laid out in fanned formation of OPD personnel whose first names were *Nick* or *Nicholas*. Two were retired, one had been on medical leave for the last five months, one worked parking enforcement, and one was a traffic cop. When I returned the folders to HR, the young lady at the counter asked, "Did you find who you were looking for?"

"No. I don't suppose we have an officer with the name *Nickel*, do we?"

"Let me check. Is that a first name or a last name?"

"Try both."

She put the information into her computer and waited. "I'm sorry, Sergeant, there's nothing. I even tried different spellings. Can you tell me why you're looking for him, and I'll check around. Someone may know who he is."

"All I know is, he's called Uncle Nickel."

"Uncle Nickel? Where did you hear that?" asked a middle-aged man in dark gray work pants and matching shirt as he emptied a trash can into a plastic bag.

"You know of someone who goes by Uncle Nickel?"

"Yeah, me. Well, not for a while. My best friend's kids used to call me Uncle Nickel."

"Would one of them be named Aubrey?"

"Yes, that's my niece. Is she okay?"

"Yeah, yeah, she's fine. What is your name, sir?"

"Dominick, Dominick Stardom. You can just call me Nick."

"Okay, Nick, would you mind coming to my office when you've completed your work?"

"Sure, I'll see you in an hour."

Uncle Nickel and I had a serious meeting of the minds. He failed to recognize the danger of passing confidential information and was sincerely apologetic. I wasn't about to destroy his career. He had been employed by the city of Oakland for nearly twenty years and had worked that entire time in the maintenance department covering the city hall and police department. However, it was made clear that any further indiscretion would be passed on to his supervisor. As our conversation concluded, I silently thanked God that it wasn't one of our officers.

I used to wonder why most cops preferred working patrol, rather than working out of the detective bureau. That question was answered this last year. For the cop on the street, every day comes with its own set of events and encounters. It's exciting, and at the end of the day, they're usually done. They arrive on the scene, sweep up the pieces of a large puzzle, shake it up real good, and hand it to a detective to try and put it together. Unfortunately, many of the pieces will be missing, a few don't fit, and some appear to belong to a different puzzle all together.

Sitting under the flickering glow of fluorescent lights, the detective will spend weeks, even months, sipping coffee that's always too cold, slogging his way through countless reports, witness statements, and mounds of evidence. He will return to the scene repeatedly in hopes of finding that one missing peace and reinterview uncooperative witnesses and spectators who won't get involved.

Over the next few months, my caseload continued to grow, and the Innocence Sold file took on a life all its own. Agencies from across the country were sending me copies of reports, fingerprints, and recent lab results in hopes of resolving their cases. The sudden influx of lab results was attributed to a rumor that had been going around.

Supposedly there's a new technology that's causing a real stir. They call it biological fingerprinting, and it's said to be better and more accurate than an actual fingerprint. Most of what we heard sounds like a pipe dream rather than reality. I asked Dr. Finch about it, and she said it's been in the works for some time, but she saw it as chemistry voodoo. Although there had been some interesting studies reported, it would need to stand up in court. They call it deoxyribonucleic acid. I can just imagine trying to say that under cross-examination. Fortunately, it has an acronym—DNA.

The case had grown significantly, and Deputy District Attorney Cooper persuaded Judge Andrews to bring the defendants to trial rather than delay it any further. It was already gaining steam in the media. It took over six months before we had a court date, and I was anxious to get this case behind me, but the way it was developing it would outlast me.

Just outside one of the county's courtrooms, I had perched myself on a wooden bench that had once been used during the Inquisition. I was about to make a break for the exit when one of the large, ornately carved doors opened and a voice echoed off the hallway walls, "Richards."

"That's me," I said, raising slowly and stretching out the kinks in my back. I straightened my tie, tucked the leather binder under my arm, and followed the bailiff into a well-populated courtroom. The high ceilings were adorned with intricate moldings, dark wood-paneled walls, and the commanding presence of the raised polished mahogany bench. On the wall behind the bench and a large leather chair hung a rectangular, tablet-shaped piece of mahogany finished to match the judge's bench, upon which the Ten Commandments were carved.

This was the Superior Court of Alameda County, the domain of the honorable Judge Samuel K. Andrews. His court was known as "Slamming Sam's Lair." Judge Andrews was highly respected and feared by those who sat at both the defense and prosecution tables. He was pro-police and expected the officers who sat on his witness stand to be honest, truthful, and prepared. Anything short of that came with consequences.

He had been known to have DA investigators do background checks on new faces in uniform who appeared in his court if something raised his suspicions. Whoever stood before him, whatever the charges might be, could be assured they'd get a fair and conscientious hearing. Of the eight judges, he was the best to draw. And of the eight courts, his courtroom was the nicest and the most controversial. The Ten Commandments that hung just over his head on the back wall had caused quite a stir. A group had filed a lawsuit against him, demanding that it be removed because it was offensive and violated the division of church and state. Judge Andrews's response was, "They'll have to remove me first."

Standing in the witness box, I scanned the room for familiar faces. Only three—the DA; the defendant, Claudia Corbitt; and Julie Corbitt. Behind them in the gallery, several angry faces glared at me. They were family of the defendant no doubt. To my left sat eighteen wide-eyed observers of justice. There were twelve jurors, five women and seven men, and six alternates, three of each gender. I'm usually good at reading people's demeanor, but these folks were hard to grasp, at least this early in the trial.

The bailiff stepped in front of me with a large, leather-bound book that required both hands to hold with the words "Holy Bible" written on its cover in bold, shiny gold letters. Judge Andrews told me that it was a gift from his grandfather, Elijah Edger Andrews, who received it from

Theodore Roosevelt, for friendship and service as the president's personal attorney. I knew I was not required to place my hand on the Bible, but I also knew "Slamming Sam" was watching and gets wary of those who don't. I proudly placed my hand squarely on the Bible and lifted my right.

"Do you solemnly swear to tell the truth, the whole truth, and nothing but the truth, so help you God?"

"I do."

Deputy District Attorney KP Cooper stood, smiled at the jury, and turned to me. "Good morning, Officer. Would you please state your name, title, and agency."

"My name is Bob Richards. I am a Detective Sergeant with the Oakland Police Department."

"Thank you, Sergeant. Were you on duty on February third of last year?"

"Yes."

"Sergeant, would you take us back to that day and tell the court what transpired."

From the side door that led into the judge's chambers, a tall thin man in a dark suit stepped in and handed a note to the bailiff, then retreated the way he came in. The bailiff in turn stepped up and handed the note to the court clerk who read it, stood, and handed it to the judge.

"Hold on for a moment, Sergeant Richards," the judge said. "Counsel, please approach the bench." After several minutes, the attorneys returned to their seats as the judge had a quiet conversation with the court clerk.

"Sergeant Richards, you're excused," Judge Andrews said. "Ladies and gentlemen, I apologize for the interruption, but it is unavoidable. Because of the Thanksgiving and Christmas holidays, these proceedings will be rescheduled.

We will resume on Monday, January fifth at 9:00 a.m. This will allow the defense the time they have requested to examine the evidence. I wish you all a happy and joy-filled holiday. Court is adjourned."

The room went still, then a stirring rose as questions began to fly from reporters, family members, jurors, and those in the gallery. The bailiff reappeared at the door that led into the judge's chambers.

"Ladies and gentlemen, Judge Andrews apologizes for this interruption and any inconvenience it may cause. He has received notice of a family emergency that requires his immediate attention. Again, Judge Andrews apologizes and wishes you all a safe and joyful Christmas."

Cooper excused himself and went toward the chamber door. The bailiff stepped in front of him. "Sorry, Coop, not right now." Looking over the DA's shoulder, he said, "Detective Richards, the judge would like to speak to you."

"Okay," I said, walking past Coop. Shrugging, I said, "I don't know, Coop."

Inside, Judge Andrews stood with his back to me, gazing out through a large bay window that overlooked the city. He didn't move and I stood silent. A sense of anguish filled the room as he turned and looked at me with eyes blurred with tears. His shoulders hunched, his hands clenched into tight fists, he stared through me into some distant place, then slowly he descended into his chair, surrendering to it without relief. I moved one of the chairs up to the opposite side of the desk and sat quietly. It was not a time for words or questions. It was a time to just be near.

Silently I prayed, retreating into a place where words aren't spoken and conversation has no sound. I didn't know what had captured his heart, and I didn't need to know, because I knew the One who did. I didn't know how long we sat together, but when I opened my eyes, I noticed that the sun was shining through his window in a different place than where it had been when I sat down. Sitting across from me was Judge Andrews with a slight, warm smile.

"Thank you, Bobby. I knew that God placed you here for me."

"What can I do for you, sir?"

"You've done it, just as I knew you would."

"Sir?"

"You gave me the hand up that I needed. Now I need to go see my family and love them as you have loved me." Reaching across the desk, he took my hand. "My dear Caroline, the love of my life, and my bride of nearly thirty-five years, is finally free from a life of fear and pain."

Standing, he stepped around the desk, embraced me, said "thank you," took his coat, and left the room out a side door. In the courtroom, I found Coop sitting at the prosecution table, along with the bailiff. Neither of them left.

"Judge Andrews's wife has been suffering from a rare, very aggressive form of Alzheimer's disease," the bailiff said sadly. "I've heard him say it a hundred times—*Uppsala deletion*. She was diagnosed when she was just forty years old, and for the last year she has been in hospice. The judge sleeps next to her every night. He comes to work in the morning, goes and has lunch with her, back to work until five, and then they have supper together. She doesn't know who he is, and it's never mattered to him."

Wiping away the tears with his shirtsleeve, the bailiff said, "Thank you for being there with him. He respects you two."

CHAPTER THIRTY-TWO

Rosie's Pet scan came back showing the possibility of cancer in the lymph nodes under her right arm. This was alarming but not shocking. Since her radical mastectomy, we knew that someday we might have to face a return of the cancer. Every six months, she had a test; and every six months, we would venture out to some culinary retreat to celebrate a clean slate. When we got home from the UCLA medical center, the boys had cleaned up the house and were watching Bear Bryant lead his Crimson Tide to an undefeated season. Sonny gave his mom a hug and proudly announced that he had already made the dinner reservations. That's when he saw the look in her eye.

"Are you okay, Mom?" His words sparked the attention of the other two. On their feet they surrounded and gently embraced her.

"I have a few things to deal with, but we know who has our back, right, guys?" she said as a tear ran down her cheek. I know my bride, and that was not a tear drawn out by anxiety or fear. It was a love tear, shed from a heart overflowing in thankfulness for the embrace of her babies.

The following eight weeks brought Thanksgiving, Christmas, New Years, and two surgeries, a season of pain, compassion, and healing. We went out to dinner the night we came home from the hospital because Rosie said she wasn't about to miss out on a good meal with good men. Tonight, Little Joe made the reservations because we were celebrating an all-clear report from Dr. Chamberlan.

On January 5, the trial resumed, and Commodore William Wilbanks stood his ground as any homicidal ship's captain would do. And after numerous warnings from Judge Andrews, he was finally allowed to represent himself. It was interesting sitting in the witness box while a man with the appearance of the Pillsbury doughboy in a suit three sizes too small proved that he had in fact had a fool for a client. The jury was out for only three hours, returning with a guilty verdict on all counts. The commodore now sits on San Quentin's death row awaiting the executioner. I'm told he has filed an appeal claiming he was not afforded proper legal representation.

Claudia Corbitt's trial was as entertaining as it was surprising. At one point it appeared that she just might get away with it. The testimonies that pointed to her guilt were all from co-defendants, or those making deals with the DA for reduced sentences, and there was little in the way of physical evidence. Then she committed the cardinal sin of jurisprudence. She took the witness stand to give her side of the story against her attorney's advice. That was when Deputy DA Cooper poured a little verbal salt into an open wound.

Leaning against the witness stand, Coop turned away from Claudia, looked out into the gallery, pointed to a boy sitting between two adults, and said, "So Mrs. Corbitt, let me make sure I have this correct. Mary Ann Avery's child is also your husband, Leonard Corbitt's child, correct?"

"No, absolutely not." I was certain she bared her teeth and began snarling.

"I guess that would make him your stepson?" Coop said and wisely stepped away from the witness stand.

Leaping to her feet in a fit of rage, she shouted at the top of her lungs, "That bastard kid will never be a Corbitt—never! Do you hear me? Never! I killed that low-life slut, and I'd do it again if I had the chance."

It took two large deputies to control her. It was like trying to restrain a caffeinated tornado in high heels. Two days later, she pled guilty and was sentenced to forty years, twenty with good behavior. There's serious doubt, however, that it will happen. She's now in solitary confinement at the Tehachapi California Institution for Women for assaulting another prisoner and biting a guard. She has certainly found a home.

Attorney Anthony Woodward, also known as Uncle Tony, or the Minted, put up a good legal battle but ultimately recognized that he had a better chance of bailing out the *Titanic* with a spoon. Acquittal just wasn't in the cards. So, he did what lawyers do—he negotiated. He pled guilty to two counts of first-degree murder and five counts of child abduction and trafficking in exchange for taking the death penalty off the table. The Minted was sentenced to life without the possibility of parole and is serving his sentence in the Federal Correctional Institution, Dublin, California. He continues to work with Oakland PD and surrounding police agencies, as well as the FBI, DOJ, and Interpol, to decipher the notes in his files and provide information that has led to the arrest of twenty-eight couples and the reuniting of twenty-eight young boys with their families.

We were able to account for all but three boys. One we know perished trying to escape by jumping overboard off the T.S. *Golden Bear*, and the other two are simply gone. We have no way of knowing if any children were harmed by Billy Kurkland when he *let them go*. Little evidence existed as to who those children may have been, and nothing as to what may have happened to them. Billy Kurkland and Chester Scoggins were the only ones who could shed light on their whereabouts, and they were dead.

I have an opinion that comes from years of experience, a gut feeling, and recognizing the depraved nature of those who market in child trafficking. It's my belief that many of the children reported missing may not ever be found, and that those *let go* have been sold into forced labor, sexual slavery, or terminated and discarded like so much garbage. The scriptures tell us that some sins are exposed here and some on the other side of death. Either way, I believe that hell has made advanced reservations for those who have been involved in bringing harm to a child.

James Corbitt and Martin Sherlie received good recommendations from both the police department and the District Attorney and were sentenced to six months with time served and five years of monitored probation. Word has it that both are seeking permission from the court to enlist in the navy.

All but two of the staff and cadets who were arrested pled guilty and were sentenced from six to twelve months in county jail and three to five years' probation. Two of the staffers were found guilty of evidence tampering, assault, and rape. Both are serving a ten-year stretch in Folsom State Prison.

Katty Louise Russell turned her heart and life over to God and went through a grueling one-year drug rehabilitation program. She did so well and showed such compassion for those going through the program, she was hired as an administrative assistant whose job is to look out for the care of the patients. She also legally changed her name, not to hide or conceal her identity, but in order to take the name of her husband, Andrew Garcia, the officer who guarded her when she was cared for at John Muir Medical Center.

Julie Corbitt and Chelsey Defo became close. After nine months of intense therapy, Julie moved into the Defo household and found the motherly love she never had. Through the Defo's encouragement, Julie returned to Stanford and finished her degree, graduating with honors and passing the bar. Within the year, she assumed the position of CEO of her father's business interests, and in the next two years, she gathered several fellow graduates and bought out the Woodward Legal Firm, that today is known simply as Corbitt Law.

Charles O'Neal continued to work at Saint Margaret Mary Church for Father Vincent. Although he was severely reprimanded for hearing confessions, the sincerity of his heart was seen, and he was forgiven. His desire to become a priest required a bachelor's degree, so arrangements were made to hire Charles as the full-time church administrator, which came with the benefits of secondary educational tuition. He was accepted and enrolled into the University of San Francisco with a major in theology and a minor in philosophy. Upon graduation he would be old enough to enter seminary.

I looked at my watch and was surprised to see that it was nearing 9:00 a.m. I had been sitting on this log bench in the Headlands watching the fog roll out and the tide roll in. For over three hours, my yesterdays had marched before me. Around me cars and tourists by the bus load were beginning to appear. The solitude I had craved was over, and it was time to go home. Sitting in the car, I watched as families gazed across the Bay, taking in the beauty that for a few hours had just been mine alone.

There are some new memories to be made, so I need to get on the road. Rosie is at home packing probably every stitch of clothing she owns and maybe some of the furniture. We are those people who wear only a third of the things they bring, but there are a couple pieces I know will get worn, such as her evening gown and my tux. Our first stop, the University of California, Riverside, where Critter (a name he loves) is studying entomology. My kid is going to be a bug doctor. Go figure. The next stop, San Diego to play with our granddaughter (the single most precious human on the planet), and spend some quality time with Little Joe and his beautiful bride. After Joe exited the military, he wasted no time pursuing a career in law enforcement. He has been with SDPD for three years. Then we're on to New Orleans, where Sonny has established himself as an incredible artist. I worried about his career choice at first, but he has been well received and his work sought after.

Our last stop will be Port Miami to board a Royal Caribbean cruise ship for ten days, bobbing around the Bahamas. If truth be told and my Rosie has her way, I'm going to be sleeping in that tux . . .

EPILOGUE

This is not just a story.

What you have read is a fictional story intended to entertain, but the account is not far from actual events. Human trafficking today generates an estimated $236 billion per year. There are an estimated 49.6 million people enslaved in the world right now—more than any other time in history.

It is my hope that *Innocence Sold* has drawn your attention to the critical issue of human trafficking—a global crisis that affects millions of lives and undermines the dignity and freedom of countless individuals. This pervasive crime is one of the fastest-growing criminal industries in the world, generating billions of dollars annually while destroying lives and communities.

Organizations like A21 are leading the charge to combat human trafficking and restore hope to survivors. Founded in 2008, A21 is dedicated to eradicating slavery through a comprehensive approach: reaching vulnerable communities, rescuing those trapped in exploitation, and restoring lives through aftercare and empowerment. Their global impact has been remarkable, with numerous survivors freed, perpetrators brought to justice, and communities educated to prevent trafficking.

A21's work emphasizes prevention, protection, and partnership, offering innovative programs such as education campaigns, safe houses, and collaborations with law enforcement to dismantle trafficking networks. Their efforts remind us that ending human trafficking is not only possible but also within reach when individuals and organizations unite in action.

I invite you to consider how you or your organization might join this critical cause—whether through partnership, advocacy, or support of A21's mission. Together, we can amplify the fight against human trafficking and move closer to a world where every person is free.

To find out more, to participate, and to support the ministry of A21, please visit their website at A21.org

Thank you for your time and consideration, and I hope you found *Innocence Sold* to be a good read.

B. F. Randall

ABOUT THE AUTHOR

An award-winning author, speaker, and pastor, Ben Randall graduated from the University of San Francisco, Global University (ICI), Berean Institute, and attendee of Golden Gate Theological Seminary. Ben was licensed and ordained by the Evangelical Church Alliance in 1984.

Following his service in the US Army and a tour in Vietnam, he served a decade as a police officer in the San Francisco Bay Area, and four years as the Assistant Solano County Recorder. Ben has served as a volunteer chaplain at San Quentin State Prison and as police chaplain, receiving training as a hostage and critical incident negotiator.

His pastoral ministry began as the administrator and singles pastor of a large Northern California Assembly of God church, and later he founded and pastored New Hope Christian Fellowship, a nondenominational, evangelical church in the Sacramento Valley, for seventeen years. Ben's ministry includes speaking at numerous churches, conferences, seminars, and retreats, as well as global and national missions.

He is also on the board of directors of The Father's House in Leesburg, Florida, and on the board of directors of Follow the Need International, Inc., a global outreach.

He has produced and hosted a weekly radio show reaching the greater San Francisco Bay Area; has written editorials, articles, and discourses; and has authored plays, vignettes, and skits. Ben's dramatic monologue of the book of James brings the Scriptures to life as he performs "A Man Called James." His work and experience have equipped him with a unique insight of human conflict and divine intervention that is clearly echoed in his writings.

www.ingramcontent.com/pod-product-compliance
Lightning Source LLC
Chambersburg PA
CBHW071201020726
47502CB00002B/492

* 9 7 8 1 5 6 3 0 9 7 8 8 1 *